MW01172260

Who Do You Love Too?

SHADRESS DENISE

Blue Indigo Publishing

ISBN-13: 978-0692566671
ISBN-10: 0692566678

Editor | Shelby Lazenby | Progressive Editing Solutions, LLC
Book Cover Designer | Dynastys CoverMe | www.dynastyscoverme.com
Interior Design | Strawberry Publications, LLC
www.StrawberryPublications.com

Also written by Shadress Denise

Disturbia
Who Do You Love?

BLUE INDIGO PUBLISHING PRESENTS

Who Do You Love Too?

SHADRESS DENISE

"There is a difference between who we love,
who we are meant for, and
who we settle for..."

-Unknown

ACKNOWLEDGMENTS

They say; *if you ever want to hear God laugh, tell him what your plans are*. When I started this journey to continue Rylee's story; I was conflicted. My emotions were everywhere. I wasn't sure if I could take on her persona again. In my head, I was in a different place. I started this story about four or five times before the beginning actually stuck. By the time I moved passed that hurdle; I started a new job and entered into my last cluster of grad school. At this point, I was in so many places mentally there was no way I could write. By early November, I had put writing on hold until I graduated (thanks mommy). Weeks went by and I started feeling like was this it? Was I going to be a one-hit wonder? Did I have what it takes to be an author? After all of that I can definitely say stress is a b$#^*! It has a way of taking on so many forms; planting so many seeds of doubt and worry. I realized this and I decided to put the pen down; take a step back and breathe. I was so used to being superwoman or being busy, I didn't take know how to tackle one task at a time. I gave Rylee a moment to gather herself so I could finish school. As the winter approached; December 7th came and I walked across the stage with my Masters. I felt excited to have accomplished one of the many things on my To Do list. So with school being over that would mean Rylee was back right? The answer would be no!

Somehow no matter how deep I reached, I couldn't find her. By now, I gave life to other characters in my head. After weeks of writing, four new women were born. Without blinking I had written and was prepared to release another book. I was excited though I felt there was something missing. To be honest, I wasn't completely happy about the finished project. It felt rushed. Over and over it played in my head. I was releasing a book I didn't feel was complete. Why? Was it because I was being forced to? Did I feel I would be left behind? Somewhere along the way I had created this competition in my head. I had formulated this idea I had to put something out or they would forget about me. In my mind, I was slowly fading away. Somewhere in mid-January, Rylee reappeared. She whispers to me and the story comes to life again. Five chapters had been written and then scrapped. Since I was now in a different head space, none of it made sense. I had arrived at a road block once again. February was on the horizon. My other new book was due to be released on Friday the 13th. To the world, my mask of excitement was convincing, though deep down inside uncertainty spread like a wildfire. When I look back, I should have taken the loss and canceled the release. I had always believed in presenting the best, but I was fighting an inward battle of quality versus quantity. Against my better judgment, I released my "3rd" official book on February 13th. Finally I could free those characters from my mind. Too many character voices attached to different storylines in your head could be chaotic. February was now closing out and Rylee was slowly tip toeing around again. Emotionally I was in two different places; however I decided to pour it all into Rylee. It seemed we were both in the right place at the right time. Chapter by chapter, I threw myself into her character. I gave her everything I was feeling at the time. She was allowing me to be naked, somewhat vulnerable as I told her story. Time went by and spring had crept up. Rylee was in full bloom as her secrets and scandals filled the pages. I wrote and wrote until I hit the corner of writer's block yet again. I figured backtracking would help, so I went back to reread everything I had written. I arrived at the end only to conclude something was still missing. I was at a full halt when it came to the direction of the book. There were pieces of the puzzle missing, but I had NO IDEA what it could be. So I did what any logical person would do, I asked my readers what they wanted to see happen in part two. We all need inspiration from somewhere. A spark needed to reignite your creativity. So I reached out to my girls (thanks you all by the way) and asked them for their honest opinions.

Thanks to them I had plenty of options to choose from. With all of my different scenarios, I was back to my keyboard. March had come and went. I had had parted ways with my publishing company and was now on my own. I had pulled the book I released to soon and kept pushing. April was here and it looked like I was gearing up for an early summer release. I had set a date, planned a sneak peek/book discussion only to end up canceling it due to other obligations. Most would never know I had about six different release dates set for this book, the anniversary of part one being one of them. I finally decided to pump the brakes. I remembered 3 things: I had no deadlines anymore (except mine), I was under no contract, and I was completely in control of my project. Once I removed the unnecessary pressure off myself, my writing seemed to flow. Rylee saturated the pages with her skepticism as the summer opened it arms to me. I was having fun, my craziness was in check and life couldn't be better. I was writing for a magazine, co-owned another one, and the book was getting close to finished (or so I thought). My original plan was to close this book out with 25 chapters. I knew I had a part 3 to write, so I needed to leave something the last book. I made it all the way to chapter 25 and guess what reappears? Yep, you guessed it......good ole writer's block! Yes once again I was stuck. This time I didn't panic. I simply opened my character journal (thanks Janel) and started writing the other characters in my head for another book down. After a couple of weeks had passed, this actually cleared my head. Before I knew it, I was back on Rylee. Three more chapters had been written, but no chapter 26. It was as if this chapter was fighting me. Finally after hopping out of bed one Sunday morning; chapter 26 was finished. Days passed and July was almost over. I had decided this book was officially coming to an end and needed a release date. With the ending almost done, I decided a fall release was best. August slid in and we both (me and Rylee) decided it was time. I typed my last period and closed out this stage of my life with 34 chapters. All of my accomplishments, my struggles and emotions during this past year were finally out. Now I could enjoy the moments that followed completing a book.

So in saying that, while I cannot thank everyone individually (it's virtually impossible), I do have a few folks I want to thank. To my family and friends, thank you all for the undying support you have given me. I love you all. To all of the media outlets (social media, radio, blogs, magazines, television, etc.), thank you for the platform you have allowed me to share my work on. To my partner, you are truly heaven sent. I thank God every day you inboxed me. You found me at the right time. I am so glad to be on this journey with you. To all of the readers, I want to thank you from the bottom of my heart. I appreciate the fact you have taken the time to buy, read and share my work with others. I hope you enjoy this one just as much as the last!

To him.....thank you♥!

Until we meet again.......
Shadress Denise
Be sure to check me out at www.iamshadressdenise.com
Facebook.com/iamshadressburks
Instagram/shadressdenise
Twitter/iShadressDenise

Prologue

This is my drug, my vice, my daily habit, or whatever you may want to classify it as. It is the only thing that allows me to function from day-to-day. It is my poison, which gives me extreme highs not even marijuana can achieve.

I craved pleasure.

At times I desired to be fucked, yet there is a small portion of me buried deep in my core that often seeks love and intimacy. Slow whispers make their way to the surface as Anais' words find comfort on my earlobe; the only abnormality is the inability to love.

I reach for it. It hesitates.

My body is content with this arrangement.

My soul straddles the fence.

My heart doesn't trust me at all.

It battles with lust, and at times it often loses.

Moments when orgasms cloud my judgment, I forget I was even fighting for love. I struggled with fighting for a balance between sanity and insanity. At this moment, what this man was doing to me clearly declared a victory for lust and a loss for love. He ravished me like a man who craved control. His touches resembled a wild being that wallowed in the mere presence of dominance. I loved dominant sex, though there was something different about this. It seemed foreign, like I had never experienced this side of him before.

It was uncivilized and untamed.

He was a predator who knew he had finally caught his prey.

I had a million things going on with my body at one time. The alcohol and controlled substances I partook of earlier with Asha at the Omega party were taking its toll on me. Initially, it started off with just a couple of shots, somehow it ended up being a few more shots that turned into a couple hits off a blunt. On top of the narcotics in my system, I added half an ecstasy pill.

Asha was a horrible influence on me. Usually I was the bad influence, however tonight she held the title. By the time she placed it in my hand it was already too late. The subdued state I was in now controlled my every move. I left the party only to show up at his place. It seemed the only reasoning I had was left at the door.

I didn't want to fight, nor did I want to argue.

My mind was in a different place from our problems.

I had come here to do everything other than talk. Talking was not on the menu tonight. I was missing him, and I needed something to take my mind off of our fight. Hence, the unnatural high I was currently trapped in. Regardless of what was said, I was wrong. I admitted it so I couldn't understand why we were still here. I realized I had hurt him. Another piece of my past showed up, and this time he showed up with a ring. We had just moved past the whole me lying thing, and we were right back to square one. I should have listened to Jay and told him the truth. I should've told him when the first set of flowers showed up on my doorstep.

Now we were at this point. Me begging for forgiveness with silent pleas of pleasures, while he showed me no mercy as he pulled them out of me.

I placed my hands on the shower door, and slow breaths fled my soul. I watched the steam cover up the handprints as ecstasy and sin were left behind. I gripped the bars as he entered me, greedily. Withdrawals had a way of consuming you. They never laid dormant for long. Eventually, you will have to feed them. You would somehow have to submit to the control they had over you.

He gripped my throat as I slid against the shower wall. The coolness of the glass made me flinch as the hot water ran down my face. I could hear the streaking sound my fingertips made against the glass. I wanted this in the worst way. In a way that was so illegal that it should be outlawed.

2

He looked at me, and I could see there was something different in his eyes. There was passion lingering upon the surface. Then there was a hunger, a possessiveness lying beneath all of it. At this very moment, we weren't making love, we were flat out fucking.

It was carnal. It was raw.

I was unconcealed, and unwilling to be caged.

It was unforgiving, and left no questions unanswered.

Our sex had never been this aggressive before. Traces of zealous violence gradually seeped through. Nonetheless, my sweet spot responded to each aggressive stroke he gave me. I was inhaling a new high that was destined to leave me with dangerous withdrawals. I was riding a wave that would soon carry me away. A new standard was being set. A new standard that I would be expecting every time we gave into our desires.

Smoke gray eyes were staring at me.

Water ran down his chocolate skin.

Well-defined muscles contracted as he forcibly held me up.

My airway was fighting for relief. My chest was pleading for me to slow down my breathing. My eyes were blurry as the water fell on my face. I wanted to wipe it away, but I decided it wasn't important. I used the strength I had left in my arms to hold onto him. He pulled out of me, and continued the assault on my sweet spot with his tongue. I stood under the water gasping for air as he lifted my legs and licked me until I yelled out in sweet surrender. My eyes rolled to the back of my head. I exhaled the deep moan I had been holding in. If that was the last breath I would ever release I would be fine with it.

I looked down as his head moved in and out. He was torturing what was left of my resolve. I blinked a couple of times to make sure I wasn't seeing things. I was tipsy and high as hell, though that mark had never been there before. It had been a couple of weeks since we had crossed paths. I figured maybe it was something new, and I could worry about it later.

I closed my eyes, drifting into euphoria as the orgasmic cloud I was on carried me away. There was something about this, about him that seemed twisted. Somehow I didn't care. I gripped what I knew to be my lover's head as he pulled out the demon buried within me. He took complete control of me.

Whatever happened after this no longer mattered.

My secrets were no longer a factor.

He held my need for pleasure in the palms of his hands.
I could die right now and be a happy woman.

December 30th

ecause we're afraid of what it may be we leave it alone. If only time could be reversed. If only God allowed us to do it all over again as if we hadn't gotten it wrong the first time. Funny thing about life is that you are sometimes given a second chance even if that second chance isn't as sweet as the first.

I stood over him. He was still as attractive as the day I met him. He was sexy with a little bit of gangsta to him. I thought of him being so full of life and uninhibited fun. He exhibited freedom by no other name. To me he was pleasure and everything in between. He was my Scorpio man.

In another life we would have been perfect together. In another moment in time, love may have won over our need for reckless adventure. I smiled at my name forever etched across his chest. The place where love crept in and somehow found a way to reside.

My cab was waiting outside so I placed the note on the pillow I had been laying on.

If time could be reversed, it would be me and you. It would be us against all odds and against the world.

I inhaled one more moment of him before leaving the chaos that inserted itself back into my life. I grabbed my suitcase, and then turned and walked out. He had rescued me. I'd ran to be free of the craziness last night and he saved me. I grabbed my stuff from Jayce's last night before she returned. I didn't want to face anyone about what had occurred. I needed time to think and his place was where I would be free to do so. No one would find me there. I could talk to him and get everything out without any interruptions. As soon as we got to his place, I told him everything about last night from start to finish.

I told him about the proposal from Trent, and how I was caught completely off guard by it all. He listened as I poured my heart out about what happened in front of my entire family. We lay across the floor and laughed about it all. We had always shared moments like this. These were the moments in life where the walls would be closing in on us. I would be Unable to see clearly and fighting for air. It was us against the world.

I climbed into the cab, and said, "LAX please."

I looked out the window as thoughts of him and last night traveled through my mind. A smiled touched my lips. There was something different about him. It was something I couldn't quite put my finger on. Something that would obviously remain a mystery to me.

I turned my phone back on. I knew everyone had probably blown my phone up by now. I didn't want to talk to anyone. I had no explanation for what occurred, nor did I feel the need to give one. Trent was wrong. He was dead ass wrong. I couldn't forgive his retarded ass for this stunt. Marriage! He couldn't be in the least bit serious. Text message after text message came through.

They read: *Call me. Where are you? Rylee call somebody! I just want to make sure you're ok.*

The texts came from my parents, Jay, Tae, Kira, and of course Trent.

I placed my phone on vibrate because I couldn't fathom what to say to him. Whatever I said, I knew it wouldn't be nice at all. I sent a group message to everyone letting them know that I was heading back to New Orleans. I told them I would call them when I felt like talking. In the midst of me sending the text, he called.

I really wanted to spare the cab driver from this drama. He didn't deserve to hear the vulgar things that were going to spill from my lips. I stared at the phone and decided what the hell. I figured it was better that it happened here than at the airport. I really didn't need to end up on the no fly list for clowning inside the airport. I swiped the answer option.

"What the hell do you want? I know you couldn't possibly think it was a good idea to call me after that shit you pulled last night. You have a lot of nerve. I'll give you that much."

"How could you leave me standing there last night?"

"Are you fucking kidding me?" I asked, looking up at the cab driver who was clearly being nosey at this point. "What the hell do you mean how could I leave you standing there last night? You show up to my parent's house and ask me to marry you after I told yo' ass all we could be is friends. What did you expect me to do? You better be glad my parents were there; otherwise my reaction may have been a tad bit different," I threatened.

"Typical Rylee. You were always afraid of commitment. I knew it, but I thought I could be the one to change that about you. F.Y.I., you can't run around having sex with different people forever. It's going to get old quick. I won't even comment on your new behavior since you've moved."

Afraid of commitment? New behavior? Was he serious?

"I guess you would know since you seem to be an expert in the area. Listen, don't call my damn phone telling me what I can and can't do, especially since you don't have the cleanest rap sheet yourself. Please don't let me refresh your memory about four years ago. I can easily help you if need be."

"I've apologized for what happened. It was a mistake and I was wrong. You should let it go, especially since you're no angel," he replied, sarcastically.

"What the hell are you talking about?"

"Oh, you didn't think I knew about him? Your little thug life fling. Well I did. You would be surprised at what I know about you. You need to be careful who you do your dirt with. I looked passed it and I forgave you so let's move on and stop pointing the finger at each other's indiscretions."

I didn't realize that he knew about Cree. He never said anything about it before so I dismissed it. Now, here he was acting like he did me a damn favor by not saying anything about it up until now. That was so incredibly typical of him! He would always conveniently bring shit up to make his flaws seems less fucked up. I needed to get off the phone with him. He was pissing me off all over again, but I was trying to be polite.

"Well, I won't ask how you knew seeing as that I already know. Guess we can say I've learned to keep my business to myself since others will use it for their own benefit."

"Wow, even after everything I've said that's all you heard. All you heard is that you should keep your business to yourself, and that's amazing Ry," he said, sounding as if that was not the response he was expecting.

"What the hell do you want from me? Didn't you just say watch who I do my dirt with? So what are you looking for me to say? I told you when I came home for Thanksgiving that I just wanted to be friends. Yes we had sex repeatedly, and I'll take the blame for it. Clearly I was wrong for thinking you could handle casual sex, especially since you had no problem with it when we were in a relationship."

I was over the coddling him. I've done nothing wrong and if his feelings were hurt. Oh damn well! I was glad to be leaving. I wanted to put as much distance between him and me as humanly possible.

"I want you to be with me. You're the only woman I will ever love, and want to make my wife. All those other women were there for my ego. I never cared for them. I used them to make you pay more attention to me. I admit I went too far with trying to prove a point. I realize you may never fully forgive me for it, but we need to move on."

"Humph," I said, thinking he had no clue.

He was an idiot because I don't play the jealousy game. I had no desire to be married. I didn't now or in the near future. Locking me down wouldn't make him feel any more important than it would make me feel secure and free. He couldn't understand that. He didn't understand me. I wasn't the 20 year old girl he met six years ago. The eight year difference between us was more apparent now than it had ever been. I was a woman now. I knew who and what I wanted, and it wasn't his ass. I was over him and this conversation.

"You don't love me, and it's not going to happen so just let it go already."

"I always get what I want. You know it and so do I. You also know you couldn't possibly find anyone as successful as I am and will be," he said.

There was the arrogant asshole I remembered. He wanted to rub the situation in my face. It was the only gun he had in his arsenal. The angry ex-girlfriend and the deceitful best friend he turned against each other. I was past it and had moved on. Whatever feelings I had about that night were left on his doorstep along with my belief in monogamy.

"Where did you go last night? Did you run to your rough neck? He likes putting you back together again because he could never fully have you to himself. I know your mother doesn't like him so you'll never be with him. Let's face it, I'm your best option. Quality over quantity baby, remember that."

We were done and this was over. I was having flashbacks of the last blowout we had. I didn't need to get worked up again.

"For the record, she doesn't like your ass anymore either," I said, hanging up on him.

I turned my phone off. I didn't want to talk to anyone else. He had a lot of nerve. I looked up to see the cabdriver trying to act as if he wasn't listening. I was too pissed to be embarrassed. I was glad he did what he did. He reminded me of why some doors should never be reopened. I could hear my MeMaw now saying, *Beware of revisiting your past. Leopards don't change their spots and neither do assholes.* All I could do was shake my head. She could not have been more accurate. Trent was definitely an asshole.

He had always been an asshole and always would be.

I had come to realize no amount of time or money would change him. He was who he was and it was the same for me. We weren't a good fit and it was ok. Some relationships were meant to end and others were not. We were meant to end. He played a part in me growing and I finally recognized that. Exes, lovers, friends, and anyone else you come into contact with were all a part of your growth. Whether good or bad, they served a purpose. When that purpose was fulfilled, it was time for them to move on. People often made mistakes holding onto people that they should have released. Our chapter was over and if he didn't want to close the book, I would do it for us.

I played a part in reopening it so this was somewhat my responsibility. We had a lot of baggage and most of it was not healthy baggage. I didn't like who I was with him. For reasons only known between him and me, we could never try again. Even though Cree wasn't the best option at the time, I didn't have deep-rooted scars from being with him.

"What airline ma'am?"

"Delta please,"

I was so caught up in my thoughts that I hadn't noticed we were pulling up to the airport. The car stopped and I handed him the fare I owed. He got out so he could grab my bags as I climbed out. In 2 1/2 hours, I would be home to peace and quiet. Micah had texted, but I would call him when I landed. I was exhausted, mentally, physically, and emotionally. I grabbed my bags and headed inside. These last two trips home had done a number on me. I needed to regroup. I wanted to get back to my normal self. I craved what I missed these last two weeks and that was New Orleans, Asha, Micah, and both of their mind blowing orgasms.

One

*10, 9, 8, 7, 6, 5, 4, 3, 2, 1—***Happy New Year!** I could hear the people yelling all around me as I looked into his eyes. I took what I believed to be my 4th shot of tequila. I was running, my mind was racing, and the tequila was what I considered to be a safe haven at this point. I didn't want to remember anything from this night other than my body being ravaged by Micah's tongue and dick. He was only a few feet away from me, and still my sweet spot was as wet as a city street on a rainy day. I could feel the intense throbbing occurring between my legs, and I needed to release and relieve it.

I wanted to fuck my frustrations away. I wanted my orgasms to rip through me like an F5 tornado.

There was only one thing I could do and that was to get the hell out of here. The New Year had come and everyone was drunk at this point, and therefore I didn't feel the need to be here anymore. I was glad Asha had invited me because it had actually taken my mind off of what occurred when I was home over the holidays. The look on her face when I told her what Trent had done in front of my entire family was priceless.

A proposal? A marriage proposal? What was the world coming to?

I was in shock then and only because the tequila was circulating through my body right now is what kept me from being in as much shock now. I was glad to be back in New Orleans, and I was glad to be here. I liked the fact that I was so far away from the craziness and madness that I had left behind in L.A.

"Hello sexy."

I snapped out of my drunken daydream to see a fine ass man standing next to me. I hadn't seen him around the campus before so I'm guessing he was a local. A lot of them tended to hang out at the college parties so deciphering between the two could be a bit difficult at times. Regardless of that fact, this fine specimen of a man standing next to me had my full attention.

"Hello."

"I saw you standing over here away from everyone so I figured I should come over and strike up a conversation. My name is Titus, but my friends call me Bishop"

I looked at him. He was confident, but there were also traces of arrogance seeping through him. He smiled and licked his lips as I looked into his eyes. I had to play this correctly. I could tell he was used to get his way with women. His way of handling himself screamed panty dropper so this would prove to be interesting for the both of us.

"Well hello Titus."

A smirked formed across his lips, implying I had disregarded the last part of his introduction.

"My name is Reece. It's nice to meet you."

"I've never heard anyone say my name the way you did. It sounds way sexier when you say it."

And so the game begins.

"Well since you say most people call you Bishop, I could see how that could make you feel a certain kind of way. Especially considering how you look so I'm sure you hear women say your name a lot of different ways all the time," I said, winking.

I could see how my response threw him off a little bit, seeing he didn't respond immediately.

"Well, I see that you're a feisty one."

He leaned in closer to my ear and I could feel the heat from his breath on my skin. I was trying to survey the room for Micah and I didn't see him anywhere.

"No worries because I like my woman feisty."

I don't think the lump in my throat made its way down before I saw Micah standing in front of me on the other side of the room. I smiled, acknowledging that I saw him. I saw a look in his eyes that I had never seen before. I wasn't sure if it was jealousy, but it definitely wasn't recognizable.

11

"Well that's good to know. Unfortunately, it doesn't matter much to me being that I'm not nor will I ever be your woman," I said, holding out my hand. "Titus, it was nice meeting you."

He lifted my hand to his mouth and kissed it. I smiled and eased past him, and made my way over to Micah. He smiled at me and I instantly became turned on. I was five shots in now and ready to go home. All I needed to finish up this night was to ride him until my body gave into exhaustion.

"Well, it seems you're mighty popular tonight."

I laughed, and then asked, "What do you mean?"

"If I didn't know any better I could have sworn Bishop was going to undress you where you stood."

"Oh, so you know him?"

"Yeah he's a football player at Southern."

That figures, I thought to myself. He definitely had the arrogance of one.

"Are you ready to go yet?" I asked.

"It depends. What are we going to do when we leave here?"

I chuckled. He wanted to play and I was all for it. I loved a little pre-game foreplay so let the games begin. I moved closer to him so he could hear what I was going to say to him. My thoughts alone were causing some serious throbbing between my legs.

"Well, I was thinking when we got home you could start by kissing me here, here, and here," I said as I pointed to my lips, neck, and the spot beneath my earlobe that made me straddle between right and wrong. "Then you can slowly remove my shirt exposing my breasts since I had no desire to wear a bra tonight. Once my nipples have given into the coolness of the air you can warm them with the softness of your lips, and the heat your tongue creates when it touches any part of my body." I could feel the imprint of his dick harden, and I knew we were heading for trouble. I leaned closer and whispered, "We're not finished."

I pulled back, looked into his eyes, and decided to finish the sexual taunting in the middle of a party that we had obviously mentally checked out of. I moved my hands against the imprint in his pants and smiled. I could feel his breathing increase, and I could tell he was fighting against his will power. He pinned me against the wall with all his might. I had declared a sexual war in the middle of this party, and the mind-blowing assault I knew was going to occur when we left made it all worthwhile.

"Now that you have my breasts exposed, you slide your hands up my skirt and move my   panties to the side with your hands. I take a deep breath as the hardness of your fingertips absorb the wetness my sweet spot has created. My clitoris throbs in sync with your finger as my moans mimic notes of a beautifully written cadence."

I stepped back so that I can see the look on his face. There was a light in his eyes. A light I knew somehow reflected a slow burning flame. A slow burning flame I had just ignited. I smiled mischievously because the ball was now in his court. He could either make the shot or pass the ball. He pulled me closer to him and I knew exactly what his decision was.

"You're going to regret every word you just said."

He grabbed my hand and before I knew it, we were headed out the door. *I caught a glimpse of Titus as we walked out and thought, Maybe in another life.* I hopped in the car and buckled my seatbelt. I could have fucked him right there, but I would play nice and wait until we got home. Until then I would give him some incentive to get there rather quickly.

He slid into the car and just like that we were off. I knew the exact spot I would instigate this already heated situation, and that would be on the highway. There was no need for conversation. We both knew what was about to occur, and nothing else needed to be said. The New Orleans skyline was clear and beautifully lit up with all of the building lights. The ink blue sky provided the perfect backdrop to the buttermilk moon that was positioned perfectly in the sky. Tonight would be a perfect night to sit on the balcony and just stare into the sky or maybe do some very naughty things beneath it.

He merged onto the highway and I slid my hand onto his thigh. He looked at me for a split second, begging me not to engage in this game that would make things so much worse for me. I gave no heed to his visual plea. I didn't believe in surrendering so I clearly ignored what he was trying to say. I unbuckled my seatbelt and turned my body so that I could position myself comfortably. I lifted up the armrest and lowered my body so that I was not in the way of his driving.

I unzipped his pants and slid my hand inside. I slowly massaged his hardened dick, creating an erotic friction against his briefs. I could see his chest moving up and down at a quicker pace. He had a serious look of concentration on his face. He was trying to focus on the road, and I was making it extremely difficult.

"Don't do this Ry. This won't be good for you," he said, smiling.

His trivial threats were obsolete at this point. I wanted everything thing he was going to throw my way. I needed it.

"Mmm, my lips hurt and there's only one thing that will make them feel better."

Before he could say anything else, I had his pleasure in my hand. I licked the tip for what seem like a few seconds before I could feel his hand on the back of my head. He wanted this just as bad as I wanted to give it to him. I moved my head up and down slowly as the moistness from my tongue mixed with his juices that had begun to seep out. At some point, we had sped up because I had to hold onto the seat as he drove. Within a matter of minutes, I could feel him braking even though I wasn't ready to stop. I fought his resistance and started to suck even faster. I wanted this first round, and we weren't leaving this car until I swallowed all of his willpower.

I took him in my mouth further and sucked him hungrily. I ravaged what little strength he may have been holding onto piece by piece. Through each stroke of my tongue, I could hear the seized air in his lungs escape. He was fighting to hold onto his pride and his willpower. The small moans seeping through sounded like whimpers of defeat. He wanted to hold onto a piece of himself, however, the warm liquid my tongue was savoring proved something different.

"Good God Ry. What are you doing to me?" I could hear the deep moans forming at the back of his throat. He had fought to hold onto them too. "Ohh Ry. Ohh."

He moved my head up and down as I licked faster. He gripped the back of my neck, and I could feel him jerking. The warmness that flowed down my throat satisfied me. I swallowed him and there was a lingering effect left behind. On my tongue and on my lips lied pieces of him. My mouth had absorbed him. My palates had grown to love his taste. I licked my lips to savor the remnants of him that I had saved.

He was delicious. I had conquered this round. The only round he would give me tonight.

I licked my lips in a defiant manner. I was bragging and I wanted to revel in it. I opened the door and got out. I wasn't finished teasing and taunting him. I needed to be sure he would come with some fire. I knew the only way to get fire is to strike the match. I walked around to the front of the car. I leaned forward and slowly crawled onto the hood. He was still trying to gather himself. I knew I was taking advantage of every moment. I lived to seize the moments when I could be in control. I was the starter and he was definitely the finisher.

I crawled closer to the front window and leaned forward.

I licked my lips and in the most tantalizing way mouthed, "Come fuck me."

I could see the flame that had grown in his eyes. It was no longer a small flicker of light. The flame was now a full-blown fire.

I motioned for him to come get it and climbed off of his car. As a show of good faith to the beginning of what I knew was going to be a night of sweet surrenders I lifted my skirt high enough to slowly slide my panties off. I stepped out of them, placed them in his lap, and then walked off. I looked behind me to see him smile the wicked smile I fell for when I first met him. By the time I made to the building I heard the door slam.

It was officially playtime.

I turned the key and opened the door. I heard him coming up the stairs and turned around where I stood. I smiled because I was ready for tonight. I needed to forget about what happened two days ago. The only thing I knew would make it happen was me coming over-and-over until I had nothing left to give. He walked in and slammed the door behind him.

"You left something outside," he said, holding my panties in his hand.

He tossed them to the side and walked towards me. It was all I could do not to buckle over from the sensations shooting through me. He reached out for me, and then pushed me against the wall.

"I warned you about starting something you wouldn't be able to finish. I'm going to give you one opportunity to beg for forgiveness. After that I will show you no mercy."

I laughed. It was all the indication he needed to realize there would be no begging for forgiveness. There would be no cry for help. There would only be the sweet sounds of me moaning in his ear. He smiled and I puckered my lips mimicking a kiss. I was taunting him now. I was definitely asking for it.

He ripped off my shirt and skirt in a matter of minutes.

I was standing there stark naked and as hot as a hell flame could burn. He removed every ounce of clothing he had on. He pressed against my body before I had a chance to move or Grasp what was going to happen. He kissed me ferociously as he lifted me up.

Our hearts were beating fast, and our breaths slowly fought to be free.

His hand firmly gripped around my butt as I caressed the back of his head. He freed my tongue as he sucked and nibbled on my breasts. I missed his lips. I missed his tongue. Yes, I definitely missed his tongue. He kissed me with such passion. The lust and horniness we felt for each other mixed with the alcohol. My body was slowly giving into submission. I held onto him and grinded my body against him as we headed towards the bedroom.

I kissed his neck and nibbled on his earlobe before whispering, "Me vuelves loco."

We made it to the bed, and he laid me down. If there was a time to beg it would have been now, though I had no intentions on doing so. He pulled me to the edge of the bed, kneeled before me, and then threw my legs over his shoulders. He placed kiss after kiss on the insides of my legs. Oh how the tables have turned. There was going to be no stone left unturned, and not a single spot would be neglected. I was going to feel his tongue touch my very core after this was over and done with.

"My turn," he said.

I took a deep breath and closed my eyes. One slow stroke turned into two, and then two slow strokes turned into three. In an instance his strokes matched the beat of my clitoris. I gripped the sheets and took deep breath after deep breath. My skin was becoming saturated with sweat as nectar dripped down my thigh. He had reached the point of no return, and I could no longer fight the inevitable. My body jerked, and I gave him what he wanted.

"Ahh!" I moaned in ecstasy.

I tried to push him off, but he slapped my hands away. I was trying to let my orgasm fully escape and he wasn't having it. I'd had my chance to run and now was not it. I was coming against his face and the feeling was insatiable. He pushed back and I was glad for the two seconds of relief. He flipped me over and spread my legs apart again.

He wasn't finished with his tongue assault. He wanted me to beg. I could feel his tongue slid back into my sweet spot, and I gripped the sheets as I let out another sweet moan.

"Ohh Micah," was all I could let fall from my lips.

I had come twice already, and he was pushing me towards the third. His kisses were soft and his breath was creating an uncontrollable fire upon my skin. This moment was sweet nirvana.

This man was truly heaven sent. I closed my eyes, and had flashbacks of two days ago as he was slowly tongue fucking me into oblivion. Every time I saw his face I wanted him to go faster and harder.

I figured if he could make me come over-and-over I would forget about the disaster that occurred in front of my entire family. My entire got damn family! I didn't even realize how fast I had gotten out of there. I had just grabbed my jacket and left. I was in shock and completely caught off guard. I never saw that coming, and right now I had no words.

I didn't have a yes or a no. There was no answer to the question that was beyond life changing.

I couldn't get to Jayce's house fast enough to get my stuff. I just wanted to escape the madness. I know walking out on the middle of a proposal was unheard of. Unfortunately, there was no way I could stay there. Everybody from my parents to Kira had been blowing me up since I had left. I didn't feel like talking to anyone so I sent them all a text saying I was home and that I needed time to think. I didn't want a million questions fired at me. I didn't need anyone making a decision for me. I was trying to convey this to her and mind had drifted off to another place.

"Rylee, are you here with me?"

I smiled at him. I wanted to tell him what was going on. I wanted to tell him someone had just pledged his entire life to me and I ran away. Maybe I would tell him later. I didn't want to corrupt what we had. This moment was perfect. This ecstasy high we both enjoyed inhaling was perfect. I wanted to leave the L.A. drama in L.A. and be here with him. In this moment, where sex had a hint of purity I wanted to keep the peace. Our pasts didn't matter, and as far as the both of us knew, this was a new beginning. This was our chance to start over and become different people.

Since we had been sleeping together, I had become a different woman. I was a sexual vixen. I was playing with fire, but at the same time I was liberated.

"Yes Micah, I'm here."

"Is something on your mind? What can I do to make you feel better?"

If he only knew those were loaded questions. I wanted to answer him, although I would rather show him. I rolled over and crawled to the top of the bed. I removed the pillowcases from two of the pillows and handed them to him. I wanted to be free of control. I wanted to submit to him and clear my mind. I wanted to escape my reality.

"I want you to tie me up and fuck me."

He looked at me and smiled. I knew I was asking for trouble and I welcomed it. I had a dark side, and he somehow ignited the fire buried within me. He was the right kind of bad. He was the bad I needed right now.

He took the pillowcases from me, and I lay back down on the bed. He took one arm at time and tied it to the headboard. He slapped me on my ass, and it was all I could do to silence my scream. He slid his finger inside me and I slightly jerked. My sweet spot was raw and sensitive to his touch. It was sensitive due to the multiple orgasms it had released. I had cum over-and-over tonight. The slightest touch easily sent sensations throughout my body.

"I see she's still wet."

I looked over my shoulder to give him a seductive look. He positioned himself on his knees, and in one swift move he slid back inside of me. I dipped my back in utter pleasure as each stroke pulled me closer to the edge. I buried my face in the sheets and moaned over-and-over again.

"Micah!"

"Scream my name baby."

"Ohh, ohh, ohh, this feels so good."

He was hitting every single spot I had and even some I hadn't discovered. He leaned in closer as he stroked me with a perfect rhythm. I could feel his lips on my back as the sweat rolled down my sides.

"We were meant to be Ry."

I turned around to look into his face. I had thought I misheard him, though every passionate stroke he made reminded me I hadn't. There was something undeniably erotic about him as I looked into his smoke gray eyes. It was as if something was hidden behind them that I hadn't seen before. There was something I recognized at the party earlier, but I refused to acknowledge it. We had moments of passion, and then we had moments of lust. Somehow, I felt the looks of lust weren't what had protruded from the look he was giving me.

I don't know how it arrived. It was now knocking on the door. It was somehow creeping in. It was love. I wanted to ignore it because it would mean I had to change. I wasn't sure I wanted to change. I wasn't sure I wanted to admit it to myself. I was losing control and I didn't like it.

I loved my freedom. I loved this life.

He kissed me softly and my thoughts faded away slowly. There was so much turmoil within my 5'6" frame. My body was enjoying the new life it was beginning to explore. The constant orgasms, which left me breathless, speechless, and without cause for movement were undeniable. I thought about him, and then I thought about her. I thought about his sweet lips, and then her soft touches. I needed the hard and I needed the soft. It was my perfect balance. They were the key to my sanity.

There was Micah, and then there was Asha. *How could I choose?*

The sound of our sweet moans smothered the echo that was going on throughout my head. I searched for an answer for him and I had nothing.

We were meant to be, is what played back. I wanted to tell him he was right. I wanted him to know my body craved him. My soul yearned for him in the worst way. It was as if she wouldn't let me say it. We were embarking on something new and changing the course of our destination was not an option. We were kindred spirits.

From the moment I met Asha in the laundry room I felt like she was seeing my life through a crystal ball. We had so many of the same occurrences that any of them could have been taken from my journal. My private thoughts were being shared with the world. My heart was beginning to betray me. It wanted no parts of this life I was creating. My body had painted this picture. It had created this mirage of ecstasy.

His warm breath on my skin reminded me I was in the center of nirvana. I wanted to run my hands across the top of his head. My heartbeat was fast but steady. My body wanted to take in this moment as if it were my last, as if there would be no more moments like this. He pulled out and pushed his tongue back into my sweet spot.

I began to grind hard against his tongue. I wanted him to taste my soul on his lips. I wanted him to swallow this fate that he seemed to be enthralled with. I needed the remnants of the corruption buried at the core to escape with the orgasm he was so desperately pulling out of me.

I wanted the best of both worlds. I wanted the freedom and love, ecstasy and passion with whomever I pleased. I wanted the ultimate form of liberation. I wanted the total absence of rules.

I closed my eyes and I could see her. It was Anais. She held out her hand to me. I knew she understood me. She could see this inward battle I was fighting. She could see how it was never meant to be inflicted on anyone. She could see the constant struggle with having the kind of love I knew did not believe in being contained. I knew initially he would allow me to fly. He would allow me to be as free as a bird in the sky, and then he would change. They always changed.

In the beginning, your sense of freedom is what draws them to you. They flock to the fact you have no desire to be clingy. It's almost as if it's an aphrodisiac. For a while everyone rides the initial high, and then like any drug you find yourself once again facing reality. The reality would be that they had partaken in the forbidden fruit. The scary part is the same aphrodisiac which drew them in could draw others in too. It was a game of control and conquer. I was in the center of it, yet I wasn't ready to be conquered. There were too many players in this game. There were too many factors that could alter the outcome.

There was Trent, Cree, and Micah. The only real question was who would be left holding the cards. *Who would fold and who would win it all? Would the winner be me and my heart?*

I had no real desire to be with Trent. Cree had captured my interest again. I don't know why, even though seeing him again had somehow provoked something inside of me. I could never forget how sexy he was. Just being within 2 feet of him certainly had an effect on me. It reminded me of all the bad we had fun doing. No matter how hard I tried, a girl could never forget her first bad boy.

Then there was Micah. He was my good and evil that was buried between my legs and making his way to the core of my soul. God this man had the most gifted tongue. It's almost as if it should be two of them just so he could let one rest and finish me off with the other one. I get lost with each stroke. I could get lost in the intensity it created upon my clitoris. The aftershocks it caused beneath the surface.

I hear Anais's words in my head.

She would whisper, "Only the united beat of sex and heart together can create ecstasy."

I could never give this up. This was a drug and a never ending high.

There were nights of endless pleasures that turned into mornings of exhaustion and satisfaction. I had opened the door. A door I knew should have never been opened. I had partaken from the tree of good and evil. I had tasted the ultimate sin. It was raw and pure. It was intoxicating and overpowering as it flowed through my veins. Everything was different and going back was not something I could easily give into. Monogamy was not an option. I had seen the other side of eroticism.

The other side was dark and it was twisted. It was also beautiful.

Our orgasms ripped through our bodies like a self-destructive tornado. My silent screams were trapped in my throat. My body poured out the very serum he needed. It was his motivation. The confirmation represented a piece of me that belonged to him. Regardless if I ever admitted or not.

He was my pusher, and I was his junkie.

We were both controlled by climatic eruptions that penetrated our souls. The after effects caused our sweet nectar to flow freely, while we inhaled the sexual air that surrounded us.

He untied me and we buried ourselves in the sheets. I could feel the tides changing. I knew feelings were now a factor. I could try to ignore them. Nevertheless they were staring at me like a reflection. I took a few deep breaths, and tried to regulate my heartbeat. I was trying to regain my senses. I gathered my thoughts so I could think clearly. I turned to look him in his eyes. The look was still there.

Shielded behind lust, it had fought its way to the forefront. I could run, even though it wouldn't serve me or this situation any good. I had already escaped one tragic scene of feelings, and I didn't have the energy to dodge another one right now. I buried my head in the pillow, and then looked at him. He smiled, and then I smiled.

I closed my eyes.

The realities I would need to face tomorrow would have to wait. All I wanted to do was submerge myself in the orgasmic high my body was floating on and drift away.

2 | Two

I had a love/hate relationship with moments like this. The ceiling fan turned silently as it cooled the dampness smothering our skin. The after effects of sex floated in the air leaving just a hint of space for intimacy to creep in. I wasn't opposed to brief moments like this, but somehow what I was feeling seemed to be something different. He was trying to make this more permanent. I could hear the possessiveness in his voice. I could see the tenacity in his eyes.

This was no longer just about sex. His feelings had become involved. He had changed the nature of the game. I could either continue playing or walk away. I wasn't completely sure of my feelings, however, I knew that a relationship was something I wasn't entirely ready to explore. I missed having moments of companionship, and someone to share personal highs and lows with. My heart felt it needed it, but I couldn't trust monogamy again. I could not subject myself to the control it required, and the illusions you had to believe in. It had only been a couple of days since I dodged a proposal. Whether I admitted it out loud or not, I was still recovering from it. Cree made me feel better about the whole thing, which only reignited some suppressed feelings I had towards him. The sex Micah and I just had was spectacular. I could see he was curious as to why I was so aggressive and somewhat outside of myself.

The sex we had was so passionate, and so full of lust infused rage.

22

I wanted to forget about the proposal and everything that came with it. As much as I wanted to I couldn't tell him what happened. There was no need to involve anyone else in this craziness. I ended up telling him some drama kicked off at home and I needed to get away. Technically I didn't lie.

I had so much going on in my head, and there were so many spirits surrounding me. They had buried themselves in me. There were hearts that I held in the palm of my hand. Orgasmic hungers I continuously fed into. I often wondered if we were truly meant to be monogamous. *Why are we attracted to so many different people? How is it possible to be so madly in love with one person, and then crave another person with such intense passion?*

Most would say it's about self-control. I would say it's an unnatural feeling you are forcing upon yourself for the sake of pleasing someone else or society. I believe there were people who yearned to only be with one person. They were perfectly happy having one person to love, whereas, there were other people who were honestly incapable of being *faithful* no matter how much they loved someone. Those were the people forcing themselves to be something they were not. I was that person at one point, and after realizing it I decided not to be that person anymore.

My sexual journey was my own. I had nothing to prove and no one to prove it too. I had grown tired of who society felt I should be. I had sexual cravings and I had become their sexual fulfillment. I was the means to an end at one point, and now the tides were changing. Now everyone had formed a habit they were not willing to be freed of. Old loves and new crushes had begun seeping through the cracks.

Micah, Trent, and Cree were all factors in this cycle of sexual lust.

Cree had come back with a vengeance, and there was no fighting him off. I had always admired his tenacity. I admired his desire to go after what he wanted regardless of how high the deck was stacked against him. He was my Scorpio man, who was sexy and on a mission. He did not care what the obstacles were, if there was a mission he was determined complete it.

I was his mission and regardless of the distance, I knew he would find a way to make it work. When I returned to NOLA, he was amongst the many phone calls that were made and wanting to talk to me. I wanted to talk to him. I just couldn't find the right words. What we did that night had brought back so many memories. I wasn't sure if I was ready to talk about them. A month ago I ran into him at the airport, and then everything changed. Things changed from the way I felt about him to the way I had felt about Micah.

I had always loved Cree, but I never realized it until I saw him again. Running into old flames had a way of doing that to you, especially when you find out what their true feelings are about you. Hearing him say I was the one who got away had done something to me. His words fueled my arrogance. They made me revisit everything in our pasts still nestled between us. Everything from the sex to all of the mischievous fun we had. I realized I had fallen for him. I had so much other stuff going on with Trent that I didn't have time to evaluate and confront those feelings. The moment I was prepared to tell him my world came crashing down. To make matters worse with him being in the streets there weren't many options for us at the time. I couldn't get caught up in the streets. My momma wasn't having it and we both knew it, however there were still questions I had been curious about. *Did we have a future? Could we move beyond our past?*

I wasn't ready for what he seemed to be ready for. I lived in New Orleans, while he lived in L.A. I struggled with monogamy far too much to commit to something long distance. Not to mention that I had started something here. I looked over at Micah and saw how he's ready for the very thing Cree and Trent are ready for.

How did we get here? What changed with him when we were a part over the holidays?

I would admit so much had changed with me. I was curious as to what happened with him.

"Rylee what's wrong?"

"Nothing. What makes you think something is wrong?"

"You seem like you're here and somewhere else at the same time. Actually, you've seemed that way since you got back from L.A. I've been trying to figure out what happened and I've got nothing."

I took a few soft breaths. I knew this was eventually going to rise to the surface. I wouldn't be able to hide the worry and frustration of everything. He would never in a million years guess what happened. Hell no one would guess what happened. Aside from my family, the only other person who knew what happened was Asha. Initially, I was a bit hesitant when I told her. I knew she wouldn't say anything and would offer some solid advice. Once she had gotten over the initial shock of it all she laughed until tears ran down her face.

I have to love my friends. I turned and looked at him. I didn't want to lie to him. I hadn't sorted through my emotions enough to tell him the truth. I hadn't answered all of the many questions in my own head.

"It was just some crazy family stuff. It's no big deal."

"Actually, it seems to be a big deal. You're in and out of conversations, and although the sex is still immaculate, you're checked out at times. If you don't want to talk about it that's fine, but telling me it's no big deal is definitely a no go."

Just as I was going to answer him, his phone rang. I glanced at the screen and saw her name, Arrington.

Why the hell was she calling him?

Everyone knew who Arrington was and what her games were all about. She loved athletes and she was dead set on being the wife of one so she was always on the prowl. The last I had heard she had dated Mario and a few other football players. She had no preference as long as it would land her in a skybox and a Mercedes-Benz in the future. I looked at him because I wanted to see if he was going to answer. He had no reason not to seeing we were just friends. For whatever reason guys were weird like that. They had the tendency to act suspicious when there was no real reason to feel that way.

He decided not to answer, and sent the call to voicemail.

"You could've answered," I said, sarcastically.

"Why would I answer her call?"

"What do you mean why would you answer her call? Isn't that what you do when your phone rings?"

I was picking a fight and I knew it. *Why?* I had no claim over him or him over me. I knew part of the reason was the fact it was her that was calling. Being a small forward and shooting guard for Xavier meant women were after him all the time, still something about her bothered me. She was always on a mission and didn't care who her next *victim* would be.

"Rylee I know what you're doing so stop trying to start a fight. I have no desire to talk to her. I'm laying here next to you so why would I answer another woman's phone call?"

I had no response. I didn't even know why I had bothered to mention it in the first place seeing we were not even in a relationship. I had a handful of men I was juggling as we speak, not to mention Asha. I was trying to change the subject and something told me he knew it.

"Are you going to answer my question?"

I looked at him. Those eyes, combined with his hypnotic smile, reflected genuine interests of concern. Both were searching for answers to questions that I hadn't even answered for myself. Part of me was saying tell him the truth. I thought I should tell him what happened and regardless of what happens, this was good while it lasted. Then there was another side that was saying shut up. Part of me was saying to just keep my mouth closed. Don't rock the boat and don't create problems where there was no need for them.

"What question was that Micah?"

He laughed, and then asked, "Really?"

"How about I make it easier for you Rylee? Maybe you don't feel comfortable telling me family stuff because I haven't done my part as a man."

I gave him a puzzled look because I was in no mood for another proposal. I didn't need any more surprise confessions, declarations of love, or anything that resembled my freedom walking away.

"I've thought about this a lot while we were separated over the holidays. We've been hanging out and sleeping with each other for the past five months. At first I was okay with this because I wasn't sure if I wanted to be with you. After this last break I realized I did want to be with you."

Once again, I was speechless.

"I'm ready for us to be in a relationship Ry. I'm ready to start building something beyond this friendship and sexual relationship that we have. I want us to be exclusive so my question to you is will you be my girl, my lady?"

"Are you asking me this because you feel I'm really upset about Arrington?"

"No 'cause I have no interest in her. I'm asking you this because I have felt this way for the past two months and I've been trying to find a way to ask you. I really like you."

I knew this was coming.

The inevitable, my reality, the decision I had not come to grips with yet. It was the question I wasn't ready to answer. I smiled and shook my head because it was now or never. I could either tell him what happened when I went home or I could not. I could tell him about the marriage proposal. It was the unanswered question I ran away from and into the arms of another to forget. I never said yes or no, which was why he and everyone else were calling me. I don't know why I didn't answer him. I think the shock of it all, and the fact that I was embarrassed, played a huge role in it all.

I should say no. I needed to say no, but somehow I couldn't get the words out.

Do I say yes Micah? There was a part of me that wanted Micah, and then there was a part of me that knew I wasn't entirely ready to give up everyone else. I knew starting this off like this would eventually put me in the hot seat. I could start fresh here. It was just the two of us. I had left everyone else in L.A. He and I were here in

New Orleans now. My sole purpose in coming here was to start over and do things my way. Yes, I had a whole bucket of issues I still needed to fix. I could and would handle them when I got ready. This moment right here was all that mattered. Trent, Asha, and Cree would be something I dealt with as they came up. I wanted this man and everything that came with him.

I smiled and leaned in to kiss him softly on his lips, and then I told him yes. He wrapped his arms around me, and I laid my head on his chest. I listened to his heartbeat and I exhaled all of my worries. It was a chance for me to see what he had to offer. It was a chance to move everything to the back of my mind. I could bury my secrets and shed my old skin.

He was my new beginning. He was my new start.

I only prayed it wouldn't be one I regretted.

3 | Three

ave you told him what happened?"

"No I haven't. I didn't see any point in saying anything about what happened at home. I came here to start over so that's what I'm going to do."

I could hear her breathing on the other end. I knew she was searching for something to say. Tae wasn't usually the one on the moral kick since at times it was Jayce's role. I called it the older sister syndrome. Even though at times when I wasn't looking, she had the tendency to switch roles with her. I was hoping she didn't go too far to the left with this conversation. I was in no mood to argue or defend any decision I had made. I came to grips with my decision and everyone's comments were simply comments.

"Ok Lee, I'm not going to come down on you about not saying anything to him. I just want you know it's going to eventually come out so it's probably best you say something on the front end instead of the back. This way it doesn't look like you jumped into this because you were running from something else. "

She had a point and I knew it. To be honest, I decided to be with him because I liked him. It had nothing to do with me running from the issues back in L.A.

"So you think I jumped into this because I'm running from Trent?"

"I didn't say that, though it's pretty clear you're running from something. I know you, and considering everything that occurred with

Trent in the past, a relationship is not something you really want. Trust me I've been there, and I know firsthand that it doesn't work. You're just adding more fuel to a slow burning fire. The only outcome to this is someone will eventually end up hurt."

Yep, she had definitely switched spots with Jayce.

When I think about it, I wasn't running from him. I just didn't want to be with him. He did exactly what he felt he had to do, which triggered the response I gave. I yelled and he screamed then we carried on for about an hour with all of that. I eventually grew tired and hung up the phone. His behavior was unacceptable, and his proposal was unforgivable. It was as simple as that.

"I hear you Tae, and when the time is right I will tell him."

She laughed, and then said, "Well, hopefully it won't be because Trent showed up at your door again. I'm not trying to be funny, but something tells me he's not going to walk away from this just yet. When you left, he looked as puzzled and bewildered as the rest of us. Yet there was still this look of intensity in his eyes. He's determined to right his wrong."

Leave it up to Tae and her psychic abilities. She was always predicting something and   sometimes she hit the nail on the head. Unfortunately, this time she was wrong. He wasn't coming back for more, and I was pretty confident about it. I was brutal when we talked, and I gave him the tongue lashing of his life so we were done.

"Well thank you Ms. Cleo. I've got it handled."

"Yeah I remember you saying that very thing after Thanksgiving, and look where that got you," she said, laughing.

I couldn't stand when she did that little I told you so laugh. She knew she was right from the beginning, and there would be more she's right around the corner. I couldn't fathom how she seemed to know him better than me at times and he was my damn ex!

"For your information, I talked to Trent the next day."

"Oh really! How did it go? I can pretty much guess for myself how it went."

I didn't really want to tell her how belligerent he had gotten. I also didn't want to admit the fact that he knew about Cree the whole time we were together. I definitely wouldn't be telling her he told me I was going to be his wife one way or another.

"Let's just say it wasn't a very pleasant conversation and leave it there."

"Pleasant huh? Ok that only means he said something to verify what I just told you. Be careful Ry. He's not going to take this laying down, and I know you know it. You don't have to admit it to me, however just be honest with yourself. He likes control and he's determined to control you," she said, laughing.

She was enjoying this way too much, and all I could do was shake my head.

"Gee thank you Tae. You're so uplifting in my time of need."

"Time of need? Are you kidding me! You manage to get a proposal and a whole new man in less than two weeks, who by the way didn't propose to you. Excuse me if I don't see any sense of need in this picture."

We both laughed at the same time.

"Ok so there is something I do want to know. You didn't stay at Jay's that night because I came back to her place to look for you with her so where did you go?"

I knew this was coming. I couldn't get anything past her. This is probably the real reason she called with her nosey ass. She didn't give two shits about Trent or that tragedy of a proposal. She didn't like him anyway so she was secretly glad I embarrassed him. All she wanted to know was where or who I ran to that night. I wasn't sure I wanted to tell her. To be honest I was surprised she hadn't guessed.

"I stayed with a friend."

"What friend 'cause Kira was at the house? You ain't got that many friends that you would spend the night with."

"If I wanted to tell you who I stayed with I wouldn't have said it was just a friend."

"Oh, so we're keeping secrets now?"

She seriously felt like she was entitled to all my business. Cree had been a complete gentleman, even though I was beyond tempted. I had fought it as hard as I could until I eventually gave in. I don't know if I could ever remember his head game being so spectacular. He had definitely had some upgrades since we last saw each other. I had told him what had happened, and he could sense I needed to relax. He wanted to go further, even though I didn't. I just wanted him to lick me into a peaceful sleep. I had a flight the next morning so I just wanted to get some rest before I went home.

"Me not telling you my business is not me keeping a secret. I just don't want to tell you," I said, laughing.

Right before she opened her mouth my line clicked, and I could see it was Cree calling. I had been avoiding him as well. We hadn't spoken since I left him sleeping in his bed. I know he wanted to check on me, and to talk about that night. I really didn't have much to say. I was in a state of shock, and a little bit vulnerable. I let my feelings for him, and a sense of bad judgment get the best of me.

"Hold on, Tae." I clicked over, and said, "Hello, Cree."

"Damn girl, were you ever going to call me back? I know you saw me calling you. Did you just use me to make you feel better, and then disappear? It's a cold game out here," he said, cracking up.

"I did, and I was going to call you back. I was just trying to get my head straight."

"It's cool. I was calling to check on you, and to let you know I was coming to New Orleans in a few weeks. I wanted to know if I could crash at your place?"

Oh shit, I thought to myself.

"Can I think about it and get back to you? When are you coming?"

"I'll be there around Mardi Gras so mid to late February."

How ironic that he would be here before my birthday. I wasn't sure if this was a good idea seeing that I had just agreed to be in a relationship with Micah. Not to mention, I was still sorting through my feelings for him. Although I had moved on, running into him in the airport, and then spending that night at his house had changed things a bit.

"Ok, I'm on the other end with Tae so I'll call you back. I will think about it and let you know."

"Cool. I'll grab my ticket, and if I don't hear from you I'll just book a hotel. Bye Ry."

"Later Cree." I clicked back over only to hear Tae screaming hello in the phone. She was forever the drama queen. "Really Tae? Is all the yelling necessary?"

"Yeah, heffa, it is. Who were you on the other end with that you had me on hold this damn long?"

"Nobody important."

"You're a lie and not a good one I might add. You wouldn't have even clicked over unless it was someone of relevance. You keep forgetting I know your ass Lee."

I didn't feel like going into this with her right now. I didn't want to tell him no. I needed to figure out how I was going to tell Micah he was going to stay here. The sane part of me knew I should tell him to get a hotel room, while on the other hand, I knew if I ever visited him somewhere he would let me crash with him.

"Tae, I'll call you later. I need to get ready for class, and you will be all day in your detective mode."

"Yeah ok. We'll talk later, and don't think I'll forget about you not answering me."

I laughed, and then said, "Oh, I know you won't with your nosey ass."

"Whatever. Oh, I forgot to tell you Jay and I are thinking about coming down for Mardi Gras."

There was a brief moment of silence because I had no words. I was already trying to figure out how I was going to accommodate Cree. Now to have him and my sisters here was never going to work. I wasn't worried about them busting me out. I needed to tell Cree I was in a relationship, and I needed to tell Micah he was staying here. I was trying to walk the straight and narrow path this time around.

I wanted to do things the right way. I had this love/hate relationship with commitment so this was a chance to hit the reset button.

"So was that a yes or a no?"

I snapped out of my daydream.

"I don't have a problem with y'all coming. It may be a little crowded here though. I only have two bedrooms."

"Well, who else is coming because that should be enough room for me and Jay?"

I was struggling with telling her. I figured what the hell since she would eventually find out. I would just throw her and Jay in the story when I told him Cree was coming. That way it would look like they would all be here together.

So much for the straight and narrow path, I thought to myself as I opened my mouth to tell her who would be staying here. I knew I was going to regret it the minute it came out of my mouth.

"Cree just told me he was coming, and asked if he could crash here."

"I knew it! I knew it! I knew something was up."

The next thing I heard was her laughing hysterically. I needed to end this call and get to class since I had enrolled at Xavier University and this was my most dreaded class. The rumor surrounding this professor was nothing short of a scene in Horrible Bosses. He was a stickler for time and borderline rude at times. Even though I was less than 15 minutes away I didn't want to chance being late. I had managed to walk out of the house and to the parking garage while talking to her about Cree. I knew if I didn't get off now we would be on the phone for another hour and then some.

"Cree huh? Well since you have class I will let you go. Oh believe me, we will be finishing this conversation hot ass! I'll let Jay know you're cool with us staying with you, and that Cree will be joining us," she said as she continued to laugh.

"Whatever. Goodbye Taylor."

"Oh its Taylor huh? Goodbye Lee, and I still love you."

I hung up on her and backed out of my parking spot. I should have just skipped seeing I would at no point be able to focus on what was being said. I decided once I walked into my class I would be hiding in the back of the auditorium. My first point of business was to send a text to Asha to see if we could talk later on. I needed to clear my head and figure out my next move.

I knew two things though. First, I needed to be upfront with Micah. Secondly, I needed to tell Cree it was ok for him to stay with me.

4 | Four

I *went up and down massaging her lips with my sweet spot.*

There was a feverish feeling that took over my body, and I felt like I was going to explode from within. Her hands guided my hips as I gyrated slowly to the rhythm her tongue had created against the insides of my walls. I was overcome with desire. All I could do was breathe in the aura the sex had somehow manipulated the air with.

The entire class was a blur, and I had specifically come here to talk. My sole purpose was to clear my head. How I ended up on top of her mouth was beyond me.

All I could think about was Asha, her tongue, and her skill in using it. It was a masterpiece that her tongue painted upon the canvas known as my sweet spot.

I was living a double life, and I didn't see a way out. I couldn't tell if I had succumbed to lust or if at some point I had fallen for them. I had tried to walk away, though somehow the intoxicating way they fucked me continued to draw me in. I exhaled the scream of ecstasy that I had trapped within my lungs, and tried to grasp what was left of my sanity. I needed a way out and I thought time would be it. I had bit into the forbidden fruit. I had seen what was on the other side of the rainbow, and there was no turning back. I couldn't choose him over her or her over him. I needed something or someone to assist me in making a

34

decision, this decision. However, I knew involving anyone else in this madness was out of the question.

I just wasn't fallible.

She smacked my ass as I held onto the headboard. I loved our freaky moments. These were uninhibited times that we shared behind closed doors. Wicked games that amounted to rounds of pleasure. I loved not being bound by rules. An outcast to those who conformed. Riding her face gave me a sense of freedom. It was a sense of liberation in its purest form.

It was like cocaine. It was me. I knew this was wrong. Somehow, it was the right kind of wrong if there was any such thing. I was being selfish and I knew it. I figured as long as no one knew the truth, no one would get hurt. Every time I came close to telling him or her an orgasm would peak, and honesty would be a distant memory as I released what I knew was my truth.

What I felt was holding me hostage.

I had come over here to talk. At some point, I ended up in this compromising position. She was caressing me passionately, seductively, and softly, which meant her high had kicked in and she was feeling frisky. She was taunting me as she licked me to ecstasy. Her fingertips created this magnetic response from within me and I could feel my body heating up.

My sweet spot was throbbing. My intent was to tell her about Micah and me, along with explaining my Cree situation. Her tongue however was disrupting my train of thought. I couldn't fathom telling her I was now in a relationship with her brother.

How would that end with us? Could we still be friends? Could we still be lovers? Or would it be every time I was near her that I would dream about those lips and her tongue, and the unexplainable amount of pleasure they both gave me.

"Ohh Asha."

I had been fighting that moan. My screams of desire indicated to her that I was close to the edge. I wanted to end this my way.

I lifted myself off of her mouth and turned around. I buried my tongue in the place that her secrets could be freed. She jumped, and then surrendered to the feeling we both had come to enjoy these past few months. She released her moans as she placed her hands on my head. The taste of her was all over my tongue. I fought back the urge to lower myself back onto her mouth. I wanted her to feel what she had been doing to me for the past fifteen minutes. She gripped my ass as she gave out a soft moan. I loved her moans. I loved the way every murmur seemed to be wrapped up in ecstasy. Pieces of her released in moments like this. Her sound was an erotic cadence that gently fell on my ears. It started off soft, and then it grew into a beautiful melody.

It motivated me as it stroked my ego. It gave me the strength that I needed to bring her to the depths of this sexual wave we both enjoyed riding. She pulled me back down on her mouth, and I squeezed her thigh when I felt her tongue caress the tip of my clitoris. It was tender, however it still had something to give. Her fingertips continued to create memories upon my skin as the vibrations from her tongue controlled the way I devoured her.

I was riding her at a steady and constant pace. I was licking her with a ferocious speed. She was almost there, and I was also close to my edge. I loved these moments with her. There were no complications and no sense of requirement. I could be myself with her. I was free.

I was a prisoner to this uncivilized pleasure, and a fiend when it came to the titillating way she drew me to the brink of insanity. I bounced softly on her tongue, and then it happened. She squeezed my ass as hard as she could and I could taste her on my tongue.

The sweetness of that taste constantly drew me back in.

I was going to put some distance between us sexually since my relationship with Micah had changed, and then realized I couldn't. I needed this. I craved an escape, and she was my mine. Things were different now with Micah so this allowed me to drift into an abyss of desire where there were no rules or limitations.

She was my secret, and I was hers.

I found my way back as the pulsations began to increase. The sensations shot through my body, and my orgasm gradually took custody of my senses. I sat up on her face and arched my back as I jerked my body back and forth on her tongue until I had nothing left to give.

I was completely satisfied.

I eased off of her. I moved to roll over facing her on the opposite end the bed. I needed to talk to her, yet I needed to regulate my heartbeat first. My breathing was quick and matched the tempo in my chest. I felt like a weight had been lifted off of me.

"You ok, Ry?"

I still couldn't breathe.

"Yeah."

"You sure? You seem a little tense. Almost like you have some stuff on your mind."

I did have stuff on my mind. *Was it that obvious?* It was Micah, Trent's proposal, and also Cree's visit. Then there was she and I.

There were so many people and so many variables. I couldn't decide which way to go. I couldn't decide which way was right or if there is such a thing. I had made a commitment to her brother and here I was with her. I agreed to monogamy when I didn't believe in it. I knew I wasn't capable of complying with its boundaries.

"Cree wants to come down for Mardi Gras and he wants to stay with me," I said, and then paused.

She looked puzzled.

I knew she that she was trying to figure out why it would be a problem or why it would be stressing me out. I was trying to prepare myself for the next question I knew she was going to ask. I wasn't sure how she was going to react. Either way I at least got my one for the road just in case she hit the roof.

She moved down to where I was on the bed.

"Why would that be what's worrying you?"

I looked at her. Just as I was going to open my mouth and tell her about me and her brother she stopped me.

"Ry, if you think it's going to make me feel a certain way because we have a sexual relationship, it won't. I know you have friends outside of me so we're good."

Friends was definitely a funny way of putting it. Micah and I were no longer just friends, and Cree was a whole other story. I knew his intentions far exceeded what we would say friends were. I knew I didn't need her permission. It was nice to see she wouldn't be going nuts if he were to stay at my house. When it came to her brother, I'm sure her response would be a little different. Telling her was going to be what it was.

Whenever that time came, but today wasn't going to be it.

I took a deep breath.

"I know and it's other things. We have a past, and it wasn't necessarily settled completely. I just pushed him away abruptly. We never really ended things. We just went our separate ways. Since I've come back I have some unresolved feelings. Not to mention, someone has asked me to be in a relationship."

"Well if you say yes to the other person then be ok with the yes. If something happens with Cree when he comes then it happens. You said he had given up that lifestyle so maybe you should give him a fair chance this time around. Hold off on the other person until you explore you and him."

She was so off base she didn't even know it.

"I guess. I'll have to think about it."

I needed to change the subject. I came over here to discuss my relationship with Micah, not my relationship with Cree. I didn't want thoughts of him running through my head. Giving those thoughts a place to sit and fester would not be good for any of us, especially Micah.

"So how's everything been with Micah?"

I was fishing for information. I needed to find a way to come full circle with my intentions. I was being strategic with my approach. I was in no way prepared for her to say we could no longer enjoy the pleasures we brought to each other. It was selfish, yet I didn't care. He was my hard and she was my soft. I needed them both to complete my circle.

It was my crazy sense of balance.

"He's fine, I guess. It's basketball season, and then you know the Greek festivities are about to start up so I'm sure he's in groupie heaven."

"Groupie heaven?"

I needed some clarification on that term.

"Girl yeah, groupie heaven. Every year the season rolls around he gets a brand new set of women who are trying to throw themselves at the players, including him. I think it's funny. These chicks know they aren't going to get anything but some hurt feelings behind it because none of them are trying to have anything serious and they still run after them."

She shook her head. I thought about what she had just said.

I knew she and brother were really close to each other. I figured they had to have times they shared information. She didn't seem to have a clue about us so maybe they really did keep their personal lives to themselves. I remembered her saying she didn't really discuss her sexual relationships with women after the scandal happened back home. Since we had just made everything official I shouldn't be shocked at the fact that she didn't know about my relationship with Micah. I was just concerned about her previous statement. I had never really dated athletes so it never dawned on me to even think about groupies. I had dated a doctor and a drug dealer, but no athletes. My sisters and friends did, still whatever they did may have been overlooked since they were always on their own missions. Not to mention, he and I were just sleeping together so whom he dated was of no concern of mine.

At least not until now.

"So you're saying your brother doesn't involve himself in serious relationships?"

"No he does. I just know he plays the field too. He had a serious girlfriend back home for a few years, and then they ended up breaking up."

"What happened?"

I was being nosey, and I knew it would be something juicy. There was always some interesting story behind Asha and her family. From her siblings to her extended family, I could always count on a good dose of drama. I had my share of family drama and stories so it was a relief to hear that somebody else out in the world had some nut jobs in their family too.

"He found out she slept with another family member of ours whom I will not name. Let's just say it was just the drama I needed to get the attention off me and my public scandal."

"So is that the real reason he came down here with you?"

I remembered her telling me he had decided to move down here with her to get a fresh start. Somewhere in there he also mentioned it was to be with her so she wouldn't be by herself. I somehow figured there was more to the story. Asha was extremely independent, and there was nothing that indicated she couldn't take care of herself.

"Yep, you could say it played a part in his decision. He wanted to get away from my parents as well. Seeing that everyone in that town knew who they were and what they did. We couldn't have too much naughty fun without running the risk of being exposed and it coming back to them. Everything makes the news in Washington D.C. The tabloids are always looking for the latest scandal to report on."

"So how did he find out about his ex?"

"She confessed. Apparently, this had been going on for about a year."

"A year!" I shouted.

"Girl yeah. She swore it was an accident, and that she had tried to tell him for the longest time. I wasn't trying to hear any of it. You don't accidentally sleep with someone for a damn year."

I was confused. How was it a*n accident? I asked myself as* I laughed.

I don't know how she managed to pull that off for a year or even why she would want to. Micah was in no way lacking in the sex area. He was gentle and hard at the same time. He made me want to do things with him that I had never done before. He was literally a drug. I would be exhausted and outside of myself every time. However, I still would come back for more. I couldn't fathom what she encountered. Whoever or whatever it was I needed to be sure to steer clear of him at family dinners. Well, if we got to that point.

"Wow that's some accident. If I ever come visit you, make sure you point him out. I don't need any part of that dick. It sounds dangerous and addictive," I yelled.

We both laughed.

"Oh he is. He's worse than Micah. I thought how women threw themselves at him was crazy. Baby let me tell you it was ridiculous. There would literally be girls at me or my cousin's locker trying to grill us about their asses."

"Damn, how many of you was it?"

"It was six of us at the same school. There were four boys and two girls, which were horrible. My parents, my aunts, and my uncles were always getting phone calls about the fights that would occur due to the hearts they were breaking on a regular. Girls were constantly acting a damn fool for no reason. Personally, I think they had some kind of game going on amongst them."

I was intrigued.

I didn't see Micah as the heartbreaker type, though you never knew when it came to dudes. I couldn't imagine being at a school with four of her relatives, and they all were fine as Micah. Tae, Kira, Zoe, and I would have had a damn field day. We had some sexy dudes at our school, but they didn't look as good as Micah.

"Micah doesn't seem like the heartbreaker type."

She gave me this puzzling look as if I clearly had no idea who I was speaking about. She looked as if this person I came to know was not the person she grew up with her entire life. I was aware of the fact that people acted differently in various surroundings. He just didn't strike me as the type. It was probably because I was bad, and he didn't seem like he was on the same end of bad as I was.

"He wasn't as bad as the other three, but he had his moments too. He sat still for a bit once he got into a relationship with Brea. They started dating at the end of high school, and went on to college. She had a bit of an influence on him so he retired his player's card for a second or at least until the *accident* happened."

She shook her head and laughed. She was in no way buying the story of an accident. I mean she knew her family and all, but there had to be another reason as to why his ex would say it was an accident.

"Wow, so are they still at odds?"

"Who? Micah and Brea?"

"No, your family?"

"Girl no, I mean they got into a fight and moved on. Men don't hold grudges over stuff like we do. I don't think they are as close as they were. I mean Micah was pissed for a while. If you brought it up now he

40

would probably frown up, though he wouldn't blow up like he did when he first found out."

"I see. So is that why he doesn't have a girlfriend?"

"I don't know. He probably does for all I know. We talk every day and we share what goes on in our personal lives, but we don't pry. I understand he needs his privacy and so do I. Besides, no brother really wants to know who his sister is sleeping with. It doesn't matter how close we are. He doesn't want to know for real. He hasn't mentioned a girlfriend, though I do know that Arrington has been sniffing behind him."

There was her name again.

"I doubt he would date her though. Now sleep with her maybe because she would gladly give it to him, but he wouldn't give her a title."

I didn't know if I was relieved or worried. To be honest, I couldn't be either. I was juggling enough hearts and sex so I couldn't add groupies to my list. I'm going to stand on the fact he asked me to be with him and move on. If time proved to be something else then I'll deal with it then. Besides, at this very moment I was in a compromising position with her.

I looked at her and I wanted some more of her.

"So what's up with you and Mario?"

She blushed.

"Nothing. We've been fucking around, but it's nothing too serious."

I couldn't tell if she wanted more or if she was okay with what they were. I guess I could relate seeing I was in her same predicament not too long ago. Changing the nature of your sexual relationship could complicate things a bit.

"Do you want more?"

"Of you, yes I do."

She licked her lips and I got wet all over again. I smiled and slid my fingers down, slowly passing my navel. I traced the insides of my thighs. I loved to tease. It was an art form and it took skill. I loved the buildup it generated. The sensual way it drew you to the edge of the cliff. It was like a tug of war.

It was seduction at its best.

I slid my finger back up my navel and drew a path to my breasts as I teased my nipples. I pushed my breast up and flicked my nipple with my tongue before placing kisses on it. I looked up to see the intensity in her eyes. I stuck my finger in my mouth and dueled with my tongue. She smiled, letting me know she was enjoying the show. I slid my finger out and did circles with my tongue until it was fully lubricated.

41

She was leaning over that edge.

I stared at her with the same intensity she was giving me. I slid my finger into my sweet spot, and I could feel the heat my body had somehow succumb to giving off again. I massaged my sweet lips, and then caressed my clitoris. She wanted to join in, but I wasn't ready for her yet. I wasn't done seducing her. I spread my legs further, and arched my back so she could enjoy the scenery in its entirety.

I went round and round, and then up and down. I went fast, and then slow. I went hard, and then soft.

This wasn't what I was supposed to be doing. I had come to talk about other things. I had come to end things and start fresh. I had deviated from the plan.

I gave her a show.

I removed my finger. I was ready for her to inflict her level of pleasure onto me. I traced my lips with my finger, and then followed with my tongue.

"Mmm, that is delicious."

"Let's see then."

She moved down to the end of the bed. She pulled me to the edge, and then knelt in front of me. She pushed my legs apart and kissed my sweet spot before taking her tongue and giving my clitoris a long, slow stroke. I thought about the pleasure she gave me, the pleasure Micah gave me, and I knew I couldn't live without either dose of it. I grabbed her head, and then slid further down on her tongue.

This was madness. It was complete insanity. It was a ride I wasn't ready to get off of just yet.

5 | Five

t had been a couple of days since Micah and I had seen each other.

We had spoken on the phone, and we had been texting back and forth. Between his basketball schedule and my school schedule we were really missing each other. I was glad we were hanging out tonight. He wanted to take me out on the town, and I was more than glad to be going. I hadn't got the chance to tell him about Cree visiting. I figured telling him in person would probably be better. Aside from other news, I still hadn't told Asha he and I were a couple. My intent was to tell her a few days ago. Somehow, I slipped up and ended up on her lips and tongue. Before I knew it, we were exhausted and the thought of having a conversation had escaped me.

Oh the flashbacks, I thought to myself.

She had a way of making me forget things. Her tongue somehow caused amnesia. I wanted to believe I was strong enough to tell her the truth without falling on her lips, yet I wasn't. She brought out a different vixen in me. A subdued side if ever discovered would find the deepest and most dangerous forms of pleasure and ecstasy. I was a devil in hiding and when called upon, I could wrap you up and consume you in the worst way.

I had consumed her and without warning she had buried herself inside me.

She lied dormant and when pleasure called, she always rose to the occasion. Asha and Micah were my life lines. They were the very essences of what my sexual liberation were made of. The overall makeup of what it had become. I think about what she said happened with him and his ex. Truth be told, we were living that very situation all over again.

The secrets, the scandals, and the sex bound us all together.

I chuckled at the thought.

They, he, she, and their family seemed to be blessed and cursed with an undeniable talent for sex. Their touch, their caress, their tongues, and those wicked and sinful smiles caused chaos wherever they seemed to go. Asha was the soft, gentle lover, while Micah was the hypnotic, aggressive drug. Alone they were dangerous, but if taken in a double dose they were addictive and a hard habit to kick.

They were good and evil all in one.

I needed to figure out what I was going to wear tonight. I wanted it to be on a different level of sexy. I needed to distract him enough so that I could tell him Cree was going to be staying with me. At the same time I needed him to want to lay me across a table and do naughty things to me. He didn't tell me where we were going, though I assumed it would be some food involved. He just said bring a light jacket so I'm guessing we would be outdoors too.

I had the perfect dress.

I remembered I had purchased a cobalt blue Michael Kors dress that was covered in the front to give you a sense of mystery, and it had a low cut back that welcomed you into a world of naughtiness. I could pair the dress with my gold spiked, strappy heels and be out the door. I had caught a couple of sales when I went home over the holidays so I had a few options. I had hoped we could make it through the date without jumping each other's bones.

Though knowing us, there were no guarantees. Luckily, my Asha fixes were holding me over until we were able to hook up. I still missed him. I missed his touch. I welcomed his sensuous kisses. I craved his dick.

I craved how the long, slow strokes sometimes became fast, hard strokes. Strokes that mimicked my ever beating heart and the erratic tempo it sometimes created when I have reached my overload level. If there is or could be such a thing. Since I met him and his sister, there seemed to be depths of my sexuality I hadn't realized existed or explored. I had found quite a few pieces of my inner vixen when I was with Cree, although never to this extent. This was unknown territory that I was submerged in. It made me want to lose myself further

44

within it. I wasn't sure where this adventure was going to end and I didn't care. I was going to ride this ride until I was forced to get off.

It was getting closer to 7p.m. so I guess I could start getting ready. I was horny. I needed a fix. I was tempted to make a quick run to his house, but I changed my mind. I decided teasing him would be a lot more fun. I grabbed my phone so that I could send him a text.

I opened my drawer, snapped a pic of my silver gifts that he'd previously given me, and then sent the text that said: *I want to feel the electricity the metal balls create against my walls as the heat from your tongue sends me over the edge. Then I want you to flip me over and slide inside me slowly as my juices soak your dick. While you have my face buried inside the pillow, I want you to kiss the nape of my neck down to the small of my back. I want to feel your breath on my back as you grab my hair to hold onto the control that is slipping away from you being buried inside me. I want to hold your pleasure hostage as your orgasm fights to be free of you.*

I squeezed my legs because I needed to keep it together.

I had gotten my own self hot from trying to seduce him. I placed my phone down and headed to my closet to pull out my dress. I had some gold bangles and hoop earrings that would put the finishing touches on my sexy yet simplistic attire for the evening. I was excited about seducing my man tonight.

My man, I thought to myself.

"Rylee and Micah," I said to myself.

It was weird to even say it even though he was my man. He was all mine. As much as I hated to admit, I was actually excited by us being a couple. I hadn't given much thought to the groupie craziness that Asha had warned me about. We were in a good space and until we weren't, I wasn't going to worry about it. I was in no position to judge right now so a little leeway was a necessary evil. He played sports and with it came attention. I was by no means an insecure woman so I felt no need to give them or the craziness any of my attention.

I was however still curious about this ex-girlfriend, and the family member incident. I made a mental note to squeeze some more juice out of Asha. I just couldn't fathom or grasp how you accidentally sleep with one of his family members. There had to be more to this story that she wasn't telling me. There was something missing.

Oh well, I thought to myself. Time would soon reveal everything and I'm sure he would get around to telling me so I won't trip off of it. Just as I laid my dress on my bed, I heard my text alert go off.

I smiled because I knew it was probably him texting me back something equally nasty.

It was Cree.

The text read: *Rylee, I just wanted to check and see if staying with you was still cool? I purchased my ticket and I will be there on Wednesday, the 17th. If not, let me know and I'll book a hotel.*

Everything in me was saying make him get a hotel. Don't put yourself in a position you will need to fight and get out of. Give this relationship a fighting chance. Walk the straight and narrow Rylee. Walk the straight and narrow. I just couldn't type the words. I figured we were both adults and my sisters was staying here too. I would be safe from any bad decisions I would probably make if they weren't here. I believed Tae said they were coming on that same date so I wouldn't end up alone with him for a long period of time.

I replied with a text that read: *Hey Cree, it's cool if you stay here. See you soon.*

I figured I'd tell him my sisters were coming when he got here. They were all cool so he didn't need a heads up. I definitely needed to be sure I told Micah tonight. I didn't want to make it look like I was being sneaky. I wasn't sure how he was going to take it, and I definitely wasn't sure how I was going to handle him saying no. Especially, since I had already told Cree he could stay.

Push comes to shove I'll just pass him off as one of my sister's friends.

My text alert went off again and I figured it was Micah this time. I placed my shoebox down and picked up my phone.

Mmm, it was him. His text read: *Ry, you have no idea the amount of trouble you are going to be in this evening. Be sure to bring your A game and some endurance. You're going to need it.*

I shivered, and bit my bottom lip.

The man could make me wet simply by texting. I had never felt eroticism on this level. Emotionally, I knew it was more than eroticism. I just wasn't ready to acknowledge it out loud yet. I wasn't ready to part with this new found freedom that I had become intimate with. I could feel it wrapping itself around me like a warm blanket. A hypnotizing pull that eventually I would give into. I could fight it, though like many before me, I would soon fall.

All good things come to an end, I would often hear my grandmothers say. I just needed to squeeze as much out of this as I could before I had to give it all up. I would eventually have to tell Asha what was going on and completely put Cree at bay. He hadn't come out of his corner all the way. My intuition was telling me he was on his way. This request to stay with me was just an introduction to his pulling me back in. He had more than enough money to get a hotel room or a suite nonetheless. He was in no way struggling so I knew there was more to this visit than he was letting on.

I could say he caught me at weak point after that whole proposal scene, however I'd be lying. I wanted it as bad as he wanted to give it. I knew it would be opening a can of worms. Especially, since he had just confessed to still having feelings for me. For once, in that moment, I had to be honest with myself and my feelings.

I just didn't care.

I wanted what wanted and that was that. I knew I was hopping on a plane the next day so there was no need to even give it much thought. Now here I am trying to tell my new man that my old lover is going to crash at my place for a few days.

In what world does this happen? Only in mine, I thought to myself.

I smiled as I texted him back, and it read: *Have you ever known me to not bring my A game? Don't worry because I will be more than ready. You just make sure you're marathon ready tonight.*

I placed the phone down and went to plug up my flat irons. I had been contemplating cutting my hair and was really leaning towards a shorter cut. I wanted something spicy. I needed a new look so I needed to find a good beautician here. Otherwise, I would be flying home to mine on the next break.

Beep!

It was another clever response I'm sure.

The text read: *Park your car on Decatur Street by 7:30 p.m. There will be a car to bring you to the Toulouse Street Wharf. I'll be there waiting and you will see just how equipped for a marathon I am. Just so you know, I will be showing you no mercy from this point on. You're mine now, and I plan to explore every crevice of your pecan-colored skin.*

Lord have mercy was all I could think at this point in time. I checked the time and saw that it was close to 6 o'clock. I had a little over an hour to get ready and meet him there. I was curious to know what he was planning since he wasn't picking me up. We hung out in our apartments most of the time. If we did step out he was a gentleman and drove so this little arrangement was new.

I was excited and I was turned on at the same time. This was going to be an adventure. This was how our late night orgasms slowing transitioned into early morning memories.

I responded with a text that read: *I will be there Mr. Cartwright with my A game and endurance.*

I placed the phone on the charger and headed to jump in the shower.

Tonight would be different. Tonight I would be breaking some more of my nonexistent rules with the man who just may tame my wild spirit.

Let the games begin.

6 | Six

***T**hank God for good genes.*
I looked at myself in the mirror and was satisfied at the way I looked this evening. The dress hugged my curves perfectly and the way it seductively showed the small of my back formed a smile at the corner of my lips. Moments like this made me feel pretty. It had been a while since I'd been on a date I wanted to be on. The beautiful blend of electric and cobalt blue within the dress created a harmonious effect with my pecan-colored skin. My choice in gold accessories couldn't have been a better selection.

I loved moments like this. The brief moments that allowed my inner vixen to shine through without very much effort. My long, brown and blond tendrils fell perfectly on my shoulder. I had some of my hair pulled back so I wouldn't be completely hidden behind it. Usually when I did this, you could see all of my Trinidadian features I seemingly managed to genetically inherit from my mother.

I smiled as I thought about my mother. Disagreements or not, I was more like her than I cared to admit.

We shared our features, personality, and everything else in between.

I strapped my heels up and stood up to give myself one more once over before I walked out. I loved these shoes. Hopefully, if the night went exceptionally well, I would end up in nothing other than these heels. The back of my dress was out and low cut so I opted out of wearing a bra. Since I was quite the exhibitionist and I didn't play fair,

I saw no need for panties either. The only thing standing between me and orgasmic bliss was the table I knew would separate us. Just as I grabbed my purse and keys, I heard my phone beep. I figured it was him checking to see if I was in motion. I opened my purse and pulled my phone out.

It seemed he wasn't playing fair this evening either. I could see it was an image file so I entered my password and clicked the message. A peek a boo pic and a message that read: *Just wanted you to see what would be waiting on I mean under the table when you got here.*

Oh, I loved how he teased. It made the sex that much more worth it and enjoyable. I decided to wait and drop the no panty news on him once I got there. I preferred seeing the look on his face while his mouth dropped opened when I told him face-to-face. There's nothing like a dose of shock and awe to give a boost to your ego.

I responded with a text that read*: Glad to know he will be in attendance and will be on the menu tonight.*

This was my game, and I loved playing it. It was probably because I was very skilled at it. We all had our ways of drawing the opposite sex in and I definitely had mine. I did it with words, looks, and of course soft touches that filled you with anticipation. I would tease you until you were at the point of exploding, and even then I still wanted you to beg for it. Tonight he will be begging for it. I headed downstairs and hopped in my car. I was still trying to figure out how I was going to tell him about Cree. I wondered should I take the honest route first or should I just throw my cover story out and let it be what it is.

I had a decision to make.

Do I go with the truth or a lie?

Whichever path I decided to take, I had to be okay with the aftermath. I had to be okay with this blowing up in my face if it went south. Telling him Cree is an old friend and will be staying with me along with my sisters didn't seem so bad. I was unclear on how territorial he may be though. He had a dominant streak. He even had times where I could see some forms of jealousy. It was never too apparent or in your face so I dismissed it.

Not to mention, at the time we were just friends.

Neither of us really had room to say too much about what the other person was doing so we didn't. Now we were in a relationship and those not so pretty hidden traits just might surface. I knew I needed to pay attention to characteristics as they appeared. It was a bad habit among both men and women to ignore red flags we see in the beginning. We would get so caught up in the new aspect of everything that we would ignore what we know to be problems. I realized this after Trent. I ignored personality conflicts between us and I looked past them. I convinced myself as time went on that he would change. I got caught up in the expensive gifts, weekend getaways, and nice dinners. I was a typical 20 year old woman. All I could see was the materialistic things, even though they never really appeased me. I had never really been without nice things due to my parents, though somehow I got swept up in his madness, and the shiny new toys that came with him. He was fine, showed me some attention, and didn't necessarily want anything from me, or so I thought. I had bought into the game without even realizing I was playing.

I trusted the wrong person, and I paid for it.

My innocence and the unrealistic belief in love went out the door with it. Now I was here was again. I was in a game that I was the starter in, while holding hearts in my hand. Knowing full well someone or some people could get hurt. I was fine when I was solo. I owed know explanations to anyone, but now things were different. Now, I had a partner and somehow I couldn't say it out loud. A part of me knew I could have eliminated this problem by telling Cree I was in a relationship. *So why didn't I?*

I guess old habits really do die hard. It was those old habits that most people found themselves losing everything over. Jeopardizing a new relationship for an old flame was risky.

That was the story of my life. I was forever the risk taker. The junkie high of being close to the edge.

Micah and I were together now. He made me happy so I didn't regret saying yes to his question. If Trent called this minute, I would gladly tell him about my relationship. Although, for whatever reason, I failed to let it come out of my mouth with Cree. That night still played over-and-over in my mind. He still had it. He still had the effect he used to have over me. I should have just said no when he came in my room. I wasn't emotionally equipped to resist him. My mind was screaming no. It was trying to keep me from making yet another bad decision. I wanted to stop before I opened another door that I would have to somehow close. Clean up another mess all because I had become this sexual vixen that was liberated and addicted to orgasms. Knowing all of this, I still couldn't find the strength to tell him no.

You can't help who you love. It was a proven fact that proved itself time after time no matter the circumstances.

He had lain next to me, and all of those nights we spent together flooded my mind as his hard body pressed against mine. I shivered. *Was I sure about this visit?* I needed to make sure I confirmed with one of my sisters when they would be arriving. I didn't need or want to be around him alone for longer than a couple of hours. Anything longer than half a day would welcome an array of bad decisions. As if I talked her up here she was. It was perfect timing. My phone rings and Jayce's number comes up. I hit the answer option on my steering wheel.

"Hi Jay. What's up?"

"No, don't hi me. You weren't going to call me and say nothing?"

"What do you mean?"

I figured Tae had already told her that Cree was coming. We didn't keep very much from each other. We all had our secrets, though for the most part we told each other everything.

"I don't know Lee, maybe something like I'm okay or I'm alive."

I laughed. She was in her mother hen mode and actually sounded concerned.

"Jay I texted you when I made it back. I told you I was okay, and that I needed some time to think. Then when you texted a week later I told you the same thing. So what's the problem? You miss me?"

I was laughing, even though I could tell she was a little annoyed. I was also sure Tae didn't make it any better by telling her we had talked a few days ago. I had actually planned on calling her. She had just beaten me to it. She wouldn't believe me even if it was the truth.

"Whatever Lee, your butt is perfectly fine and wasn't too shaken up. I mean, you're the same person who can dump someone on Monday and be on a whole new date by Wednesday. Cut it out!"

Dang, I wasn't that damn bad or was I?

"You make it sound like I don't have feelings."

She laughed.

"Really? Are you acting offended? You and Tae crack me up with this convenient sense of being offended. You know as well as I do that you don't get attached to people. It's a gift and a curse if you ask me."

I rolled my eyes. I would never give her the pleasure of saying she was right. She was the more sensitive one. Whereas, Tae and I let stuff roll off our backs. We had moments where our feelings got hurt, not nearly as often as hers did though. She was more like my father's mother in that aspect. She was a gentle soul who absorbed everything around her. I had one of those too. It was just heavily guarded by a barbed wire fence.

"Yeah okay, well if you're done being the older sister, what's up? You seemed to call wanting to chit chat so spill it."

"Well aside from me calling to scold you, Tae told me we would be having a certain someone join us while we're there. So you can say I was trying to get the scoop about who our mystery guest would be?" she asked, laughing.

I knew it. Gossip was the real reason her ass was calling. She wanted to be nosey just like Taylor, and get the scoop on Cree and me. We always had this thing about who would get the scoop first so that's probably what really had her panties in a bunch.

"So now we get to the real reason why you called, huh?"

"Oh don't get it twisted, I called to chew your ass out about not calling me. Make no mistake about it, it just so happens I wanted to know about your company you plan to have while we're there. Especially since I'm trying to figure at what point you mentioned the two of you were even cool on that level again."

"Oh my company, huh? I know flapjacks over there told you everything so do I need to repeat any of it?"

"No, I just want to know what your new beau said about this arrangement?"

Damn, she really did tell everything. I'm glad I didn't want to save that piece of news to tell myself. Tae had managed to spill the beans quicker than I threw them in the pot. I couldn't blame her though. I may have let the juice spill just as quick. It was no secret I still felt something for Cree.

"Actually, I'm on my way to meet him for dinner. We haven't really seen each other since he has games and practices to juggle, along with school. I wanted to tell him in person versus over the phone. I figured if he could see my face then he would see where Cree and I stood."

She laughed again.

"Where you and Cree stand? Well first of all who knew you two stood anywhere. I'm not buying it. You're stalling and you know it. Telling your man your old lover is coming to stay doesn't require a hand holding session in case you didn't know."

I rolled my eyes again. I hated she wasn't getting any of these facial expressions I was giving her and her smart ass comments.

"First of all, I just told you we've been busy and have been missing each other. Next, he's not my lover, we're friends and friends are what I will be telling him we are. Thank you very much."

"Oh ok. I know you Lee. If you haven't told him it's because you haven't figured out how to get around not telling him. Save the friend lie, it's me you're talking too. I know better or did you forget?"

I hated she knew me. Dammit.

"Whatever Jay, I'm going to tell him."

"Well then that only means one thing."

"And what's that smarty pants?"

"Me and Tae are your alibis," she said, belting out a laugh.

I rolled my eyes once again.

"Well, since you seem to know so damn much I don't need your permission to use you as a cover then."

"When have you ever?"

"I'm glad you know. Well I'm at my destination so I'll call you later, chick."

"Okay, just one more thing."

"I'm listening."

"You will eventually have to make a decision."

"A decision about what Jayce?"

"Your heart or these unlimited orgasms you seem to be enjoying. Eventually you will have to decide which one is more important. It's going to be love or lust. I'm not saying it's today or tomorrow. However, I am saying the day will eventually come. Just don't make a mess out of everything before you have to make that choice."

I loved my sister. She was my voice of reason at times. She was that even when I gave no attention to what she may have been saying at the time. It always came a time where I remembered and applied it. She believed in love. I believe in present day emotions. Somewhere in between there was a happy medium. Someday I would be content in it. For now, I will continue on in my own way. Her advice was solid, but it wasn't as simple as she made it seem.

The heart was a tricky organ. Love was a complex emotion, and a broken heart was a disease that often times went undiscovered.

"I hear you, sis. I will let you know if you and Tae are my cover story."

She laughed again.

"Okay, and Tae wanted me to tell you our tickets are bought. We'll be there on Friday, the 19th. She got super early flights so you're going to have to come get us. I told her to do afternoon flights. She dismissed it, and said she wanted to come early."

I couldn't remember when Cree said he was coming. *Was it Wednesday or Thursday?* I had hoped it was Thursday. I didn't want to have to hide out for two days before they got here. I scrolled through my phone to find where he texted me his arrival date.

Shit, it was Wednesday, the 17th.

I took a deep breath. They were definitely going to be my cover stories at this point. I was still going to tell Micah. For my sake, it would be a modified version of what I was going to say at first. No way was the old friend approach going to work now.

"Okay, I'll call you later."

"Okay, goodbye Lee Lee," she said in her ghetto girl voice.

We hung up and I added some more lip gloss. I needed to make sure the sexy was on high for this conversation. I got out of the car and saw a black Chrysler 360 parked with the driver standing outside. I walked towards the car.

"How can I help you this evening ma'am?"

"Reservation for Cartwright, I'm Rylee."

"Yes ma'am. Right this way please."

The driver held the door open and I got in. It was a do or die moment at this point. I wasn't sure how this news drop was going to be received. Either way, I would be ending this night with a bang. Tomorrow would be a new day for whatever decisions I would have to make.

7 | *Seven*

*O**n the way, I thought about what Jayce had mentioned.*** She always had a valid point. Though sometimes I felt she wished Tae and I always saw things from her perspective and acted on it. She was the golden child who walked the straight and narrow. The one who never really colored outside of the lines. Sadly, life didn't work that way. We were sisters with our own identities. I saw love and sex differently than the two of them. It's our differences that made the world go round. If everyone was the same we'd all be living in a state of boredom. I knew my time with this game of sex, lust, and love would be short lived. Micah, Cree, and Trent all proved to me that feelings were now a factor. Hell, when I thought about it, the only person who wasn't acting all emotional was Asha.

Go figure. They say women aren't capable of being sexual beings absent of emotional feelings. Clearly, we were examples of how evolution is constantly changing. How woman are able to retract their feelings and place them on shelves. Broken hearts and emotionless sex had a way of molding you to be a robot.

A person who only wanted to possess feelings only benefiting them.

I still hadn't quite wrapped my head around how I was going to tell Micah about Cree. I really didn't want to lie, but desperate times would call for desperate measures. I also knew he wouldn't be entirely on board with him crashing at my place. I wanted advice from Asha, though I knew that was a dead end too. She was either snatching my

56

soul out through every orgasm or we were floating on cloud nine from being high. Regardless of the two, nothing I set out to talk about got mentioned. My sisters had pretty much weighed in so it was pretty much all on me.

I hadn't even realized we had arrived at my destination due to me being so lost in thought. I couldn't see much of where we were since the windows were tinted. I heard the driver get out of the car so I grabbed my purse and jacket.

"Here we are Miss. Just head in the direction over there," he said, pointing.

I stepped out of the car and saw a huge cruise boat that read *Steamboat Natchez* in front of me. *Wow,* I thought. I was even more excited to get this unforgettable night that was ahead of me started. As I headed towards the boat, I noticed the sky was beginning to blend into a beautiful array of colors. Pinks, oranges, and yellows danced across the sky as traces of blues created reflections of purples. I looked for Micah. I thought he would be outside waiting.

When I didn't see him, I headed up the ramp and onto the boat. It was beautiful inside for it to be a boat. The tables were beautifully decorated for what I assumed would be dinner. There was a band setup area so it looked like some live music would be getting played.

He had really outdone himself on this one. For it to be our first official date, he was off to a good start. I saw people walking upstairs so I followed suit, hoping he would be up there. When I reached the top, I saw him leaning over the balcony rail.

Damn he was fine. I was mesmerized by this incredibly sexy man leaning over the balcony with this beautifully painted sky as his backdrop. Everything looked perfect, including him. The rails were romantically lit and the sound of the water moving was entirely relaxing. I was in complete awe of how the entire scene looked. He had put so much effort into how this date would go and I couldn't be more impressed.

I wasn't sure what was fated in the stars for me and I had no complaints. I saw he had some flowers in his hand, and I smiled as I headed towards him. He looked over my way when he saw me coming towards him. He extended his arm to hand me the flowers. They were beautiful and also my favorite soft pink peonies. I hadn't realized he even remembered. They weren't the usual favorite flower most people had so I was shocked.

"Thank you."

"You are quite welcome," he said with a devilish look.

"Why seven? Is that your lucky number or something?"

"You could say that, or how it actually stands for the time in which we've known each other. Seven months to be exact."

Wow, I hadn't realized he was keeping track. When I thought about it, it had been seven months since I bumped into him coming into my building. I would never forget walking into *930 Poydras* that day. Life as I knew it began when I moved into my building.

"Well Mr. Cartwright, I must say you outdid yourself with this. I should've jumped at being your girlfriend months ago."

He laughed, I laughed, and then we smiled.

"Oh the night has just begun Ms. Coltrane. I have yet to keep that promise I made to you earlier."

My heart was beating and my insides were heating up. Somehow in the midst of all of this the throbbing had started. I was trying to keep it together long enough to enjoy the date he planned. He turned me on in the worst way. I wanted to make him beg for it. I walked closer to him and slide my hand up his thigh where I could see the imprint peeking through.

"Well by the looks of things you may be fulfilling that promise sooner than you think."

He flashed that wicked smile and leaned close to my ear.

"Careful Ry. Otherwise I will be forced to take you downstairs, bend you over one of those tables and give everyone a show they will never forget, including you."

"You wouldn't dare," I replied.

"Try me."

I loved a good dare as much as the next girl. It was my adventurous side I loved to feed. Just as I was going to call him out on his dare, the announcements started. The person speaking was letting everyone know dinner was going to be served soon and the boat would now be taking off. He held out his arm for me to slide through so that we could head back downstairs. I wasn't ready to part with what seemed to be a beautiful sunset on the horizon. The colors were really blending together and the light was bouncing off of the water perfectly.

"I'm not quite finished with this sunset," I said to him.

He knew I loved sunrises and sunsets. I always felt they were so tranquil. The way God would throw splashes of colors above us so we could see how majestic he was is beyond incredible. There was no other way to describe it. When I was back home, my sisters, and I would lie on the grass and just stare into the sky. I would close my eyes as the cool, summer breezes blew across my face. Those moments were so peaceful and allowed me time to clear my head. Most people would do yoga, exercise, or other activities to clear their head. Not me, I would simply find my spot in the grass lay my blanket down and just look up into the sky.

Simply, watching God paint a beautiful canvas. A canvas that was never the same each time appeared.

"Okay, I will check on the exact time dinner starts and then grab us some drinks. Would you like a glass of red wine?"

I gave him a devilish grin.

"Careful, you know what red wine does to me."

"Do I? Well, refresh my memory. What exactly does red wine to you? I mean I know what tequila does to you and I'd have to say I quite enjoy that side of you. So tell me Ms. Coltrane, what does red wine do to you?"

I moved close to him so no one could hear or see what I was going to say. I moved closer to him and placed his hand on the exposed part of my back. I looked up at him and licked my lips. Since he wanted to start this night off with teasing, I figured I would keep it going. All was fair in love, war, and the seduction it was wrapped up in. He pulled me closer and gripped me with some intensity.

"See the thing is when I drink red wine I become the ultimate temptress. Not the bold and brazen version of me who climbed onto the hood of your car, and then removed her panties. No, that's not who I will be tonight. Tonight I will be vixen that will slip slowly as I contemplate what is going through your mind once I tell you I have nothing on under this dress all the while you run your fingers over my ass like this."

I breathed in the cologne he was wearing and it was intoxicating. I didn't recognize the scent, but it still was definitely taking over my senses. I looked up into his eyes, and they were full blown smoke gray. The gray that meant I wasn't far from being bent over the table he threatened me with. It looks as if I had won this round of teasing.

One for me, and zero for him.

"You know Ry, if we were not already floating down the Mississippi those words would have you tied up right now. I'm guessing you knew that which is why you told me."

I gave him a look acknowledging I was aware of what I had done.

"So you thought wearing this dress that accentuates your body perfectly, while leaving just enough mystery and nothing under it would keep you safe in public?"

I stepped back so he could get a good look at me. I had no intention on saying anything else. This move spoke volumes and no other words were needed. It was my way of letting him know it's your move. In a chess game moving in silence proved to your opponent it was his turn. He gave me a small nod, and then turned around to get the drinks and dinner information. I leaned back against the rail and watched him walk away. I looked out into the sunset as it became more beautiful. I realized I could tell him about Cree another time. I had a couple of weeks before he got here.

There was no need to ruin a perfect date night.

8 | Eight

n hour had gone by and dinner was beyond delicious. I wasn't sure what they had in that creole mustard sauce nor did I care. It did wonderful things on my palate with the pork loin I smeared it on top of. I was picking off of Micah's bread pudding and as much as I wanted to stop, I couldn't. It was simply melting in my mouth. I was officially stuffed. His meal looked and smelled just as good. I was torn between my choice and the rib roast he had. I'm a sucker for horseradish sauce and beef.

The band had played jazz selections during dinner, and a few people even got up to dance. I was tempted to join in when he asked, though I figured we didn't need anything else to spark this already slow, burning fire. As I started to ask if he wanted to head back up to the deck to hang until the boat docked I saw someone heading towards us. I couldn't place where I knew her from, and yet she was definitely heading towards our table.

She gave me a once over and then spoke to him.

"Hi Micah. It's funny seeing you here."

I looked her up and down. I needed her to know this was not a party she wanted to attend. He turned and looked at her, and then looked back at me.

"Hi Arrington. What are you doing here?"

Arrington? There was her name again. I looked at him, and then back at her. She was pretty, but not threatening. I could see what Asha was saying in regards to her though she seemed somewhat average to me. I was waiting for her to answer, as well seeing it was awfully funny she was here. Or how she even knew he was there. I mean I was from L.A. and the groupie quota was at an all-time high there. However, it was for already established athletes and businessmen. I guess she wanted to sink her claws in him early so it wouldn't look like she was an actual groupie. She probably wanted to get in early so she can reap the benefits later. I remembered hearing a girl say that very thing at one of my mother's casting calls. I shook my head at the thought. I didn't hate on those types of women. I just didn't have the patience to deal with all the nonsense for it.

I've been there and did all of that with Trent. The bags, clothes, and jewelry all had an expiration date with men in those arenas, and sadly so did you.

"Oh, I was on a date with a friend," she answered.

Not even five seconds after she answered he walked up. I was trying to hide my facial expressions so no one could see them. Micah looked up and saw him coming towards us so he stood up. I guess Asha was right about the groupies. They come from all angles.

As soon as he reached our table, Micah said, "What's up Mario?"

"What's up Micah? I see you're here with the one and only," he said, giving me this smile that screamed please don't bust me out.

I had nothing to say about any of it. For one, Asha had made it clear they were only friends or bed buddies. Secondly, I knew Arrington was a temporary fix so why even trip. Not to mention, none of it was my business to begin with. I had my own secrets to juggle. The more time you spent exposing other people's secrets meant you had to work twice as hard keeping yours buried. If Asha knew Arrington was chasing Micah so did Mario. The problem was he didn't care, and was going to enjoy his time with her however long it lasted.

"Hi Mario."

"What's up Ry? You look nice."

"Thanks, and you clean up pretty well yourself."

She looked puzzled. I knew she was trying to figure out who I was seeing both of them knew me. I did the usual campus activities, hung out at the bars on Maple Street, and other fun stuff. My only thing was I did not run behind the ball players. Meeting Micah was by chance since we lived in the same complex.

"Hello, I'm Arrington. Are you from around here?"

The way she asked that question almost made me chuckle. Figures she would think I'm a local since she didn't know who I was. The typical popular girl who tries to make you seem irrelevant if she didn't know who you were. Or maybe she was just simply being nosey.

"Hi, I'm Rylee. No I'm not from New Orleans."

"I see. Do you go to one of the universities?"

"Yes, I'm enrolled at Xavier. Micah and I have the same major."

I knew she didn't ask for the last part, and I could have cared less. I was the wrong one to be subliminal and territorial with. I was honestly ready for them to leave so that we could return back to our evening of seduction we were emerged in before she pranced her tail towards our table. Mario was chatting with him and she was trying to get a consensus of who I really was. I had no intention of broadcasting it to her, seeing she was of no importance to me. I would let her curiosity eat away at her. If that wasn't enough, she could grill the hell out of Mario for the information. Hopefully, he didn't know too much. I really didn't want or need information getting back to Asha anytime soon.

"Oh, well it was nice to meet you. Hopefully, I'll see you at the games sometimes."

She was still fishing for information.

"Yeah sure you will. It was nice meeting you."

She smiled and Micah dapped Mario again before they walked off. I wish I could tell Asha about this situation. Unfortunately, there was no way to do that without telling on myself and blowing everything up. As far as Asha knew we hadn't really hung out since her house party.

"Well Ms. Coltrane has the red wine taken effect yet?" he asked, grinning like a mischievous kid and I smiled.

"It depends. Will your little cheerleader be joining us?"

I took another sip of my wine and looked back him. He was sitting there trying not to laugh at the fact I appeared to be jealous. My statement may have come off a bit more aggressive than I intended. He chuckled and stood up to hold his hand out. He led me back up to the deck. The air was chillier due to draft that was coming off of the water. The sky was a deep shade of indigo blue and the crescent shape moon gave off just enough of a glow on the water. The skyline was lit up as we passed under the bridge that was lit up with lights intertwined with the beams. L.A. was always lit up at night, but this was different. The skyline that the buildings created along with sky in the background and the water in front was beyond picturesque.

He leaned against the railing and pulled me close to him. His cologne mixed with the cool breeze was doing a number on my senses. He kissed me softly, sensually. It was different from all of the other times we had kissed. It was almost as if he felt he could relinquish control of the untapped passion he kept hidden from me before. My gentle lover who could ravage my body when need be. He placed a peck on my lips, and I looked up at him. I wanted him, yet it was a different kind of desire. As hot as I was for him, I wanted tonight to be different.

I wanted slow and sensual. I wanted him to explore different parts of me. Different parts of my soul.

He squeezed me tight and stared into my eyes.

"Rylee, if I wanted to be with Arrington I could be. She's not my type, therefore there is no need to worry about her. You're the only cheerleader I want or need."

He sounded so sincere.

I wanted to believe him. I wanted to dive knee deep into him. I just wasn't sure I could give my all quite yet. I wanted him to slow down, though I felt I was too late. He was already close to edge and there was no way I would be able to pull him back. I would just have to be careful. Careful with all of my secrets. Careful with his heart.

I placed a kiss on his lips. He rubbed his hand up and down the opening of my dress. I   shivered. His hands were warm and felt good upon my skin. Most of the people had cleared the deck since the cruise was heading back to the dock. We were ducked off in a corner area so we could have some privacy. He spun me around and pushed me again the rail. The cold metal pressed against my skin. I wasn't bothered by it since there was enough heat brewing between the two of us. He leaned down to place a kiss on my neck.

"You really shouldn't start something you can't finish," I whispered in his ear.

He turned his head enough for me to see his eyes, and the smirk that matched the look buried beneath them. He sucked my earlobe softly and I did all I could not to give into the buckling my knees were beginning to feel. I knew this was payback for the taunting I had dished out earlier. He wasn't going to let me off this boat before he made sure he was one up on me. He lifted my left legs just enough to caress the outside of my thigh. He wanted me to beg for it. He wanted to hear the silent pleas hidden and laced within my breathing.

"See the thing is Rylee, I'm a closer. There has never been a time I start anything I can't finish. For instance, the way I am rubbing the outside of your thigh right now. If I were to move my hand like this, my fingers would simply be tracing the outline of your hips."

I swallowed hard. He was pulling me in, and I was willingly allowing him to.

This was seduction. It was my favorite game.

"I would never be satisfied with small amounts of tantalizing you.

So my fingers would then find their way to the back of your thigh. The place I love to grip when you are sitting on the tip of my tongue. Then we come to the place that makes me weak in the knees. I would move my finger up and down like this until I reach the curvature of your derriere. Once I left enough fingerprints along your beautifully carved body, I would then need to hold you like this."

Before I knew it he had me lifted and pinned against the rails. If my mother could have seen me right now she would've died. My legs were wrapped around this man on a boat in a dress. I had thrown caution to the wind and everything else along with it.

He wasn't playing fair. I needed to regain some control. He was about to go in for the kill when we felt the boat come to a complete stop.

"We'll finish this when we get home Ms. Coltrane."

"Indeed we will sir," I said as he lifted me off the railing.

I threw my jacket on and we headed downstairs. We walked down the ramp and across the parking lot to his car. He opened the door and I slid in. I watched him walk around to his side. I contemplated another round in the car, and then dismissed it. I had something so much better in mind. I would give him a memory he would never forget. A memory I would pay for later on down the line. He started the car and opened the sunroof. I leaned my head against the headrest and closed my eyes. The night air was perfect and the cool air fell wonderfully upon my skin. My jacket warmed my arms, while the rest of my body welcomed the refreshing night breeze. I felt him squeeze my hands as India Arie's *Beautiful* allowed me to drift off.

I thought about tonight. I thought about how perfect everything was and I could not have asked for a better date. From the food, to the music, to the beautiful sunset, I was captivated by it all. It was as if he'd been waiting in the perfect moment to plan it. I had no idea how I was going to tell him about Cree. I knew I still needed to put it out there. Jayce's words played over in my mind, *Your heart or unlimited orgasms.*

Why couldn't I have both?

I opened my eyes and looked at Micah. I did have both, though I wasn't ready to dive all the way in just yet. I had opened that door for Trent and I saw where it led me, which is right to Cree. I knew Micah was different, and I knew he was nothing like Trent. Then I reminded myself everything appeared to be different when it was new. Once the newness wore off, it wasn't too far from what you knew it to be.

He pulled into the parking garage and found a spot. He placed the car in park and looked over at me. Sometimes he never had to say a word or even touched me. Sometimes the way he looked at me spoke volumes.

I smiled at him and unbuckled my seatbelt. He continued to look at me, while watching my every move. I realized what he was doing and decided to play along. I gazed into his eyes and bit my bottom lip softly.

There was no reaction.

I traced the outline of my lips with my finger, and then slowly licked the tip. He was fighting the arousal that was forming in his pants. I didn't want to do this here. I needed room to move around and his car didn't provide that kind of space. I grabbed my purse, leaned over to trace his lips with my tongue, and then got out of the car. I headed towards the elevators. I pushed the buttons and heard his door close. I chuckled and turned around to see him leaning against his car.

He wanted a show. He wanted me to make this hard for myself once again.

The elevator opened and I walked in. I turned around so I could hit the button to my floor. As the doors were closing, I waved him goodbye. I knew he wouldn't be too far behind me. I would have quite the surprise waiting for him when he walked off. The door opened once it reached my floor and I got off. I could hear the other elevator coming up so I didn't have much time. I opened my door and threw my purse and jacket on the table next to the door. I left a small crack in the door so he could open it. No need to turn on any lights. The light from the hallway and the moonlight coming through my sheer curtains would be just enough.

I slid my dress over my shoulders and let it fall to the floor. I heard the elevator chime and the doors open. I stepped out of my dress and stood in the middle of the floor with my hands on my hips. I could see his shadow as he got closer to the door. He pushed the door open and stood there watching me.

"I was thinking about what you said on the boat. How you were describing the various ways you loved to touch me. I mostly loved how you said you would start here, and then you would very gently move here."

I rubbed the top of my thighs, and then traced the outside of my hips.

"Then and I want to get this correct. I believe you said you loved to caress this part, while gripping this part as I slide down on the tip of your tongue like this right?" I asked as I turned around to bend over so he could get a full view of my butt.

66

He closed the door, and then moved a little closer. He kept enough distance so he could continue watching the show.

I stood back up and rubbed my hands over my derriere, then up the sides until I reached the back of my neck. I gripped my hair, and then peeked over my shoulders. I was far from done. I turned around to finish the frontal show.

"I guess when I think about it, you left out a few spots."

He crossed his arms across his chest. I knew that was a defense mechanism. He was trying to hold onto his self-control. Well, what was left of it any way since it was swiftly slipping out of his reach. He'd give me a little longer, and then he would shut all of this down.

"See I'm curious to know how you would touch me here? Would you caress them with your fingertips or would your lips create small sensations to aid in sending me over the edge?"

I looked up for a response and he gave none. Wow. His resistance was definitely improving.

I smiled as I moved my hands down towards my navel, and then to the top of my sweet spot. I moved towards him a couple of steps.

I still had my heels on so of course they were doing wonders for my legs and curves.

"Now that we've established what your lips do to me, we should discuss your tongue and the places it invades. I always loved how you would start here right beneath my navel and slowly move down. I always found it quite arousing how you would never go straight for the kill. It's not you and that would be too easy. No, you like unpredictable and erotic. You're all about the anticipation and the yearning for the unknown. You like to hear the sporadic, yet deep breaths I make as you kiss the insides of my thighs. It's an ego booster to some. I personally like to call it romantic torture. You pull me back and forth until you have me right where you want me. At that point, that's when you—"

I smiled and stopped in mid-sentence. He looked at me and waited for me to finish. I had him right where I wanted him. I turn around and walk towards my room.

I looked back at him, and said, "I would finish, but unfortunately it seems I had a lapse in memory. I may need to be reminded of how you close."

67

9 | Nine

ast night couldn't have been better. I was still wrapped up in the deep sleep I fell into after our passionate rounds of sex when I heard the knocking on my door. I rolled over to check my phone. It was 9 a.m. so I had no idea who could be on the other side of my door. I didn't have any missed calls and Micah was lying next to me. I prayed it wasn't Asha or otherwise this would definitely be awkward. I stretched across the bed while lying still a little while longer. I had hoped they would get a clue and would go away.

"Did you want me to get the door?"

"Nope, whoever is it didn't call first. Therefore, they will eventually get the hint," I said, rolling back over.

After Trent's surprise visit I was done opening my door to unwanted visitors. I had no tolerance for pop-ups at this point in time. I had enough secrets to keep buried. I didn't need anything or anyone exposing them sooner than I cared to explain them. Besides, I had no idea who it could have been anyway. Other than my family, Asha, and Micah no one knew where I lived. Cree wasn't due to come for another two weeks. Therefore, anyone on the other side of that door was clearly at the wrong address.

"Ry, I'm not going to lay here while somebody bangs on your door. I'll go see who it is."

"Suit yourself, but I'm not getting up," I said, pulling the covers back over my head.

I wanted to hop up and stop him. I should have, but unfortunately I had no energy to do so. The last round I won and it took everything out of me. I figured whoever was at that door was about to get the surprise of a lifetime. Hopefully, this didn't backfire on me. I heard the door open and close without much conversation. Maybe it really was someone at the wrong address.

I waited a few minutes for him to come back to the room, but there was nothing. I rolled over to see down the hallway, but I still couldn't see anything. I was listening to see if I could hear voices, and there didn't seem to be any sound coming from the front. I wasn't sure if this was a good thing or bad thing. I figured either way I needed to see who or what was up there. I grabbed a t-shirt and slid it over my head.

Please God let there be no more surprises.

I said a silent prayer as I walked down the hall and into the front room. I stopped midway and they caught my eyes. He was just standing there trying to figure out what was going on. I was too. He looked up when he realized I was standing there. He waited to see what my reaction would be and I drew a blank. All I could think was clearly my prayer didn't reach pass the ceiling. I was tired and searching for an explanation was not something I wanted to do right now.

"I guess I'm not the only person who knows what your favorite flower is," he said, placing the card on the table.

I wanted to move to pick up the card, yet somehow my hands wouldn't move. I had to admit they were beautiful. I searched his face for some type of emotion and couldn't see much. I detected a bit of disappointment in his voice when he made his last statement. I looked at the bouquet of white peonies and wondered who they were from. I'm guessing they were from a guy since he sounded like the world was coming to an end. The card looked like it hadn't been opened, though from the way he placed the card on the table they were.

Then the drama begins.

I walked over to the table to pick up the card. I looked down and the words were written plain as day, *I will never give up.* I stared at the card then I looked up at Micah. He was leaning against the island as if he was waiting for me to explain. I wanted to say something, anything but I couldn't figure out what to say. Honestly, I had no explanation because I had no clue who these could were from. I had an idea though no concrete proof. There were only two people who could be responsible for this.

I wanted to rule Cree out since this didn't seem like his style. He was more of a, *I want you to know this is from me type of guy.*

Romantic surprises didn't really happen too much when we were together. Not to mention, I couldn't remember ever mentioning peonies were my favorite flower to him. To be honest, I may have. Since he was on this newfound life path, and my head was everywhere, I really wasn't sure. Then there was Trent, whom I prayed they weren't from. Though the message on the card clearly indicated it was him, which would prove Tae was right. Despite my suspicions, there was no name on the card which meant whoever sent them automatically assumed I would know it was them.

They were so wrong.

With all that was going on in my life, it could literally be anyone other than the person standing in my front room looking at me sideways. I could call either of them to find out the truth. In doing so, that would mean I would have to say thank you and be forced to acknowledge reasons for sending them. I had no energy or emotional space to argue with Trent anymore since I was done with him. Now as far as Cree was concerned, I would address him when he arrived. At the moment, I needed to clean this up. Fighting over flowers was the least of my worries at this point. I still needed to slide Cree's visit in.

He kept quiet as long as he could. I figured he was waiting for me to kick off the conversation.

He looked at me, and said, "So you wanna tell me who is sending you flowers or no? I mean, I would think it's a random person if they weren't peonies. These aren't typical flowers to send someone unless you know the person likes them. Oh, and let's not forget the card."

He had a point.

I kept staring at the card. I figured now would be a good time to tell him about what happened over the holidays. How I had one ex propose to me in front of my family and completely embarrassed me. Then after all of that happened, how I ran to the guy I cheated on him with for comfort. Now would be a great time for it all to be laid on the table.

I could bare my soul and start fresh. No secrets and no lies to get caught up in again. I could lay it on the line so that if anything else popped up he would be prepared. There was a piece of me begging and pleading for the truth to come out. A piece that wanted so badly to be loved the right way. I remembered her at one point. I recognized her smile and the way she believed in love. Then I thought about the girl I was today. How betrayal and the abuse of her trust formed the cynical outlook she now has. It was that girl who caused me to keep quiet and let the chips fall where they may. I looked up to say something, but he beat me to the punch.

70

"Rylee, if there's someone else just let me know. I realize me asking you to be with me was kind of sudden and out of the blue. So if you have someone else whom you were dating keep it real with me. I don't want to get too far into this only to find out you're going to break my heart."

"What do you mean? Are you having second thoughts?"

"No I'm not. I just want to know if there is or was something you need to end before we move any further with this? I'm asking simply because I don't want to look up in six months and someone is at your door, ready to fight because you are stepping out on them."

I laughed, and then said, "No one will be showing up at my door, Micah."

"Are you sure? You seem a little distant and somewhat different since you've been back. It's like something is on your mind, and you haven't fully come to peace with it."

I thought about what he said and part of it was true. Coming back from a proposal, and then jumping into a relationship did seem like I was caught up in a whirlwind. I realized I should have probably taken a moment for myself before I said yes. A moment to give myself a chance to really process what had actually happened in L.A.

I needed time to process Trent and Cree.

I smiled at him, and said, "Micah there is no one. I had an ex who I bumped into recently. We're cool, and it's been over for years. At this moment, it's just me and you."

I ran my fingers through my hair. The straight and narrow path seemed so feasible yesterday. Today, it was becoming a distant thought that I see drifting away. I stood up, placed the card on the table, and walked over to him. I wrapped my arms around him and looked into his eyes. He was a gentle soul even though he had a ferocious side to him at times. His eyes had hints of vulnerability hidden beneath them. I stood on my tiptoes and placed a kiss on his lips.

"I don't want to be with anybody else. I only want to be with you."

He wrapped his arms around my waist, and he placed a kissed me on my forehead.

"Good. I thought I was going to have to rough somebody up to prove my love for you."

We both laughed and I laid my head against his chest. I looked at the flowers on the table and the note I had placed in front of them. Words somehow connected to a life miles and miles away. A life I was fighting to put behind me. I closed my eyes as the sound of his heartbeat slowly thumped against my ears. I could hear the words I said to him replay in my head. I held him tighter and exhaled.

I missed my opportunity. I missed my chance to be free and start over.

Hopefully, I could keep this under control.

10 | Ten

few days had passed since the flower incident. Micah was gone for a couple of road games and Asha was busy studying. I was glad because it gave me a chance to clear my head and think. Even though I had already committed to Micah, there was still time to reconsider. Yes, there were feelings involved, but I could still get out before any further damage was done. I still had time to tell him I needed more time. He had already suffered a broken heart. I couldn't be the reason he had two.

I could hear myself thinking out loud, "Why did you say yes? Why did you complicate this?"

I had no answers. I had no reason as to why I jumped into this other than I liked him. I felt like we had such great chemistry, and just maybe I could have the best of both worlds.

I wanted to have the sex and freedom. I wanted love and unlimited orgasms. I wanted it all wrapped up in one person.

Maybe I was fooling myself or maybe I was allowing my feelings to lead me. Either way I was going to be okay with the outcome. Whether I caused its demise or it happened naturally. In the midst of my clarity, I realized I hadn't spoken to my mother since the whole proposal fiasco. She had called a few times like everyone else when I initially got back. Like the rest of them, I told her I didn't want to talk right now. I told her would call once I'd gotten my head on straight. Coming from a proposal gone bad to a new relationship needed processing. I needed time to put things into perspective without judgment.

Sometimes my mother was incapable of not passing judgment. Her need for control and the appearance of perfection clouded the fact she just needed to listen. I appreciated her raw and blunt way of giving advice. I knew because of it I was strong and able to take some hits. Sadly, this was not one of those times. I needed a sounding board I could pour into, and for her to just listen to me. I knew I could have called my father and talked through it. The only thing about that route would be I'd eventually end up at this exact point, and having to figure this out for myself. He would listen, and give me some advice. Once he finished, he would leave me in a state of bewilderment. Unlike my sisters, I figured out long time ago the method to his madness.

You would have to figure it out for yourself. You got yourself into it so do the work and get yourself out of it. He liked his method. It forced us to be accountable for our actions and decisions. It put all the responsibly on us. This method, his method, forced us to be independent thinkers. This way we could pass no blame on anyone for the advice given. I didn't mind his way seeing I was going to end up doing what I wanted anyway. He knew it and I knew it.

There was no need to put myself through this rigorous amount of conversations. My mother on the other hand, would offer her advice whether you asked for it or not. I could hear my father now, *Marita, stay out of it. Let her figure it out.* She never listened, which was a clear indication where our rebellious streaks stemmed from. I picked up the phone to call her. I knew I didn't have too much time left on the clock before she showed up at my door. For a brief moment, when Micah went to answer the door the other day I thought it was her. I thought she had hopped in her car or on a plane. Showing up on one of our doorsteps was not beneath her. If it had been her, she definitely would've gotten quite a shock. She would have definitely concluded he was the reason I made a mad dash for the door. I never believed my mother thought any of us were angels. Most well versed parents who knew better never let it cross their minds. Something tells me she would never fathom just how close we were to the other side.

It was actually funny when I thought about it.

Oddly, Jay would be somewhat safe. She only has a couple of potholes on her road to heaven. Tae and I on the other hand, have parlayed in the devil's playground so long we probably wouldn't even get directions to the road to heaven. I picked up my phone and decided to get this over with. I took a deep sigh and pressed the button that called her. I prayed this would be a simple conversation. We could catch up with each other minus the five million questions. I knew that was like praying for a miracle so I prepared myself.

Ring! Ring! Ring!

"Well hello my lovely daughter. Seems you've decided to come up for air and call your mother. I'm glad to know there is still air in your lungs."

I laughed. She could never resist small moments of sarcasm.

"Hi momma. How have you been?"

"I'm fine Lee. How are you?"

"I'm good. I've been getting back into the swing of things regarding school. I need to shake this procrastination bug since being on break kind of put me in a lackadaisical mode. How are daddy and everyone else?"

"Everyone is fine. You know your grandparents were sad that they didn't hear from you before you left. I thought you would have come back to at least say goodbye to them."

Now I felt bad. I loved my grandparents. Since they lived on the other side of the country, I didn't get to see them very often.

"I know and I'm sorry. I'll call them later on. I never intended to rush out of there like that. I just felt like I was suffocating, and I needed an escape."

Suffocating was an understatement. No matter how many times I replayed that night over in my head it never made sense. I never saw it coming and by the looks on everyone's faces, they didn't either. When he first started, my first instinct was to locate my mother. I knew I had told her what happened between us and somehow I still felt she may have been a part of him doing this. She liked Trent. Yes, he cheated on me, yet I felt she was still rooting for him. When I realized no one could have helped him execute this, I ran.

"I understand. Well how do you feel now? Have you talked to Trent since it happened?"

"I'm fine and yes we've talked. Well it was more like we argued. Hopefully he understands why I do not want to marry him. I also told him I didn't appreciate him embarrassing me in front of my family."

I figured I would leave out the other parts of the conversation. She really did not need to hear about Zoe, nor the extreme use of profanity the cab driver endured.

"Well you have to admit it was rather bold and courageous considering this is Trent we're talking about. I mean your father and I were shocked. I couldn't imagine what would prompt him to do something like propose. Your sisters on the other hand found it to be rather amusing."

I'm glad they thought so.

Personally, I couldn't find one ounce of courage in what he did. I would give him stupid and well planned, but definitely not courageous. He was hoping putting me on the spot would force me to say yes. He also hoped the 4.5 carat diamond ring was going to be even more convincing. It was a beautiful ring and if he had been the right person, I would've said yes in a heartbeat. Unfortunately, he wasn't the right person. I mean on paper yes he was the right person.

Trent had all the right credentials that any parent would find great and suitable for their daughter. He was a doctor and a very good one. He was eventually going to branch off into his own practice. He had a couple of properties and a nice portfolio. Regardless of all those pros, it wasn't enough. I mean, if I didn't mind dying of boredom, occasional emotional abuse and sexual frustration, he would be my first pick. He had financial security and I knew I could get away with just about everything other than murder. Sadly, I was in no way looking forward to my sweet box not being used properly. Nor was I interested in being married to someone I would eventually try to kill.

Where was the fun in that?

"I don't know if would call his little stunt bold and courageous, "I said, laughing.

She laughed too.

"Honestly Lee, I didn't think he had it him. I would've expected something like that from that little rough neck you liked, but never Trent though."

Geez, clearly rough neck was Cree's identifier. She was fishing and I knew it. Everyone saw me run out after he proposed. Seeing as though my sisters, cousins, and Kira were there the question was where did I run too? *Better yet, who did I run too?* I knew she didn't approve of Cree. Therefore, I never saw the need to defend his honor. He would never be good enough in her eyes so I saw no purpose in trying to convince her of such. When I thought about it, he could care less if I did or didn't defend him. I felt like it was that very attitude that made us click. He had a rebellious side to him as well. He never cared what people thought of him. You were either for him or against him. Either way he felt no need to validate either of the two. Oddly, Trent was just as much of a mess as Cree, though somehow his wrongdoings were forgivable.

"He has a name momma. It's been four years now. You could at least call the man by his name," I said, laughing.

I really didn't mind the fact she wasn't a fan of his. I would, however, prefer she call him by his name. Cree and I happened because I allowed it to happen. He didn't deserve to bear that cross by himself.

"Fine, I expected something like that from Cree not Trent."

"Why is that? You never met Cree and are only judging him based on some conversations I had with Jayce and Taylor. I won't say he was a saint, but a surprise proposal I can guarantee he won't do."

I knew saying his name made her want to leap off a cliff. I actually found it humorous and paid no attention to it. None of the men in my past were innocent, including Trent so I moved on. Her expecting him to do a surprise proposal versus Trent showed just how little she knew about either of them. Cree was daring and all, however, he wouldn't do a surprise proposal in a room of strangers. Trent on the other hand, well we see what happened. His arrogance always seemed to leave him looking stupid. When I ran everything through my mind that night, I realized I played a small part in this madness.

Yes, I slept with him multiple times. No, I didn't stop when I should have, and now I was paying for it.

Sadly, I wasn't sure I needed too. We were two consenting adults who were occasionally breaking each other off. How a proposal became a factor in any of this was mind boggling. It was so like him to go from zero to a hundred overnight. His confidence had always been sexy. It was when it became more than confidence I began having problems with it.

"Speaking of Cree, have you spoken to him? I know Taylor still talks to him, which is weird since he's your ex. Is it because you asked her too?"

I wanted to correct her about the ex-comment, but decided it wasn't worth addressing. I couldn't believe it. Five minutes ago she couldn't call the man by his name. Now she was asking me if I was having my sister spy on him.

She was unbelievable.

I looked at the flowers sitting in the middle of my table. I'd be lying if I said I didn't want them to be from him. A part of me missed him. I missed all of the crazy filled days and late nights full of forbidden sex. What we had was left unfinished, and sometimes I felt like our chapter needed to be played out. He was the bad boy I dated to get over my cheating boyfriend. He then evolved to the guy I dated to piss my mother off. Through all of it there was this void left unfilled because we went our separate ways. I never got a chance to date him for the right reasons. We never had a fresh start. Now he was back in my life and fighting to be a contender again. Only problem was I was no longer in the game.

"Mother, I would never have anyone spy on anyone. Taylor speaking to Cree has nothing to do with me. I didn't even know they were still cool until she mentioned it. They had gotten cool when we all were hanging out, and they stayed in touch. None of which I had to be updated about."

"You still didn't answer my question?"

"I did. You asked if I was having Tae spy on Cree, and I said no. Which part did I leave out?"

"Oh, you know which part. I'm your mother Rylee, therefore I know you better than you know yourself. I also know you are a master at avoiding questions you don't want to answer. Chopping off part of the question doesn't mean you answered it. So since you are going to act like you forgot what I asked let me remind you. Have you talked to Cree lately?"

Why did she want to know?

I wasn't in any danger, nor were we even within a close range of each other. I shook my head because she was right.

I was purposely avoiding the question simply because I had no desire to hear her reaction to my answer. I also wanted to avoid her going on and on about how he was a bad influence on me. If she only knew we were equal in the bad influence department she would let it go already. Hell, it was the exact reason why I walked away. I would never forget the night I knew it was over. The night I cried because I had to make the hard decision.

One of us had to be responsible. One of us had to see the downward spiral we were on.

Whether it was passion, love, or lust, one of us had to get off the uncontrollable ride.

I figured I would tell the truth since I'm sure she somehow found out we had spoken recently. I doubt my sisters would've said anything. They knew how she felt about Cree. No one was crazy enough to throw fuel on that slow burning fire. She may have accepted my stance regarding Trent, but she was nowhere near that evolved.

"I bumped into Cree at the airport when I came home for Christmas. So yes I guess you can say I've spoken to him recently."

Answered, and now it was case closed. She wasn't getting any more than what I gave. I needed to change the subject and quick. I was trying to block him out. The longer I sat on the phone and talked about him it would make it that much harder. I was focused on Micah, and I needed to stay in my lane. Cree was ancient history even though he would be on my doorstep soon.

"Where's daddy?"

"He went golfing with your Uncle Ryan. They decided to have a guy's day so I'm here relaxing."

And being nosey, I thought to myself.

I was glad she went along with the subject change since she knew me so well so I'm sure she got the hint. I was already dealing with the decision of if I was going to even say anything about Cree visiting. Her scrutiny was not welcomed at this point.

"Okay, well I have some running around to do so I'll call you all a little later on."

"Alright, one last thing though."

Of course she had one more comment.

"Yes mom."

"Please don't fall back into Cree, Rylee."

Too late, I thought to myself. I could hear the concern in her voice though I didn't understand why. She always spoke of him as if he was this dark presence hovering over me. I wish she could see he's nothing like who she has made him to be in her mind.

"What are you talking about momma? Cree and I are just friends."

I tried to sound convincing, seeing as though I was telling partial truths.

"Staying in touch with your sister all this time is no coincidence. They may be friends and all, but I know there's more to it. I may have never met him, still I know his type. He's always moved with an angle and he still does. It's his hustler mentality. You placed some distance between you and your so-called past when you moved. So keep the distance from all of it. I'm not sure where you went when you left though my gut tells me it was to him. Whether you realize it or not, I know what he does to you. Falling back into that bad habit, regardless of how much he says he's changed, is never a good thing. Take it from me, I've dated his type and they never change. They only present the appearance of change."

"Yes mom, I hear you."

"I hope you do, Lee. No good will come from re-opening another door to your past. Let well enough alone and move on. You live in a new city. Meet a nice young man and enjoy being somewhere different. Both Trent and Cree have caused you enough trouble. Close those doors and start fresh. Do you hear me, baby?"

I sighed. I knew she only wanted what was best for me. I wasn't sure what place of experience she was speaking from seeing my father was a different man. I acknowledged the fact we all had our secrets. Untold stories never to be spoken of. We said our goodbyes and I hung up. I had one thought and one thought alone on my mind. I was going to kill my sisters.

11 | Eleven

gathered the stuff I needed and headed to the door. My keys were on the table by the door. I glanced at the flowers before I walked out. I exhaled so I could inhale a whiff of their sweet aroma. Even though she was somewhat off base, my mother had a point. Cree did have an effect on me. He always had, and he always would. I was playing with fire by having him here. I knew it deep down. Somehow, my mind felt confident it was in control. It believed there would be no issues, and we would get through the two days before my sisters arrived smoothly. My body on the other hand was a different problem. It responded differently to Cree, which was the effect my mother was forewarning me about. She had no clue about Micah so it had nothing to do with my current relationship. I swiped my passcode on my phone to call out.

My sisters had some serious explaining to do.

The mere fact my mother uttered the very words I had spoken to them was no coincidence. She had her moments when she would hit the nail on the head, I'd give her that much. Though, this didn't seem to be one of those moments. I wasn't sure if my sisters' blabbing my business to her was what bothered me or if it was what she said. She hit a raw spot when she said what I may have been thinking about Cree.

Ever since the flowers had arrived I couldn't shake it. I gave no thought to the flowers being from Trent since in my mind they were from Cree. There was an internal change my body morphed into around him. I could never explain what it was exactly. I always felt he was the one person I could be carefree and uninhibited with. No cares and no worries, just enjoying the moment for what it was and nothing more. I saw life in a different way with him. I realized with him I desired so badly to run free. I embraced the fact monogamy was not something I wanted. I was a slave to the word once since society and my mother frowned upon anything else. I allowed myself to be imprisoned by a relationship because *I love you* was whispered.

Youth had a way of betraying you. Worrying about the opinions of others aged you. The acceptance of self was the only true lifeline.

I dialed Taylor first.

The phone rang twice before she answered, and said, "Hello."

"Hold on," I said, and then clicked over and called the other one.

"Hey Lee, what's up?"

I merged the calls, and said, "So which one of you blabber mouths told momma about Cree?"

"What are you talking about?" Taylor asked.

"Yeah Lee, nobody said anything to momma about you and the secret love affairs you seem to be having again," Jayce said, laughing.

I was so glad she thought this was funny, especially since she was probably the one who told. Everyone knew if my mother wanted to know anything about either of us, she would ask Jayce. Mainly because she knew Taylor and I were lost causes when it came to spilling the beans. Taylor would play crazy and I would simply redirect her to the person she was inquiring about. Maybe it was the oldest kid thing, who knows. With the way my life was right now, I hadn't had a lot of time to be nosey. I was in a relationship when I was allergic to monogamy, and yet part of me was ok with it. I wasn't sure how long this calm before the storm would last. It was a vicious cycle I knew would eventually come full circle. I hoped I didn't hurt Micah in the process. I prayed I didn't lose control. He was no Trent, and this would be no easy hurt to overcome.

"Glad you think this is funny, Jay. What did momma bribe you with this time to get you to spill the beans?"

"Wow I'm actually offended you felt I was the one who cracked. It could've been Tae you know. Besides last we talked you and Cree really didn't have much to talk about. So what could I possibly tell unless you were lying?"

I wished she could've have seen my face. My whole mouth was turned up at the very thought she was trying to act offended, surprised, and then got smart. I didn't lie about what happened between Cree when I ran out. I just chose to keep some of my business to myself. There was no harm, no foul.

Tae laughed, and said, "Well that's because everyone knows you're momma's go to for gossip chic."

We all laughed. She knew it was true so she saw no need to deny it.

"For your information I haven't spoken to momma, and if I did I wouldn't have said anything about you and your extra romances you got going on over there."

I pulled out of my parking garage and headed to the bookstore. It was the weekend, and I needed to grab a book. I hadn't had a chance to read for leisure since I was back in school. I wanted something to take my mind off of my own craziness. Reading offered me an escape, and I definitely needed one, right along with a glass of wine. My balcony was calling me, and it was a pretty nice afternoon.

"Well somebody said something because she seems to know I was with Cree when I ran out the house. The only two people who knew that were you two. So who was it?"

"I think you're going crazy," Tae said.

"Lee we didn't tell momma anything," Jayce replied.

"Right, I mean it wouldn't take a rocket scientist for her to figure it out though. We all were there so where else could you have gone. On top of that she knew we had seen him at the club so she probably figured you ran to him," Tae said.

"Oh," I replied.

I had totally forgotten about seeing him when we went out. I thought she was gone by the time we had even talked about seeing him. It was almost as if she had a Cree radar, and anytime his name was brought up she was within an ears reach to hear it. She didn't care for him and I often wondered why. I mean, I knew the whole street life wasn't a pro for any parent so I understood the concern. However, there was something else to the disdain feeling she harbored for him. Her earlier mention of knowing *his type* led me to believe she wasn't referring to my father. I had heard of his dealings with that lifestyle from my grandmother. He was no angel by any means. Unlike one of my uncles though, he got on the right path. My grandmother told me my mother saved his life. Her no nonsense attitude with that lifestyle forced him to walk away. It was her or the streets. I knew her warning was not in reference to him. The silent plea buried beneath her advice belonged to another. I was curious about my mother's past loves. I wanted to know about all of the men who may have had her heart at some point. She didn't seem to hand it over easily so I was interested in knowing about the men who tamed my mother's wild spirit.

She was a stallion. She was the one who ran free. The one who only slowed down for those who were worthy. We were similar in many ways.

"I don't think she knows anything. You know momma will act like she knows something to get you to tell on yourself. I do have to ask though. Why does it matter if she knows? Are you having second thoughts about him being there in a couple of weeks? I mean, it sounds like you're a little panicky. Why don't you just tell him to stay in a hotel? It's not like he can't afford it," Jay said.

She had a valid point, but I couldn't retract the invitation now. I would be fine and so would he. At least I was leading myself to believe I would be. I hadn't been alone with him since Christmas and even that didn't go too well. This time would be different. I would use Micah as my defense if things got too heated before my sisters got there.

"I already told him he could stay here so it would be rude to change my mind now."

"Is that the real reason or is there something else? Sounds like you want him to stay there more so than him. Better yet, are you trying to see if there's still anything between the two of you?" Tae asked.

Leave it to Tae to point out the obvious. She was so annoying! A fly couldn't hide in the room without her drawing attention to it.

"I don't care either way to be honest. He asked and I said yes. Seeing as if I were to ever visit him somewhere, he would let me crash with him. We're friends so I don't see the big deal."

Dead silence lingered for a few seconds. I was throwing this *friend* term around like they had no knowledge of our past. I knew they were digesting what I had said and trying to figure out how they should respond. We weren't afraid of being honest with each other. We would be real about whatever we felt despite if the other person wanted to hear it. We vowed a long time ago to always be honest with each other regardless if it hurts. I felt this was one of those times.

They were being strategic, and their approach had to be delicate. Despite our honesty pact, I was known to be defensive. I would easily turn everything off and walk away.

"Well, if you want to keep telling yourself you two are *just friends*, then I'll just leave it alone. I'm good with your decision either way. Just let me know if I need to bring some real pajamas or if I can walk around with my butt out," Tae said, and we all laughed.

None of us really wore clothes around the house. The very thought of three half naked girls running around the house used to drive my mother nuts. She was old school and believed in robes and the whole nine. We, on the other hand, felt like we were home so why wear all of these unnecessary clothes. My father would advocate for us sometimes, though when it got too crazy he would side with her.

"Have you told Micah yet?" Jay asked.

"No, I was going to tell him the morning after our date and didn't get a chance to get it out. Somebody had a bouquet of flowers delivered to my house."

"Someone, but you don't know who?" Tae blurted out.

"If she did she wouldn't have said someone crazy," Jay replied, sarcastically.

I laughed, and then said, "I don't know who they are from, although they can only be from Cree or Trent seeing Micah was looking at me crazy when they arrived."

I pulled into *Barnes & Noble* parking lot, found a spot upfront, and parked my car. I could hear them talking amongst each other and I just listened. Tae was going on about how she felt they were another desperate attempt from Trent. Jayce disagreed with her and told her it was Cree getting me warmed up. I leaned my head against the headrest, while they continued to debate. None of this was helping me. I didn't need their rationality. I just needed an answer. Usually, I was perfectly fine with making my own decisions. For some reason, this time I wanted someone to do it for me. I opened my door and headed into the store.

"Well, I'm glad you two detectives are on the job. When you figure it out let me know. Until then, I'll call you once I finish running my errands."

"Bye," they both said at the same time.

We all hung up and I reached for the door.

I wanted a good book so I could sit on my balcony and get lost in it. I wanted to free my mind of the mini cluster-fuck it was in. The love triangle my mind was begging me not to go deeper into.

I wanted to be free of all the madness.

12 | Twelve

I *floated around the bookstore undecided on* *what I was in the mood for.* I was definitely horny so erotica may or may not be a good idea. Micah wouldn't be back until tomorrow so if I got too hot he wouldn't be here to put out any fires I may have. Asha was probably home. I could always swing by there if I really needed someone to give my sweet spot some much needed attention. I hadn't realized with it being basketball season that I would be on a sex ration. That is not a good position for me to be in. I was trying to be good, and it was hard.

I liked sex, actually I loved sex. I always have if I thought about it long enough. I always had a curiosity that extended far beyond what a normal person should have.

I was no longer in denial about it. Seeing my sex drive was at an all-time high, rationed sex would not work. I knew if he were here we would definitely be going round for round. Unfortunately, he wasn't and I or shall I say my sweet spot would only wait so many days. I knew I needed to make sure we got in a few good hot and sweaty rounds before Cree arrived. It was the only way I would survive until my sisters showed up. I grabbed the last of my book selections and made my way down the aisle to check out. I was excited to dive into *Decadence* by Eric Jerome Dickey. I fell in love with his character Nia Simone after his novels, *Pleasure and The Education of Nia Simone Bijou.* Her desire to explore her sexuality without the concern of judgment intrigued me. She was a free spirit. I understood and related to her on that level. I headed out the aisle when I managed to bump into the one person I had no business running into at this point. I was horny and although his arrogance was over the top, it was somewhat sexy and damn near a turn on. It was almost challenging if I'd had to really label it. He was the type I took pleasure in breaking down to his knees. The perfect position to reach the only area his tongue needed to be moving in.

"Well, well, well, if it isn't the seductress herself. Didn't think I would run into you again, though I will say it's a pleasure."

I fought so hard not to roll my eyes.

I looked at him, trying to fix my face of the annoying look I know it reflected. He couldn't just say hello. He had to lace it with some form of game that I had no real interest in hearing. I moved to walk around him, however his incredibly large frame was blocking me. He was attractive face wise, though he had a nice caramel complexion. Between his body and his swag, I was sure it was how he pulled women. I could tell football is what held his body together, otherwise his body would probably go to hell.

"Hello Titus. It's nice to see you again," I said, trying to disguise the lie I was telling.

"Oh Reece, you say that like you don't mean it. Besides, I told you everyone calls me Bishop."

"Well lucky for you I'm not everyone else so Titus works just fine for me," I snapped back.

I tried looking for a way around him but it wasn't happening. He was solid so the only way I was getting away from him was to turn around and walk all the way back the other way. I had a feeling he would block that too so I didn't bother even starting the game he seemed to want to play. He looked me up and down, and then licked his lips before smiling.

"I like the way it sounds coming from your lips anyway."

I shrugged. Oh, that was the mouthpiece that made panties of the naive fall quickly. He actually had a nice set of teeth. I was big on teeth, white teeth. I liked a man that had his own set of teeth in good health and not fifty million colors. I never understood with all the different types of over the counter dental products how you could be missing teeth or that they would be falling out. Major turnoff! A man could be fine as hell, but if his teeth were jacked up I would pass. I was not into projects. Fixing another grown person up was of no interest to me. I was my own project. Taking on another one, only for it to probably end, did not excite me. I figured if you couldn't manage something simple as brushing your teeth I was definitely too much to handle.

"Glad to hear it. Well, if you don't mind, I would like to check out and go home."

"Home? Why would you be inside on this beautiful day? Where's your man at? He should be taking you on a picnic in *Jackson Square* or at least a nice walk through the *French Quarter.*"

He was fishing for info and I knew it.

He remembered the slight diss I showed him at the New Years' party we met each other at. I knew it wouldn't be the last time I bumped into him. I had only hoped I wouldn't be by myself. He was an Alpha male and Alpha males were my weakness. I loved a man who was strong, assertive, and intelligent. They were the only kind I knew and would be bothered with. I had no attraction to men who let women run over them. I needed a balance like my parents. My mother was a strong woman and my father knew it. He knew she needed the room and freedom to be strong. Aside from that, she needed to be right 90% of the time. Regardless of how it may have looked to the outside world, we all knew who really ran our household. My father had a strong, yet silent presences. When he was done talking about it and a decision was reached the conversation was over. We all knew it and acted accordingly, including my mother. They respected each other's strength and role in their marriage. It was a balance, and once I finished my sexual exploration whenever that was, I would need and had to have it.

There was nothing more and nothing less.

"My man is where he's supposed to be, and I have every intention on enjoying this beautiful day on my balcony with my book and wine as soon as you move out of my way."

"Or could it be that your man is on the road, and you're reading because you're bored. If boredom is the case, I have plenty of ways to excite you and keep your interest. I mean if you were my woman I would not be leaving you unattended in a city full of available men. I mean you are incredibly beautiful. I know firsthand how many men would hop on the opportunity to be walking hand-and-hand with you," he said, while licking his lips again.

A smirk formed upon my lips and I chuckled.

Clearly, the lips thing was how he pulled them in. As tempting as riding his tongue appeared to be I couldn't give in for so many reasons. One being he would work my nerves for more knowing full well I had a man. Secondly, he would make it his business to rub it in Micah's face. I couldn't be a part of something I knew he would use to intensify the rival our schools had formed. The risk was too great so I would stick to my secret sex sessions with Asha. I had no fear that she would open her mouth and reveal anything.

"Titus, as much as I'm enjoying this cat and mouse game you like to play, I would really like to go home. I am perfectly happy with in my relationship. I could care less who else was interested in me. Now, you're in my way and I have no intention on walking all the way around when you can move. So move," I said, ushering him to the left.

"What are you afraid of?"

"Excuse me?"

My face reflected every ounce of the attitude my voice had just projected.

"You heard me. What are you afraid of? Is it the sexual energy transferring between us? I know you feel it and maybe you're afraid of it. It's cool if you are, but just admit it. I won't bite. Well not hard anyway."

Wow, he really was that arrogant. Hell at this point he was a borderline asshole. I would admit there was some sexual attraction though I was nowhere near afraid of it. If anything I was doing him a favor. I had enough men I had to deal with right now. Adding him to my list was not in the least bit attractive. I looked at him, raised my eyebrow, and swallowed before I responded. I could feel my accent surfacing, and he wouldn't comprehend me once I started down that road. My sweet spot was slightly throbbing. I couldn't give into her right now. Focusing on the feeling would lead me down the wrong path. I had to stay strong, and resist the challenge to be superior over this man who I know would crumble at this slightest taste of my nectar. He used his size as intimidation. I could see it clear as day. He couldn't have been any taller than 5'11", though his frame seemed to have given illusion of a taller statute. Sadly, none of it had any bearing when it came to skill.

"What makes you think I enjoy biting?"

He looked me up and down, licked his lips, and then he winked at me with a smile.

"Oh Reece, I'm sure there are a lot of bad things you enjoy doing and having done to you. You have this good girl exterior, but I'm not fooled. You like getting dirty don't you?"

"You will never find out, Titus."

"Be careful, never say never Reece. I've had the pleasure of breaking down quite a few never walls in my day."

He could talk a good game. To a woman who was unsure and lacked confidence he would prevail, however, I was neither. To me he looked to have a solid 15 minutes before his world came crashing down. I could feel my inner lioness coming out. She was sharpening her claws and her predatory nature was seeping through my pores. She wanted to go in for the kill, show no mercy, and give no second chance. Only for the opportunity to prove she could reign supreme if need be. I opened my mouth to rip him into shreds when in a matter of seconds he had me pinned against the bookshelf, covering my mouth with his. His hands pinning my waist to the shelf as our tongues dueled aggressively with each other.

He was trying to prove a point and so was I.

Our tongues dueled and fought with each other. He wanted to show his Alpha male and my Alpha female was not backing down. After what seemed like an eternity, I pulled my head back. I lost control and I needed to regain it fast. I looked around to make sure no one saw what just happened. I wanted to slap the shit out of him. I wanted to give him a clean, hard palm slap across his entire face. I'm sure he would enjoy it so I decided on a different route. He thrived on his ego so I would dig into what I knew would piss him off.

"First off all, back the hell up!" Completely forgetting I was in a public place, I let him have it while I was out of breath and all. "You have a lot of damn nerves putting your mouth and tongue on me. I have no clue where your tongue has been and you put it in my damn mouth! Newsflash jackass you can't go around kissing people unwarranted. You know I have a man so why would you do that? You know what just move out my way. Ah chuts! Chupidee!"

He looked confused. My Trinidadian side had surfaced unfortunately. I only spoke the language when I went to visit my family on the islands, and at home with my sisters when we didn't want anyone to understand what we were saying. The only other occasion was during a pissed off moment. We looked at each other. I was glad he was quiet. Finally! It seemed nothing would be able to silence him. Just when I thought he was done for good, he plastered that slick ass smile back across his face.

"Ohh you're an island girl, huh? Well, you being this angry could only mean one thing. You enjoyed it as much as I did and you're in denial."

"I'm not in denial about anything. I told you I had a man and you kissed me. It's just that simple so don't make it out to be more, Titus."

"You didn't immediately push me off so obviously you wanted it too. It's ok Reece. You'll eventually see things my way," he said, moving out of my way.

I scurried past him, turning up my mouth in the process.

"The day I see things your way is when hell freezes over, melts, and refreezes again. Goodbye for good, Titus."

I turned around and walked towards the checkout counter. I wanted to get home to my wine. I needed to rinse his taste out of my mouth. It was beginning to linger too long, and making me question the strength I was fighting hard to maintain. I placed the books and my purse on the counter. I wanted to turn around, though I knew he was still staring at me. The girl at the counter handed me my receipt and bag. I said thank you and turned to walk out, only to see that he had disappeared. *Thank you God for small favors,* I thought to myself. I made my way out of the store and to my car.

Temptation seemed to always find me, even at a damn bookstore.

13 | Thirteen

he drive home seemed too distracting. My lips seemed to still feel the tingle left behind from Titus's lips. I could still feel his hand around my waist as my heartbeat steadied itself. His scent invaded my senses as the feeling left upon my lips began to bury itself beneath the surface. The wine tasted sublime as I swallowed it slowly. I had a gorgeous view of the sky as the evening wind gracefully touched my face. I softly bit my bottom lip, hoping to erase any sign of Titus. A smile formed across my lips at the thought of his daring behavior. I had no feelings of guilt because I had no idea he was going to do it. It was unexpected and unpredictable. Totally and completely, this was not my fault! I knew I did not immediately fight him off. I was taking no blame in this one though. *More secrets,* I thought. I looked back down at my book. I had made it to chapter three with no interruptions before I heard my text alert.

It was from Asha.

I could use a dose of her right now. Titus had awakened the desire I was trying to contain until Micah came back. I wished my balcony was a little more enclosed or in a different spot. This would definitely be a good day for some outdoor sex. Just she, I, and the elements as we reached our climax and nectar flowed from our sweet spots. I contemplated the balcony sex as I texted her back.

The text read: *Not doing much here. At home, sitting on my balcony, and reading a book. Now that you have texted, I'm trying to decide if I want to ride your face as the wind blows across my skin.*

I pressed send and buried myself back into my book. Whether she came or not I was content with being here. I would love to release a few orgasms since it seemed I was becoming tense. If I couldn't have it my way, I would just wait until Micah returned tomorrow. My phone chirped again.

Her text read: *Will my balcony suffice?*

I answered: *Well damn. Sure, be there shortly.*

I really did not want to move from my spot even though she was just upstairs. I thought about it long and hard. *Riding her tongue or sitting my house? A night full of countless orgasms or my book and wine?* I had promised Micah there was no other man. Never did I say anything about a woman. I placed my book on my table, slid my flip flops on, and went into the house. I told her I would be down in a few and headed to the shower. I had been running around and needed to wash Titus' fingerprints off of me. I needed the cool water to relieve me of the dimly lit flame he sparked; that was buried beneath the surface. I had to control the fire. My inner lioness who was daring to be released. I was spoken for. I could no longer run free. The wild, my wild, now contained boundaries. Boundaries I'd hoped would be strong enough. Otherwise, she would run free and anyone in her path was fair game, and up for the taking.

Asha fell within my boundaries, I thought to myself as the water ran over my face. I missed her touch. I had dipped back when I supposedly went to end things with her. I had worked it all out in my head. I was going to tell her about Cree, the engagement, and then end our relationship. I went to tell her Micah and me we're together, and therefore she and I could no longer give each other pleasure. She could no longer disrupt my insides with her sensual tongue massages. I was going to tell her all of those things.

Somehow, it had slipped my mind. I realized I wasn't strong enough. Her lips and her touch persuaded me to give it just one more time. My willpower betrayed me. My resolve and self-control wavered in a time I needed them the most. I turned off the shower. I needed this tonight. I needed her. There was no other way for me to make it through Micah being gone or Cree being here without Asha. She was my bridge between sanity and insanity. She was the fix that would keep me afloat.

She was above water, and completely within the boundaries.

I just wanted to be in my happy place. Somewhere between ecstasy and freedom. I wanted to be uninhibited and flying high. No worries of broken hearts and hurt feelings. No concerns with judgment. I dried off, threw on shorts and a t-shirt, and headed for downstairs. I debated on taking my phone seeing I would have no interest or ability to answer it. I sent Micah a, *I miss you,* text then dropped it on the couch. I grabbed my keys and walked out the door. I took the steps since her apartment was two floors down and close to the end of hall. I knew he wouldn't see that text until later so I figured I had some time to burn.

I knocked on the door. I heard her yell come in so I opened the door. Her house always smelled of some scent that was extremely pleasurable to your senses. I could hear *The Weeknd* playing from the back. I closed the door and walked towards her bedroom. I could see what looked like candles flickering against the wall. Her balcony was connected to her bedroom. Mine was off of my front room. I would have preferred my bedroom. I turned the corner and saw her standing naked in her window.

She was totally uninhibited. She was a complete exhibitionist to her core.

From here her silhouette was perfection. It was moments like this and when her tongue was all over me that caused me to forget I was supposed to be ending this. I peeked around to see she had placed three big mirrors around the railing. I noticed her mirror that hung over her bed had been removed. I couldn't fathom how she'd gotten it down and I didn't care. It looked like sex on a balcony watching each other cum was the theme for tonight.

My kind of night.

I removed my clothes and slid out of my flip flops.

She looked over her shoulder, acknowledging she heard me come in. I moved closer to her. I wanted to feel her against my skin. I wanted to smell her womanly scent. I had never been attracted to women, nor had the desire to be with one, however she was different. There was something about her, her aura and sensual center. I traced my fingertips down the center of her back, only to stop at the top of her gorgeous ass. Whether it was sports or genetics, she had a beautiful ass. Holding onto it when she rode my tongue in pleasure sent me over the cliff. I could see traces of Micah within her, though there was someone else too. There was a wilder spirit, daring to break free. It was the side that drew me in.

She was a gentle soul mixed with a ferocious spirit. There were dual personas that made her completely and totally a Cancer. The mirrors reflected the glow the candle flame flickered as I traced the silhouette of her hip with my fingertip. I placed a soft kiss upon her shoulder and she moaned. Her skin was soft and smelled like lavender and vanilla. I placed my hand over her stomach as I moved my finger up and down her stomach. She worked out so her stomach was incredibly flat, which went perfectly with her curvy hips and rounded ass. I kissed her earlobe as my fingers began to draw circles around her breasts. Her nipples were hard, which meant she was just as ready as I was to get this show rolling. I turned her halfway around, positioning her so we could both stand in the window frame.

Those eyes, her eyes, Micah's eyes were my weakness.

The fact they went from slightly dark to a full stormy gray depending on their mood intrigued me. They enticed me so to speak. I pulled her arms above her head and moved to kiss her. Our tongues dueled round and round as our bodies pressed against each other.

She was my soft to his hard. She was the sensual, yet delicate side to our twisted love affair. I had thought about what it would be like to not have her to kiss and lick on me and I couldn't fathom it. We started this journey together, and to have to move on without her would be unacceptable. She softly bit on my bottom lip and I smiled. I playfully licked her lips as I released her hands.

"Lie down and turn over on your stomach," Asha requested.

I stepped outside and lay down on the palette she created. Surprisingly, it was really soft. I wasn't sure what she was about to do, though I was excited. I loved how there was always something new with her. As soon as I laid my head on my arms, I felt warm oil on my back. My initial reaction was to jump, but her hands gliding over my ass and up my back settled me. *The Zone* was playing through the speakers. I took a deep breath and watched her hands go up and down my body through the mirror. My sweet spot hadn't reached full throb quite yet. Usually I was ready to feel her tongue, make figure 8's within my walls by now, however her hands seemed to be extremely relaxing. It was as if she knew what I needed. With all the craziness I had going on in my head, Micah, Cree, her, and now Titus this was right on time. My shoulders, my back, my legs, and my feet had all been evenly rubbed down. My body was now relaxed. All I needed now was for my mind to follow suit. It wasn't two seconds after the thought escaped me that without warning she slid her finger inside me.

"Mmm," I moaned as she moved her finger inside my wet, yet warm center.

The contrast of hard and soft blended beautifully and she played with my clitoris. The throbbing had begun to increase. I was ready to ride her face until the night sky swallowed us. She lifted my hips, spread my legs, slid under me, and then pulled me on top of her mouth in a matter of seconds.

"Ohh God," was all I could mutter as her tongue flickered, vibrated, and sucked my clitoris.

I could feel my juices running down onto her lips. Her hands massaged my breasts as I watched my hips grind back and forth in the mirror. Watching her turned me on more. I could see and feel what she was doing to my body at the same time. I was on the verge of cumming. I could feel the intensity mounting as she pulled me down harder onto her lips.

She was truly gifted. Her lips were skillful. Her tongue formed a masterpiece upon my sweet spot.

Most people didn't realize there was an art form to this. Yes everyone had a tongue, and yes everyone was capable of licking. Sadly, very few were blessed to do both so well that it was all you could think about or even dream about. I started bouncing against her tongue until I could no longer contain the tornado brewing within.

"Asha, you are ammazing," I muttered.

Her hands moved over my breasts, down my side, and then she gripped my ass creating the perfect combination to send me plummeting over the cliff. I screamed out in pleasure. I knew it was the first of many so I saved my breath. Between the two of us, we could reach six or seven orgasms in a night. I slid down so she could catch her breath. She licked her lips. I leaned forward to lick the rest of me off her lips. She wrapped her legs around me and we rolled over so I could be on the bottom.

It was my turn.

It was my turn for her center to invade my senses, while I licked her until she surrendered her nectar to my tongue.

"Be right back," she said, getting up.

I looked up into the sky. The nighttime had begun seeping in and a mixture of dark and light blues began blending in as the moon peeked through. The night air blew across my skin. I was curious to what she was retrieving. I knew whatever it was that it would only intensify the night.

As soon as the thought escaped me she reappeared.

She stood over me and my heart skipped a beat. I had never seen a metal dildo before. It was long and silver. The tip had a curve, which I presumed was for hitting the g-spot. I immediately got hot all over again from the excitement of what was about to occur. She kneeled over me and lowered herself slowly onto the tip of my tongue. I wanted to taste her.

Her center was warm. The aroma of lavender and vanilla was inhaled and I took a slow, yet long stroke. I moved my hands to grip her behind as she moved her hips in a slow motion. I drove my tongue in as deep as I could. She moaned in sync with each stroke. I teased her clitoris, while I entered my finger into her core. She was not prepared for the entry. She was savoring the erotic waves my tongue created with each lick. I licked, and then sucked. Licked and sucked, each time pushing my finger further inside her. I moved it back and forth as she leaned her head back, moaning with pleasure.

She looked over her shoulder, and asked, "Are you ready for this?"

I nodded since there was no other way I could respond. Being she figured I was all in she leaned forward and licked my sweet spot. A few strokes of her tongue, and then I felt it. The cold, vibrating sensation of the metal dildo against my warm flesh. I lifted her up and moaned in bittersweet pleasure. She must've placed it in the refrigerator because the chilling feeling created a shock I had not expected. The vibrations and the hardness were beyond arousing. I was trying to steady my breathing and regulate my heartbeat at the same time, while she moved it in and out.

My sweet spot was on overload as she lowered herself back onto my mouth. She had become jealous of my moans and wanted some of her own.

She needed them.

I increased the speed of my strokes. I licked her intensely. Greedily and hungrily as if I needed this to survive.

Ferociously, until she had no more willpower, until her strength gave in and bowed out. Her nectar saturated my lips as she continued to rock against my lips. She wasn't through. She had more to give. I slid my finger back inside of her as she softly bounced against it and my tongue. Her tongue was buried within the lips of my sweet spot as the dildo touched my soul. I would never have thought to try a metal dildo since I figured it wouldn't feel good. Somehow she has definitely proven me wrong. I spread my legs a little wider. She pushed a little further. I rocked with the movement her body was creating upon my tongue.

She went back and forth, slow and fast, and then up and down. We were fighting the end. The inevitable we knew would eventually come. We wanted to live in this state of pleasure forever. Our orgasms were ready to be free. Our bodies could no longer contain them. We were dreading the bittersweet end. That would be the moment when our orgasms escaped us, and all we had left was the ecstasy we were to inhale. I could feel her clinching my tongue. She wanted to savor the moment.

She was giving it all she had.

I pulled her down harder as I rocked my hips against the vibrations. I was ready to be free and I needed her to be free too. These internal explosions were on the brink of combustion. I dug my fingers into her cheeks as I came in shockwaves.

There was one after another. Orgasm after orgasm, and all of them plummeted throughout my core.

I could feel the juices running down my thigh onto the palette. She sucked me softly, wanting to savor the very essence of my center. She was nearing the end as she sat up to wrap herself further around my tongue. She wanted the depth of my strokes to resonate throughout her body. I watched her back move back and forth as she watched herself in the mirror. It was her turn to watch the beauty of cumming. She ran her fingers through her hair as she gripped the strands and leaned her head back. The curvature of her back, collecting the sweat beads as they gently rolled down.

"I'm cumming," was all she could whisper as her moans took over.

Ecstasy possessed her and her mounting orgasm was now in control. She returned to the soft, up and down bounces before it took over. Pound after pound, moan after moan, she was on the verge of being freed. I relished in the sweetness of how she tasted as the scent of lavender and vanilla mixed with her nectar and flowed down my throat. I could still feel her throbbing as I finished her off with slow strokes.

Her body had surrendered. Her orgasm was waving the white flag. Pleasure and nirvana had declared a victory.

She moved to lie at the opposite end. She reached for what I knew to be her nightcap. She lit it and inhaled. I smelled what I assumed was a grape flavored option this time. She handed me the bong and I joined her in the state of bliss we seemed to be in. I inhaled twice and handed it back to her. I lay back down and looked up into the sky as I reveled in this erotic trance I was in. I closed my eyes and let the grape flavored substance nestle its way into my senses.

I had one thought and one thought alone. I was never giving this up. I wasn't giving up him or her ever.

14 | Fourteen

*"*ou did what! With who exactly? Rylee Reece Coltrane are you serious!"*

I was laughing hysterically through the phone as Kira was ranting and raving. We hadn't had a chance to really talk since everything happened. I ran out of there like a bat out of hell. Now that I think about it, we hadn't really talked in depth since I moved. I missed our Saturday morning conversations as we chatted about our dreams, our new loves, and the many other things going on in our lives. I also missed just lying across her couch with a glass of wine as we reminisced about the fun and crazy times we had. Every woman needed a friend she could do those things with. You need another woman, whether friend, or family member to share those intimate, yet private thoughts that you wouldn't tell another soul. I was prancing around the house cleaning up while talking to her. Micah would be back tomorrow and I had let my house go to shits for a few days. It was actually one of the things I loved most about living alone.

I could clean when I wanted to.

"Kira, you are cracking me up!"

"I'm glad you're getting a kick out of all of this. I see I can't let yo' ass go three feet without supervision. You move away and go completely buck wild."

"What are you talking about? I was wild at home. "

"Chile please, you know damn well Marita wasn't having all of that nonsense in L.A," she said, laughing.

She knew my mother oh so well. She, Taylor, and I had some wild nights, but still within certain boundaries. My mother had a reputation, and we didn't need our ruckus getting back to her. She would be mortified. We laughed together as we remembered our little street fight. It was me, Kira, and some girl who felt like she had rights to Kira's then on again, off again boyfriend.

"Whatever, you seem to be confusing me with my sisters. I was a free spirit or did you forget?"

"Oh I remember quite well grasshopper. I also remember how we almost got killed a few times because of your need for freedom. You could never dance on the line of trouble. You my dear always had to cross it, and then run ten miles out. It was madness sometimes dealing with your crazy butt."

I laughed again because she was right. I was never one for rules. They had no place in my life. Everyone else's idea of what I should and should not do blew in the distant wind as far as I was concerned. I lived my life my way. Anyone else would have to move on to the next willing soul. I could never be a victim of conformity. I was a rider for rebellion. I listened to her as she told me about the married life. I was still shocked she was married. Kira was similar to me and free until the day she died. Somewhere along the way, she jumped ship and fell in love. I was happy for her though. She loved him, and despite his crazy antics in the past, he loved her too. When it was all said and done, it was the only true and real thing that mattered.

"Well, I always had you there to be my voice of reason," I told her.

"Yeah a voice you rarely listened to."

She had a point seeing I never gave much ear to the voice.

"Well just know I heard you even though it never seemed like I did."

"Ok well, that's nice and all but I want to hear about this five-way split love affair you have going on missy. Spill the beans since you've been holding out on a sistah. I can't believe you've had all this exciting drama going on and you haven't told me. You know I live vicariously through you and Tae now. Start talking!"

"Well first of all I'm not in a five-way split love affair or whatever you want to call it, heffa. I'm engaging in sexual activities with two people. Get your facts straight," I responded, laughing.

"I'm sorry. It seems moving away has somehow affected the way you count. Let's see there's Trent who showed up at your door two days before New Year's and proposed to you. Now it doesn't take a rocket scientist to figure out there was some type of motivation behind him making that much of an ass out himself and you know it. You've been dipping in the cookie jar so don't try and deny it."

"Yeah, yeah, I dipped back twice. Let's not break out the pom-poms or anything. Who was I to think that the person who cheated on me numerous times couldn't handle having casual sex without catching feelings so go figure."

She busted out laughing.

"You're kidding me right? When you broke up with him he begged you take him back for months. You know damn well he wanted you back so don't play like you didn't. You took advantage of it and him so keep it real heffa."

"Well honestly I didn't until he showed up at my door five months ago. I had given no thought to Trent still having feelings about me whatsoever, nor did I care. I knew I didn't want to be with him, therefore nothing else crossed my mind. Besides, Trent isn't in love with me. He's in love with an idea of me, which doesn't push you to propose. He's older than me and he knows better. He hasn't found what he really wants and thinks going backwards is the answer."

"Is that right?" she asked.

"Yes, you know it as well as I do that he's not in love with me to the point of marriage. I believed a lot of his little stunt had my mother written all over it."

"Chile you took the words right out of my mouth. I was going to ask you if you already asked her about it. I didn't want to throw it out there, but we all know your mother is a Trent fan until the end. Why she still is baffles me, but hey we're all entitled to root for who we want to win."

I thought about what she had just said, *Root for who we want to win*. I wondered who she was rooting for or my sisters for that matter. To be honest, I wasn't sure who I was rooting for, but I knew damn well it wasn't Trent.

He and I were done in this world and the next.

"No I didn't, though her responses to it led me to believe she wasn't a part of it. I ended up telling her about what really happened with us before he did it so her doing that would have been ass backwards."

"What do you mean? What did you tell her?"

"I told her how he cheated on me and that for many reasons he and I could not be together. Now I didn't get into the whole tearing up his house and stuff. I didn't think she needed or wanted to know about all of those issues. I just explained how we had a lot of drama and going back to it was not an option."

101

Kira got quiet.

I knew it was because she was shocked I told my mother any of what had happened. I was private and kept my relationship issues to myself. I knew how my mother felt about him. I knew her love for me would never waiver so I saw no need to paint him in a bad light. I had already moved out by the time all of the madness kicked in so she was oblivious to the inner workings of the monster she seemed to love so much.

"Well we all know your momma. She knows what's best for everyone. So I'm just glad to hear her hand wasn't in it this time."

"Right, because I would've been pissed."

We started laughing again.

Not only did my mother know she was the best agent, she also thought she was a matchmaker. I loved her and valued her opinions at times, though my love life was off limits. I needed to keep that to myself, otherwise she'll fix me up with someone like Trent. I mean he wasn't a bad person. There were far worse men to date. He just wasn't for me. He had qualities I wish could mesh with someone else, just not him as a whole. Now when I think about it, if I could pull qualities from all of them I would have the perfect man.

"Okay, so what about you're other lovers?"

"What other lovers, Kira?"

"Are you really gonna make me front you out, and have all your business yelled across L.A. traffic?" Now she was just being dramatic. "Ok let me help you out since you've seemed to have forgotten. I guess you're on sex overload and your brain cells aren't working properly. Since we've covered your ex whom I can't stand and would gladly run over with a semi-truck, let's talk about your new boo in New Orleans."

"Semi-truck, really Kira?"

"Girl bye with the shock and awe. I'm listening so start talking. You know I don't like his ass not one bit so don't get me started."

I knew why she didn't like Trent and I wasn't going to touch it. We both almost got arrested for the fiasco that occurred. Even to this day I didn't see any of it coming. *You gotta to be careful who you bring around your man, baby. Everybody who says they are your friend ain't always your friend.* I remember my MeMaw telling me those words as I buried myself in her lap and cried my eyes out. I had given my heart away. I had trusted the wrong people. I wasn't hurt at the fact that Trent cheated on me. Men will always be men. It had happened before, and I wasn't being faithful either. I was hurt and angry at the fact Zoe was supposed to be my best friend.

We had grown up together. It was the three of us. It was me, Zoe, and Kira in addition to my sisters. We were The *Fab Five* who everyone loved to hate. We fought together and we laughed together. No matter what we had each other's back. Above all we had a code that said, *You never slept with the other person's man.* Considering neither Kira nor my sisters cared for Trent, I assumed she was on the same train. *It was foolish of me to assume,* I thought to myself. Walking in on them had to be the worse. I stood there as she was kneeled on the floor sucking him off as he moaned in utter pleasure. I watched her head go up and down as I stood there in shock trying to rationalize my next move. Somehow I had stepped outside of myself, and within seconds I snapped and was all over her and him.

After I had whooped her ass, she ran out in tears while apologizing. I knew her leaving before Kira got there was her way of trying to avoid a second ass whooping. She knew Kira would've dragged her all over his house. There wasn't a corner of his house I didn't destroy. I remember him freeing himself from my grip long enough to call Kira to come get me. That was the wrong move. She came over to help me finish tearing his shit up. Broken glass, holes in the walls, and furniture turned over was how we left his house. No stone was left unturned. Chaos was all that we left behind.

We were riders until the end.

Once he realized Kira was no help, he decided to call 911. I was so full of rage I didn't even think to leave. Had it not been for Kira calling Jayce to rescue us and Trent not wanting to press charges, we would have been sitting in processing at county. Walking to the car, I left everything on his doorstep that night.

Trust, betrayal, forgiveness, and the idea of me believing in monogamy ever again were destroyed.

As I drove myself home, I promised myself I would never fully give myself to another person again. Especially a man! *If he would go so far as to ruin a friendship of more than ten years, why should I be all in?* Trent standing there with a ring had somehow brought all of those memories back. I could block the memory for the sake of an orgasm since it benefited me. Now as far as marriage was concerned, it wasn't happening. I could never marry the man who slept with one of my best friends. The image was forever engrained in my mind. I hadn't talked to Zoe since it all occurred. She called and apologized time-and-time again. Regardless of our history, I couldn't move past it. She hurt me deeper than he ever could. Forgiveness was something I couldn't offer her at the time.

She had stolen something from me and for that we would never be what we were.

"Have you talked to Zoe?"

I knew asking this was pushing it, though part of me was somewhat curious. I knew I had cut her off, but I wasn't sure where she and Kira still stood. I never bothered asking her after everything blew up. I didn't want to make her feel uncomfortable about being both of our friends.

"Actually, I saw her not too long ago. She has a little girl now who I must say is adorable. I was shocked to see she had a kid since she was so hell bent on not having any. She looked just like her."

"Wow, that is something. Zoe swore on twelve bibles and the Koran that she wasn't having kids. How old is she?"

"I believe she said she was four or five. She didn't look very big so she couldn't have been much older than six."

I leaned against the wall. The time frame seemed to be a little too convenient. I, for whatever reason, wondered if there was more to this story.

"So are you going to say it or should I?" I asked her.

I knew she was thinking the same thing, but she just didn't want to open up old wounds. I wasn't sure why I cared, however I was definitely curious. Especially since he stood in my parent's house two months ago proposing to me.

"Honestly, I wasn't sure I wanted to know. Hell, it might have pissed me off all over again," she said, laughing.

I knew Kira was put in an awkward position when everything was exposed. We were all so close and I never wanted her to feel like she had to choose between Zoe and me. I knew that my sisters would cast her aside because technically she was *my friend* so ignoring her was no problem for them. Kira, on the other hand, had a different position with her. The three of us asides from my sisters were best friends. I always felt Zoe was ashamed of what she had done, and had just separated herself from all of us. I guess she figured Kira would automatically take my side so she didn't want to stick around for it.

I really didn't think Kira would push her to side. I knew she would be pissed for a while, but I figured they would move passed it. The damage and betrayal was done to me, not her. With Zoe putting the distance between them, Kira eventually gave up. Despite the fact Zoe and I would never be friends again, I had always hoped the two of them could fix things. Since Kira knew how I felt about her, she would never bother telling me they had patched things up. Now hearing her tell me Zoe had a child, it was clear the reconciliation never took place.

"Yeah, well we know he isn't very forthcoming with information. If it were true he wouldn't have told me until after I said I do just to be sure I couldn't go anywhere."

"So let me ask you, did you even consider saying yes? I mean just for a single moment did you consider being Mrs. Trent Young?"

"Hell no I did not. You remember what I went through with him!" I yelled.

"Okay, I just had to be sure. You know sometimes we change what we want because it seems so farfetched and we settle. I know that may not necessarily be you, though it does happen. Time evolves, we get lonely, and we figure it's easier to settle with the known versus the unknown."

I listened to her and she was right on so many levels. So many women gave into the pressures of being lonely. Whether it was an emotional or psychological reason, misconceptions about being single would somehow manifest into bad decisions. Hooking up with an ex or someone not worthy would seem more attainable. They would give up hope that there was someone out there that was actually looking for them. Someone who wanted to love them the way they wanted to be loved. I had seen it so many times before. At one point, I worried Jayce would succumb to it. She loved being in love so much I was afraid she would fall for someone who was selling a quick dream instead of the lifetime she truly deserved. No matter how much positivity was engrained into us, there were two true facts that remained.

We were women, and we needed and wanted love.

"Well I see your point, but the answer is still no. I've made enough bad decisions with Trent in the past. There is no need for me to infect my future with any of them."

"Well I'm glad to hear it. I would hate to tear up some more of his shit. So now on to your new boos," she said, snickering.

Just as I was about to tell her about Micah, somebody knocked at my door. Nobody had called or texted so I didn't know who it could be. Cree wasn't supposed to be here until Wednesday and my sisters on Friday. I looked through the peephole and all I saw was pink.

"Hold on for a second Ki, somebody is at my door."

"Who is it?" I called out.

"I have delivery for Ms. Rylee Coltrane."

"Who's at your door, Ry?" Kira asked, impatiently.

"I don't know. It's a delivery for me."

"What is it?"

"Dammit, hold on woman," I said, opening the door to yet another bouquet of peonies.

Not again, I thought. This time they were a beautiful shade of pink. I looked at the delivery guy. He gave me a confused look as to why I was hesitant to accept them. I needed this to stop. Whether it was Cree or Trent, it wasn't funny anymore. I held out my hand so he could give me what I needed to sign. I signed for the flowers and walked back into my house. I saw there was another note tucked between the petals. I was going to have to stash these somewhere out of sight. I didn't need an argument two days before Valentine's Day.

"Dang, is it a bomb or something? You seem awfully quiet," Kira said.

"It's another bouquet of flowers," I said, trying to figure out who I was going to text first.

I opened the card and once again another message but no name. It read: *Someday, somehow I will have you in my arms again.* I couldn't understand the games, and frankly I was tired of it. I thought to just send Trent a text since Cree would be here soon. I could tell Cree face-to-face.

"Another bouquet, what do you mean? Well who was the first from? When did the first one come?"

I started telling her about the first bouquet, and how Micah intercepted it the morning after our romantic date. I told about how I was completely caught off guard, and had absolutely no explanation as to who sent them or why.

"So have you told him about the whole proposal and everything? I mean, seeing you're in a relationship now and receiving flowers from an unknown person. I think you should be honest. I wouldn't start this relationship off with a bunch of secrets Ry."

Now she was sounding like Jayce.

"I didn't tell him anything about what happened over the holidays. It happened before we got together so what's the point? I didn't want him to think I said yes because of what happened."

"Well did you?"

I thought about her question. I had told myself over-and-over again it had nothing to do with me saying yes. I really liked Micah and me running away from a proposal was completely something different. I felt to everyone around me it appeared to be something different. I figured they knew me well enough to know I wouldn't use a new relationship as a Band-Aid.

"I will agree that I ran out on a proposal, however me being with him has nothing to do with it. Trent and Micah are two totally different situations."

"Well, other than Trent, who else could they be from?"

I remembered I hadn't told her about Cree or the fact that he was coming to visit soon. They had always gotten along so I didn't anticipate too much of an outburst.

"I suspect Cree could be sending them."

"Cree, why would he be sending you flowers? You haven't mentioned him in God knows when. If my memory serves me correctly, you were trying to distance yourself from his lifestyle. Have you recently changed your mind?"

"No I wouldn't say I changed my mind. I ran into him when I was coming home for Christmas. We've started talking again, and he says he's doesn't deal with that lifestyle anymore. He actually owns *Halo* and is trying to go legit. He's who I stayed with the night Trent pulled his little stunt. He's coming to visit me in a few days. We've always been friends so we're just picking up where we left off."

"Wow, you are really pushing the boundaries Ry. You've already dipped back once, and you see where that got you. You know I'm not one to judge or tell you what to do, but this is pushing it. I like Cree and all, but why is he coming there? You already know how things were when you were around each other. . Once you're within five feet of each other, madness breaks out. Normally, I'm all for you dancing on the wild side still I think you're playing with fire having him coming down there. Have you told your new man he's coming?"

"No I'm going to mention it on our date tomorrow."

"Well, I hope so because if you fool around and get mixed up with Cree again that will be a mess. You know Cree. He won't stop until he gets what he wants. You remember how you had to move and change your number when you ended it. I don't know how you find them, but you always find the ones who don't like you to walk away."

She had a point. He was and could be very persistent when he wanted something. It was actually what I found most attractive about him.

"I know, and I'll be careful," I told her, trying to sound reassuring.

I wasn't sure if I was trying to convince her or myself. We talked and gossiped for another hour. I heard her hubby come in, which meant we had exceeded our girl talk time. I promised her I wouldn't let things get out of control, and that I would come home soon. She promised she would visit too, and we said our goodbyes.

I thought about what she said, and what my mother had said. I thought about Cree and the laws of attraction nestled between us.

Either way I was all in at this point. Two days wasn't going to be long and I would be fine. Micah would understand and all would be fine with him. I picked up my phone to text Trent that I got the flowers and to do me a favor and stop sending them. I started to inquire about Zoe and if he was the baby's father then decided against it. He wasn't my concern and neither was she. As much as my curiosity may have wanted to know, decided to leave well enough alone. Sometimes re-opening certain wounds can be far worse than before.

I was beginning to realize that very thing live and in color.

15 | Fifteen

*A*bsolutely not Rylee! I don't care if y'all took baths *together as kids. He's a grown man and you're my woman so hell no."*

"It's just for two days, and we're friends Micah. It's really no big deal," I said, trying to sound convincing.

Yesterday had come and gone. Micah had decided to reschedule until today since he was exhausted from the road game. They were having a great season, and it looked as if they would be continuing into the tournaments scheduled to come up. He had already explained the schedule if they continued on into the March Madness portion of it all. With all of that being said we were celebrating our Valentine's Day early. We were having a picnic in *Jackson Square* since it was such a beautiful day. He had gotten beignets from *Café du Monde* and prepared food for lunch. I was quite impressed. I lay across the blanket under the oak tree, and processed what he had just said. *I should've kept my damn mouth closed*, I thought to myself.

"I'm not sure if you heard me the first time. My answer is hell no Rylee. You're in a relationship. Regardless if you're just friends with him, staying at your house is out of the question. Tell his grown ass to get a hotel room. Why would he be cool staying with you, while knowing you have a man?"

Truth be told, he didn't know. I never let the words fall from my lips. My plan was to tell him once he got down here. I needed to put my guards up quickly, and telling him about Micah would be definitely it. I convinced myself it would create boundaries I knew we would need.

All I could say was, "Probably because we're friends, and he would put me up if I visited him somewhere."

"Well good for him, but unfortunately it's a no go. I'm not cool with my girl's male friend staying with her. I heard the part about your sisters too. My answer is still the same. You hanging out with him because of Mardi Gras is one thing. Overnight bunking won't be happening."

I had heard him loud and clear. It didn't still matter. He was leaving for another game so he wouldn't be here anyway. By the time Cree left Micah would just be getting back. Their paths would never cross. I was playing with fire and putting myself in a sticky situation. I had done my part and mentioned it to him. I never said I was going to comply if he objected. If it blew up in my face which it wouldn't I would deal with it then. There was no need to worry about something before it happened. I gave him a convincing nod. He needed to be reassured. I wouldn't verbally say or agree with anything. Therefore he couldn't say I lied later on if it resurfaced. I knew it was a play on words and his intelligence if you really looked at it. However, at the end of the day, no lie was told.

"So tell me more about you?" I asked, trying to change the subject.

I wanted to know more about the situation Asha had mentioned regarding his ex. My curious mind needed something to focus on other than Cree coming and me covering it up.

"What do you mean? You know a lot about me. I don't keep anything from you."

"Tell me what really made you move down here."

I was trying to inquire without being obvious. I knew he was aware Asha and I were cool. I didn't want to tip him off with the fact she had already told me bits and pieces. I wanted to hear his version. I wanted to hear the real, raw, and uncut version. The parts shared between him and his ex that no one else knew. I knew they existed because I had them with Trent and Cree. I had moments with Trent neither my sisters nor Kira knew about. I had memories of self-hatred because of his arrogance and emotional abuse. Times when the reckless behavior I was involved in with Cree that kept me sane. I had cried many nights before the Zoe incident even occurred. There were so many moments where our verbal fights danced on the edge of becoming physical. Many days came and went with me thinking this was as good as it was going to get. My mother pushing me further into his arms, completely unaware I was on the verge of falling off the cliff. The cheating, the STD, and the emotional abuse were my daily drugs as I digested them one after another. On the outside, I looked happy and full of life.

I was a true Pisces and equipped with the ability to hide the truth. We were private and full of secrets. It was a gift and a curse.

The only person who had a clue was Cree. We ran the streets, tearing up the town and releasing all of our cares together. It wasn't until things became life threatening that I had to be free of both of them. Seeing Zoe and Trent together was a minor part of the insanity. Cleaning blood off of Cree in the middle of the night, and him hiding out at my house was the last straw. I never knew what had occurred that night and I didn't ask. He wasn't shot, yet he was covered in blood. He was standing in my living room with no wounds and eyes completely blank.

After we pulled orgasm after orgasm out of each other, I held him all night. Tears were running down my face, and I knew I had to let them go. The Scorpio and the Gemini. The pleasure and pain I became succumb with. Reality had finally set in and I knew I couldn't save them. They were lost, and I was lost. Together, the three of us were causing more damage to each other. I was a sinking ship. I was drifting further into deeper waters. We were all drowning. It was time to me to find my way back to shore. I craved freedom, and somehow this was no longer it.

I needed air. I needed to breathe again.

"Well, Asha coming by herself bothered me so I came too."

He was being guarded. I needed to motivate him to open up. Yes, I was being nosey, however I still wanted to hear it from him.

"Yeah she told me what happened back home with her and how it affected your family."

"You mean my parents because the rest of us weren't in that much shock."

"What do you mean?"

"Asha was always a wild card and we knew it. My parents did too. They had this persona they wanted to keep up it so it was ignored. I wasn't shocked about ole boy at all. I'm a man so I saw him coming a mile away. Not to mention, Asha seemed to always find herself at home when she knew he would be there. She lived on campus and purposely moved there to get some freedom. Her conveniently popping up at home all the time was no coincidence."

"I see. Well, it seems her reasoning for moving made sense. You obviously didn't like the school either if you came too. I'm not buying the whole protect my sister story though. Your sister seems more than capable of taking care of herself. Hence, the wildcard label," I said, laughing."

"You're right. There was more to me moving here. I had an incident with a relative which resulted in a fight and caused me to move."

I just stared at him.

He wasn't getting off that easy. I stretched across the blanket and propped myself up. I wanted him to know he needed to keep talking. He was worse than me when it came to being vague. It was a beautiful day and he'd found a perfect spot under this tree. We didn't have oak trees like this back home. All we had were palm trees and other bushes that could survive L.A. heat. It was majestic and beyond picturesque. I wondered how much history this tree held. How many wars and lives had been lost around it? Nature, despite what people may do, always transcends throughout time.

"What was the fight about? Must've been pretty serious since you moved to the other side of the country."

"Actually it was. A few broken ribs and a broken jaw came out of it to be exact. Our parents were pissed once it was over. My cousin slept with my girlfriend of three years and had been for a year of it. He was doing it right under my nose, and I never saw it happening. I walked right across the football field and punched the shit out of him. He looked stunned, even though he knew what was happening. A whole year of them as if she and I weren't together one day. As if I wasn't going to ever find out about what they were doing."

"Wow, how did you find out?"

"She ended up pregnant and confessed. I had found the test in the trash, and she said she was waiting to tell me. It was ironic how it happened because I was getting ready to propose to her. We were about four months into the pregnancy when she started acting weird. I thought it was because she had figured out I was going to propose to her and she was nervous. Sadly, two days before I was going to pop the question she confessed. She broke down in my dorm room and told me everything. For those few moments, I was glad she was pregnant. I would've been afraid of my reaction otherwise."

"Did she end up keeping the baby?" I asked.

I wanted to know if it was possible to forgive someone after they cheat and conceive a child with someone else. His situation was different than mine because they were family. I didn't have to deal with Trent or Zoe anymore if it turned out to be their child.

"Yes she kept him. I believe he's around four years old now. "I was processing everything. Mostly, the part about him almost proposing to her. This moment would have been a good point to slide in my recent disaster of a proposal that had occurred. Telling him would have cleared the air. My only fear was he would question my reasoning behind saying yes to him so I said nothing and continued to listen.

"So you went to find your cousin?"

"Yep, I sure did. I called his brother to find out where he was and went looking for him."

"So his brother went to the school too? What school was it?"

"We were all enrolled in Howard, and yes, they were twins."

"So I guess multiple births run in your family, huh?"

"Yes my grandfather was a triplet and my great grandmother on my father's side was a twin. It skipped my father and uncles and landed with us. My mother only has sisters though. None of them are twins or anything."

I laughed, and then asked, "How big is your family? I mean, I thought my family was big, but yours clearly tops mine."

He laughed too.

"We're pretty big. On my dad's side, my great grandmother and her twin had about six children apiece. Her brother didn't have twins, although she did which is where my grandfather stemmed from. His brother only had four children, while he had eight. He had three girls and five boys. My dad and one of my uncles had the multiple births. The rest just had individual kids, which amounted to a gang of us being spread out. Two of my aunts moved to Philly, an uncle went to Atlanta, and another uncle moved to New York. The rest of my family stayed in D.C. It's about six of us within the same age range. The rest were either older or younger mixed with boys and girls," he said, shaking his head as he added them up. "As far as my mother's sisters, it's four of them including her and she's the second to last. Only two of my aunts have kids and the baby decided children were not in her future. Her oldest sister still lives in D.C., one moved to Seattle for work, and the baby lives in Dallas. I literally have family spread out everywhere, which is a good thing. At least it gives us somewhere to visit and get away too. So what about you? You said you had a big family too. Are they all located in L.A.?"

"No, my immediate family lives in L.A. My parents and sisters all still live there. Both of my parents are originally from Brooklyn. They moved to Cali once they finished college to start over. After a while, my dad's youngest brother moved out there with us. Both sets of my grandparents still reside in New York, while my aunts, uncles, and their kids are spread across the east coast."

"Okay, so how many sisters do you have?"

"I have two sisters named Jayce and Taylor. They don't have kids as of yet."

"Are you're parents still married?" he asked, smiling.

I wondered what the smile was for. It seemed as if he was searching for something beneath the answer I was going to give him.

"Yes, my parents are still married. I don't see divorce anywhere in the future, which is something I admire about them."

"Ok cool. Are you close to your parents?"

I laughed because close was definitely a sketchy term. Despite our relationship, I guess I could say we were close.

"Well, I have a different relationship with my mother and my father. They are two totally different people, but yes I am fairly close to them. More so my dad than my mom, which I think is because we are so much alike."

"Yeah, I can feel you on that one. It's the opposite for me. I'm closer to my mom versus my dad. He and I are close, though we bump head's a lot due to the testosterone and personality similarity."

"I see," I said, giggling.

"So do you and your family visit New York a lot?"

"Yeah we trade off holidays so everyone gets a break from the airfare. This year we did Thanksgiving and Christmas in L.A. so next year it will be the east coast. Usually, in the summer, we would go to Trinidad since my mother's mom is from there and she spends most of it there."

"Oh wow, your mother is from Trinidad?"

"Partially, she was born there. Then they moved to the states when she was seven. She was raised in Brooklyn. My MeMaw and Pa Pa are from there though. My dad and his parents are New York to the core."

"I can totally see some different features in you," he said, caressing my cheek.

"Yeah the island girl met and fell in love with the b-boy from the block. They fell in love, moved, got married, and had kids. It almost sounds like a fairytale."

"Well, it's nice to see love like that does happen in real life. Do you want to get married Ry?"

I looked up and him and smiled. He was truly sexy to the core. It was damn near erotic how he believed in love. I wondered if any of it would eventually penetrate me. I wondered if he had any idea how I turned my back on love the day it showed its ugly side. I didn't hold grudges, but their betrayal cut me deep. I swallowed what he had asked me. I wanted to answer and wasn't really sure how. I tried to think back to a time where I wanted to get married, and I couldn't remember a single one. I was never against it, but I still couldn't remember being an advocate for it either. I always admired my parents and the love they had. I knew it was perfect, but it was theirs. In my mind, I had set the bar to the level of their marriage. If I was to ever get married and that was a big if. It would have to be pretty damn close to my parents' relationship.

"I don't know Micah. I've never really given it much thought. Even when my best friend got married, it wasn't something I felt drawn to do."

He looked at me as if he was searching for something in my eyes. He was staring at me as if he was searching for who or what caused me to have this outlook.

"Do you want to get married? Do you want a family? From the looks of it you all have a strong sense of family, and you seem to have a lot fun," I said, laughing.

"Actually I do want to get married one day. I want to share my life with one person. I will admit I've had my wild moments, but still in the end I want that one special girl. Kids are up for grabs to be honest. My family is so big if I didn't have any I wouldn't be crushed. Now as far as the fun part we're a wild bunch. I'll say that much," he said with a laugh.

"Well, I'm sure your family functions are a blast if nothing else."

"Yeah, well a blast is putting it lightly. Speaking of family, this is Asha calling now."

I had heard the vibrating. I ignored it because I thought it may have been mine. It was two days before Cree was supposed to come so it could have been him calling to make sure staying at my house was still cool. I also considered that it may have been Trent responding to my text regarding the flowers. Either way, I couldn't entertain either of them right now. I was hoping he would send her to voicemail. I was enjoying our conversation.

"Hey sis, what's up?"

I rolled over on my back and closed my eyes. The trees gave off a nice breeze and it blew across my face. I was saying a silent prayer. I hoped he would refrain from mentioning I was here.

"Yeah he's back. He's probably sleeping since we had a game and have to turn around for another one."

She was asking about Mario. That was a relief in itself so far. I think she was feeling him a little more than she was letting on. I would have to ask her about him later. For now, I was focused on his mouth telling too much. I had managed to keep this double life a secret so far. I didn't want him professing his love to mess it up.

"No I leave out Wednesday so I'll bring you the money later on. We have practice tomorrow so I'll tell him to hit you up. Well, I'll call you later. I'm on a date."

Damn, there it is, I thought to myself.

"What do you mean with whom? Who else would it be? It's Rylee. We're a couple now. She didn't tell you?"

I cringed. If God had a sense of humor, I was now the punchline. I just took a deep breath and ignored the rest of his conversation. The damage had already been done. I would deal with the fallout tomorrow. If she was pissed and things between us ended at least this was fun while it lasted.

He finished talking to her and rolled on top of me. He ran his fingers through my hair and kissed my forehead. He placed a kiss on my lips as he ran his hand up my shirt.

"Rylee Coltrane I just may be falling hard for you."

I pulled him closer and placed another kiss on his lips. He had no idea what he had just done. I wrapped my legs around him as he pressed against my sweet spot. My mind was racing at what Asha could be thinking as this very moment. *I questioned myself as to whether she was angry or if we could continue being secret lovers?* Whatever her decision, I would have to be fine with it.

If nothing else, I got my one for the road.

16 | Sixteen

Her text message read: Call me. We need to talk. The message was clear as day on my screen. I wasn't avoiding her, though it would appear I was. Two days had gone by and we still hadn't talked. She called and texted a couple of times asking me to call her. I knew we needed to talk. Micah had pulled the lid off, and now I had some explaining to do. I wasn't afraid of her reaction. I knew at some point this was going to stop. One of us would grow tired of each other and move on to something different. I had already begun to do it. My head was in so many different places that the only time it seemed halfway clear was during sex. Honestly, I was glad it had happened this way. My biggest fear was that I would be caught in bed with one of them. Now since that it was out I could breathe.

Wednesday had finally arrived and Cree was due to be here soon. I had no plan or idea how these two days would go. I prayed he would be on his best behavior. I was looking at yet another bouquet of flowers. A dozen yellow peonies this time. Trent never responded to my text. Either he was still upset about our last conversation or he had no idea what I was talking about. I still found it odd he hadn't said something ignorant to me telling him to stop sending them. I figured since Cree was coming today, I would soon find out. The messages left on the card could apply to either one of them.

Again they were vague and left me in a state of bewilderment.

I grabbed all the notes sent with the flowers. I had two classes today, and then I was done. By 2:30 p.m., I would be headed home to do homework until Cree arrived. He was renting a car so I didn't have to pick him up. I was glad he had decided to go that route. Residing under the same roof for two days would be hard enough. Having to drive in the same car would only prove to be more difficult.

He had some business to attend to while he was here so I would have some alone time while he was out and about. I know I needed to get this conversation with Asha out of the way before he arrived. I didn't want her popping up while he was here. The last time she did that when Trent here it got a little too hot. She knew he was coming this week so I figured that may be the reason why she hasn't pressed me about having a conversation with her. I picked up my tea and headed to the couch. I had a couple of hours to clear my head. Mid-terms were coming up and I didn't need any extra baggage clogging up my head. I had a presentation in my history class today, and I was actually looking forward to it. I needed to focus and this was causing me not too. I spread all of the notes across my coffee table.

One after another, message after message, the mysteries before my eyes.

One of the messages read: *I will never give up. While the other read: Someday, somehow I will have you in my arms again.*

The last one: *It was always you.*

Each note could easily belong to either of them. The last bouquet came when Micah was here. I had managed to snatch the note out of them before he came out of the bathroom. I lied and told him they were from my dad. I made up a whole story about how he sends all of us a bouquet of our favorite flowers for Valentine's Day and mine apparently arrived late. He seemed to buy the tale so I left well enough alone. Another lie and another secret I was keeping. I hoped I would get to the bottom of all of this before it blew up in my face.

The flowers and how Asha and I would end, and all of my unresolved feelings for Cree.

I had to come to a consensus about what I was feeling for him. I smiled, thinking about Trent telling me he knew about him. He sounded so agitated. It seemed like he was expecting me to apologize or something. We both knew that wasn't happening. He slept with my best friend, and to me his actions were far worse than anything I could do to him.

I thought about Zoe and the fact she was now a mother. The thought that it could be Trent's saddened me. There was a point in time it would've been me being a mother to a fantastic little boy or girl. Sadly, a miscarriage ended that dream for me. I had hid my pregnancy secret for three months. I hadn't told a soul as I battled back and forth with if I was going to tell him. I had found out two weeks after I caught him with Zoe. I thought I was sick from all of the stress my body was going through. It turns out that the stress was only one of the causes. My heart was in shambles, and my mind was a complete fucking mess. I was all over the place and my stress levels were through the roof.

I was fighting for my sanity, while trying to decide if I was ready to be a mother. I was done with Trent, yet I felt compelled to hold on to him because of the baby. I wanted Cree to get his shit together, though I knew that was a dream and not my reality. I was surrounded by people and felt completely isolated at the same time. I was alone with a child growing inside of me. I had a child, my child, by a man who was absolutely no good for me. I was at the point where an abortion was no longer an option. I was all in.

My only decision was with who I would be all in with; Trent or Cree?

I knew it was Trent's child because sex was the one thing Cree and I played it safe with. Despite who the child belonged to, I still wanted to be a family with Cree. The idea was madness which explained my state of mind at the time. Regardless, of who they were I had decisions to make for myself and my baby. The answer to my silent prayer seemed to have come two days later when Cree stood in my apartment covered in blood. The tears ran down my face as I silently cried myself to sleep that night. I was drowning and for the sake of my life and my child's life I needed to jump ship. After everything with Zoe and Trent, he didn't seem like a viable option either. A week later, I released them both. I made my peace with God and started moving forward. I knew I had to tell my family about the pregnancy. I would worry about telling Trent later. I still needed time to figure just how involved I wanted him to be. He wouldn't accept just being a baby daddy so I needed a game plan. The night the miscarriage happened was the first night I had fully accepted the fact I was going to be a mother. I had climbed in bed with a hand over my stomach. I was excited about the face I would see in six months. Whether it was boy or girl, I would love the baby unconditionally.

The extreme cramps and pain of that night were still etched in my mind. After returning from the hospital, I cried uncontrollably for two days. Thoughts of how God was punishing me raced through my mind. I thought about how I apparently wasn't deserving of being a mother. My recklessness and the choices leading me to this position played over-and-over. The mounting heartbreak over a man I had grown to hate, and another I still wanted but couldn't be with. My life was a repeat version of Jazmine Sullivan's, *I'm In Love With Another Man,* song.

I blamed myself, Trent, Zoe, and anyone who had a hand in my stress levels being on an extreme high. After a while, I came to understand everything happens for a reason. It just wasn't my time. Being pregnant by a man I didn't want to be within 5 feet of was not a good situation for me to be in. I knew there would be no peace between us so it seemed to be for the best. I never mentioned it to anyone and until now I hadn't thought about it. Kira telling me Zoe was a mom brought back lots of memories. It brought back painful memories I never wanted to remember. A part of me wondered if her daughter did belong to Trent. The other part of me didn't give a damn.

There was a lot of bad blood there. A lot of wounds I knew didn't need to be reopened.

I sipped on my tea and stared at the notes. I was beginning to feel like I did before. I was choosing between my heart, my desire for freedom, and sex. Being with Trent was not an option. I had opened a door I should have left closed. Jayce was right in saying I knew he still had feelings for me, and he always would. He realized he messed up, and it was as simple as that. His wanting me back had levels to it. Control, ego, and appearance were all factors in his sudden interest in me again. Love and my mother were also ingredients in the mix too, but not high up on the list. My mother had given him the courage and reassurance that he still had a chance. A fact so far from the truth that it didn't exist in this world or the next. The world could come to an end and Trent still wouldn't be an option.

I already had a front row seat to what life with him would be like. Aside from everything else, I could never forgive him for the loss of our child. He had no idea about the baby, but that fact didn't matter to me. Regardless of how much time may have passed, he hadn't strayed too far from that person. His proposal was proof of it. If these flowers were from him, I would once again have to bring his world crashing down. If they were from Cree, it may end up being my world that comes crashing down.

Cree respected boundaries. I knew that much. How long he would respect them when there was an objective in sight, I couldn't say.

I stretched across my couch and stared out my window. It was a beautiful day outside. Since Cree wouldn't be here until this evening, I figured I could stop by *City Park* and enjoy a piece of the sunny day. I turned on my iPod and closed my eyes as it played track after track of

Souled Out. Her voice and her lyrics traveled through my mind. Melodies of love, the desire to be free, and her search for inner self discovery fell upon my earlobes. I wanted love just not in the conventional way. Not in the way society felt I should have it.

I didn't completely trust love or my feelings while in love. There was no safety net, or end to the uncontrollable falling you slip into.

I felt it offered you a false sense of security. It pulled you in and created some kind of illusion of perfection. You believe in the fairytale. You buy into what appears to be a drama free- happily ever after. At one point, I was a consumer of it. I sold everything I owned for a piece of it. I gave it all I had, including my soul, my sanity, and somehow my peace of mind. Somewhere in there my self-esteem and my unborn child became casualties. They became a part of the price I eventually paid. Now years later, I realized I would rather rent than buy. I would settle for temporary satisfaction until the excitement wore off. When I no longer desired it, I could return it and move on with my life.

Expiration dates reminded you that nothing last forever. They are constant reminders of how all good things come to an end including love.

17 | Seventeen

wonder do people ever really change or do we evolve?

Do we somehow trick ourselves into believing we have become a different person when in reality we are still the very person we've always been? Is it surface versus core? Is it fantasy over reality?

The unsolved mystery surrounding it all.

My grandfather always had the impression people don't necessarily change. They simply become better or worse versions of themselves. Beneath it all, if the right circumstance presented itself, you would see how they were the same person they had always been. I contemplated the concept when I thought about the men I had attachments to. *Had Cree really changed? Is Micah really this amazing person? Was the ball floating around waiting to drop again?* My mind was going in a million directions and I needed to focus.

What did I really want? Who did I really want to be with?

"Ms. Coltrane! Ms. Coltrane! Rylee!"

I looked up, and then said, "Sorry Professor Collier, I got lost in thought. I'm ready."

"Please proceed to the front. We're waiting for you to begin," he said in an almost annoyed tone.

I was so in my head I hadn't heard my professor calling my name. I got up and proceeded to the front. It was my turn to present my history presentation. I was in Greek history and our assignment was to pick one of the Greek characters and do a project on them. I was always fascinated with this topic because to some degree there were pieces of fantasy buried within. I had chosen Aphrodite, the Greek *Goddess* of love, beauty, and sex. Her story fascinated me. The way she controlled her heart and the hearts of the men she loved left me enamored.

I was always curious as to how she kept them all at a distance, yet within arm's reach. What intrigued me about her the most was even though she used her beauty and sex to manipulate them, she still loved them. I thought about my feelings for Cree and Micah. In my own way, I had love for them both. I loved different things about each of them, however, it wasn't enough for me to throw myself completely into either of them.

I loved my freedom.

I pondered on my feelings for Cree. *Did I desire him because our story had been left incomplete? Was there really something buried within me trying to show me we were meant to be?* I knew my feelings for him were different from my feelings from Micah and Trent. It's funny how we often think love is going to be the same each time around. We look at it as this one constant thing, and feel it will be the same with each person we encounter. As a woman who is evolving, I now see how untrue that fact is. I remembered hearing one time, *Love is like the ocean. It's constantly moving and it's different on every shore.* Hearing those words helped me understand how there are different kinds of love. Although I may want to group that love together, it will never be the same.

They were different shores. Miles and miles away from each other.

Different pieces of me they all seemed to gravitate too. I often searched for similarities among them, and came up empty handed. Nothing about them was the same. They were honestly polar opposites. I was the only constant in this equation, and even I was all over the place. I gave my presentation, answered the necessary questions, and found my way back to my seat. I had another ten minutes of class left. I would be grabbing something to eat, and then it was home to finish up another project before my guest arrived. Micah stopped by before class and gave me a see you later kiss. Had it not been for this teacher and his desire for being on time, I would've got a one for the road. I needed something to keep my sex drive at bay until he returned this weekend.

I needed a little something to keep me sane.

I rambled through my phone until I heard my teacher dismiss class. Even though his being punctual to class rule sometimes worked my nerve, I liked the fact that he released us on time. I grabbed my stuff and headed to my car. I was hungry and wanted to grab something to eat. I figured Cree and I would grab a bit to eat later, but for now I just needed a snack. I made my way to my car. A few seconds after I had thrown my stuff in the car, I heard my name being yelled.

"Rylee!"

I looked around and couldn't pin point where it was coming from. It sounded like Asha, but I didn't see her so I turned back to get into my car.

"Rylee!"

I looked around again and saw Asha heading towards me. She didn't look pissed off, though I knew it had been a couple days since Micah had dropped the relationship bomb. For a moment, I felt guilty about not telling her first. Sadly, it all faded away once the tip of Micah's tongue stroked my sweet spot. Yes, I could've come clean about me and him. However, I wasn't ready to give them both up just yet. I was being greedy and there were no if, ands, or buts about it. I was mesmerized by the pleasure they both gave me. I was caught up in the constant highs of ecstasy, and the waves of eroticism we floated on.

These were moments I was not ready to file away as memories.

"Hey chic, I was trying to catch you when I saw you walking out of the communications building. You heading home?"

I knew we needed to talk, but I wanted to do it somewhere other than my car. There was no way for me to escape if I needed too.

"Yeah I'm going to grab a bite to eat, and then head home to finish up before Cree gets here."

"Oh yeah, I forgot your old flame was coming this week," she said, laughing.

"Whatever! No just get in," I said, smiling and shaking my head.

I hoped it wasn't that obvious since I was in a relationship with her brother. I knew we were cool, but not cool enough to where I could trust her to not sell me out. She was my friend, nevertheless she was his sister first. I slid in the car and started it up.

"So should I put you on blast now about avoiding me these past few days or wait until we get home?" she said, cracking up.

"Not put me on blast," I said with a laugh.

"Well, I mean you did go ghost right after Micah told me you guys were a couple and all. I mean you do realize I knew we were casually sleeping together, and you were not necessarily into women right? Don't get me wrong, my mouth dropped when my brother said it since I felt like we are friends and you could've told me."

I listened to her closely. She was right on all ends. We were friends, and what we had was casual so I didn't have to be with one person. I guess I figured it was just too much to say I'm sleeping with your brother. To top it off I was being outright greedy.

"Well, I didn't know how to say I'm sleeping with your brother. Let's be honest, there's no easy way to say it."

She looked at me, and then said, "Well yeah there isn't, though we could've talked about it. I can't imagine what kind of crazy stuff you had going on in your head. How do you keep secrets like that hidden?"

"Girl you have no idea, although you guys were what kept me sane. Especially after coming home from the holidays. I was like what the hell."

"I bet. So have you told Micah about all of it?"

"Not yet, but I will once the season is over. He has enough to worry about with all these games so I don't want to add to it."

"Well, my lips are sealed about all of it. Like I told you before, we are close and have a great relationship, still we don't cross certain boundaries. Relationships are one of them. It never ends well when you get into people's relationships, regardless if they're family or not."

I took a deep breath.

For the moment, I felt relieved though I wouldn't get too comfortable with them minding their own business. Depending on the situation or mood, I knew those words would change at the blink of an eye. Outsiders never won when it came to siblings. I knew that to be one true fact. I pulled into the drive thru to order something quick, and then head home.

"Well I'm glad to know our friendship is still solid. I didn't want to give it up, though I knew it would ultimately come down to how you felt. I would never want to come between you and your brother."

I turned to order my food, and then let her order hers. I pulled up to pay and grab our food. She checked the bags and we pulled out of the lot. It was quiet for a few blocks before she turned to and looked at me. Her face held this sinister look of seduction I had never seen before. I was confused since I couldn't make out what the look meant. She slid her hand over my thigh and moved it up and down.

I wanted to move her hand. I should have moved her hand.

The truth was out and we could finally just be friends. I could have a clean slate and actually be faithful to her brother. I would be able to leave all my past indiscretions behind me and Micah would never know. Somewhere in between those thoughts, I realized her hand felt good on my thigh. It was soft. The way she caressed it sent vibrations throughout my center. I arched my back so I could control the minor throbbing I could feel making its way to the surface. She moved her hand further up my thigh, slowly creeping up my skirt.

I knew her destination, and yet I did nothing to prevent her arrival. I wanted to feel her fingers go in and out. I wanted to feel the stimulation they gave my clitoris as the temperature of my center rose to pleasurable levels. I wanted more, but the position we were both in caused me to hold tight to my steering wheel and enjoy this moment.

I was close to home, and I could wait a few more blocks. Although, every single parking lot I passed up became more tempting by the minute. I wanted her to go deeper. I wanted to feel her tongue on my lips as her stroke pulled orgasms from my soul. I thought this would be the end of us. The final moment, and then our sexual relationship would come to a full-blown halt. Instead, she was taking what she felt was hers.

I had the pleasure of her first. I had the honor of her tongue, and the wicked smile it hid behind it.

It was pleasure and ecstasy all wrapped up in a 5'7", brown-skinned frame.

She had placed the food on the floor. She turned her body so she had a better position to move her hand around. I took deep breath after deep breath as I tried to maintain my composure. I wanted to close my eyes, and enjoy the moment as I felt my orgasm mounting. I clinched my muscles as I fought to hold onto what I knew was an inevitable end.

I came to the light before our building. I had looked over to see the sneaky look still remained on her face as her eyes grew darker. She was on fire, and they reflected the passion buried beneath them. I pulled into the parking garage lot. I found a spot closest to the wall and out of sight from anyone pulling into the lot. I turned off my car so I could lean back in my seat. I wanted this no matter how wrong I knew it was. I silently promised myself this would be my last time.

There was no turning back. There was no more one for the roads. There would be no more momentarily lapse in judgment.

I had to be with Micah and only Micah. Anyone else was just trouble. I moved my seat back further so I could have more leg room. I leaned my head against my window. The temperature inside my car was heating up. She moved her hand from my sweet spot. I slid my panties over my butt and down my legs. I wanted to feel more from her. She repositioned herself, and I placed my feet upon my window. I had pushed my armrest up to give us more room. I pushed my sweet spot closer to her mouth. She grabbed my hips, and slowly slid her tongue inside me. I placed one hand on the neck rest and the other on the steering wheel.

I needed something to hold onto as her tongue removed what was left of my resolve. Pieces of the righteous path I was secretly fighting to stay on were slipping away. The hard, yet soft circles the tip of her tongue made gently broke me down stroke after stroke.

"*Ohh Asha,*" was all I could manage to utter as I controlled my breathing.

The windows had developed a layer of dew as the heat we created to cover our secrets.

I wanted to come. I wanted to give her the orgasms my body was holding captive.

My sweet spot had come close to the edge, yet I wasn't ready to give in. I wanted to savor every moment, every stroke she gave to my swollen center. The throbbing was intense as my nectar ran down my thigh and covered her chin. She wanted everything and to leave nothing. My nectar had been hers first. She was my first bite from the forbidden tree.

My eyes opened, and we were as naked as we ever could be. I had pieces of her spirit buried within me. She had captured a fraction of my soul. I wanted to free myself from her hypnotic stroke, though somehow the pieces remaining fought to keep me here. I was addicted to the euphoria. The orgasms I constantly exhaled. I pressed my feet hard against the window as I lifted to release the orgasm I could no longer hold onto. I lowered my body as I smeared my hand across the window. I glanced at my hand print. It was proof of my rebellion against monogamy. The smeared marks expressed my blatant disregard for boundaries and the rules aligning them.

I looked at her eyes. The darkness had subsided. Traces of passion still wallowed within them. The intensity had somewhat faded. I moved so I could place my legs back onto my side. She opened the bag and grabbed her food. I was still trying to calm the storm between my legs. She opened her door and I glanced over at her. I opened my mouth to tell her we had to end this when she placed her finger over my lips.

"Shh, I know what you're going to say and we're not ending this. What Micah doesn't know won't hurt him. It will be our little secret. No worries your other life is safe with me."

My door slammed.

I watched my idea of do the right thing disappear as she walked away.

18|Eighteen

hat Micah doesn't know won't hurt him It will be our little secret. No worries your other life is safe with me.

Those words played over in my head as I sat on the couch and stared out of the window. I wanted so badly to erase those words from my mind. I needed to forget my hand and footprints all over the windows of my car. The unforgettable strokes that lead to my juices flowing onto my car seat. The sky was a beautiful array of blues. The light and dark shades were tussling with each other as the sun went down, and the moon gave off just enough light to illuminate the skyline.

I had taken a nap after our little car rendezvous. I planned to finish another project before Cree got here. The idea faded because I passed out once I got upstairs. Cree had called and said he was on his way so I had managed to pull myself up out of the bed. It was 6 o'clock. I thought he was coming a little earlier, but he ended up switching to a later flight. It was something about some unfinished business that he had to take care of and couldn't leave out until later. When I think about it, the late flight was perfect timing.

Seeing Asha earlier had me in a very uncompromising position. I was still tingling, and to be honest I wanted more. My phone broke my train of thought. I went to pick it up. I figured it would be Cree telling me he was downstairs. I had given him my address for him to plug into his GPS since he was driving a rental.

It was Micah.

I figured he was through with his practice and wanted to talk before he called it a night. I was glad he had called before Cree had gotten here. The conversation may have been a little awkward before I had the chance to tell Cree I was in a relationship.

"Hello," I answered.

"Hey baby, what are you up too?"

I missed him. Hearing his voice reminded me how much I really did. I was thinking about surprising him at one of his road games not too far away from school. I figured I could get Asha to go along since she was always up for a chance to see Mario. We had fun on our last road trip so another one was definitely up for the taking. I had no plans for spring break yet so I could probably attend a game during that time.

"Nothing much, just waking up from my nap. What are you up too?"

"Just finished with practice and going to head out with the team. I was missing you and wanted to hear your voice. How are midterms coming along?"

"Oh they're going ok. I finished a test in one class and a presentation in another one today. I need to wrap up another one to present on Friday. I want to get done before everyone gets here."

I figured I would mention everyone as a whole so it wouldn't seem like I was waiting for just Cree. My phone beeped and I saw it was Cree calling. I figured he was downstairs and needed me to come grab him.

"Hold on for second, baby," I said before clicking over.

"Hey Cree, are you here yet?"

"Yeah, I just landed and I'm on my way to grab my car. What's your apartment number?"

"It's 1906. I'm on the 6th floor."

"Okay, I'll be there shortly. Have you eaten yet?"

"No I was going to cook."

"No need, just get ready. I'll be there to pick you up in a few. We can grab some food out."

I said okay and clicked back over to Micah.

"I'm sorry about that."

"It's cool. I thought you forgot about me. Who was it anyway?"

My first instinct was to say Asha, then I remembered I had mentioned to him about Cree coming so it was no big deal. I just had to remember the no slumber party rules he insisted on when we were out and again before he left. I guess he figured I would try to slide him in hoping he forgot.

"It was Cree. He's landed and was calling to let me know he had touched down."

"Oh ok," he said, sarcastically. "Well don't forget to tell his ass he needs to get his own room. I hope you mentioned it before he got there. I'd hate for you to have ole dude sleeping outside on the streets."

I waited for a slight laugh to follow, though I knew there would be none. He wasn't playing and I knew it. It only worsened the fact that things would go really bad if he found out he was staying here. I figured I would placate him enough to ease his fears. This way it keeps me from telling a whole lie.

"I hear you, baby."

It was all I needed to say. I would not provide any extra information, and there would be no lies to remember.

"I'm not playing, Ry. Don't have that dude up in there."

I laughed. He was really trying to sound serious. His tone sounded so goofy so I couldn't even take him seriously. I knew he wasn't playing. I knew I needed to lighten the mood. The longer we talked about it the more he would try and turn into the detective he could sometimes be. I didn't want to add on to the deception I had planned. Cree would barely be here two days. On top of the time, he would be in his own room. I hadn't told him my sisters were coming too, though the minute I did he would be on his way to a hotel in a second. He was cool with my sisters and all, but he wasn't trying to be shacked up with three women for a weekend.

"Boy bye and I heard you. Go enjoy yourself, and I'll see you when you get back. How many games do you have again?"

I wanted to make sure he wasn't coming back earlier than he should.

"Two, but we may come back late Saturday night."

I made a mental note and told him goodbye. I needed to get ready for dinner. I didn't feel like dressing up too much since it was just Cree. I had the perfect place to take him since it was probably going to be a late night. I was sure we would be drinking, not to mention acting a fool so I had the perfect spot. I felt like dancing, hearing some good music, and catching up. I had heard about a new hole in the wall on St. Claude. I wanted to check it out.

I hopped in the shower. I stood under the water, hoping to cool my body temperature off. I was playing with fire going against Micah's wishes. I was tempting fate once again. The Gods had granted me solace when it came to Asha. I had managed to slide through the cracks without him finding out. I thought Asha would have ended it, and make my life easier. She could have forced me to cope with the withdrawals of her tongue, yet she did the opposite. She gave into her greed. Her lust ruled as she devoured all of my unspoken words and willpower. The invisible fragments I had hidden and reserved to fight her off.

I rubbed my hands down my stomach and over my hip as the water ran down my skin. My body temperature seemed to stay just below overheated these days. Hands, tongues, and wicked smiles controlled the peaks and valleys my body traveled upon. I wanted to introduce Asha to Cree. I paused, remembering what happened with Trent. I didn't need a repeat of crazy so I decided against it. I didn't want Cree to know that version of Rylee.

She was a different woman. She was much different from the girl he knew in L.A.

I turned off the water and climbed out of the shower. I rubbed lotion over my body and threw on my clothes. Ripped jeans, a superman tee, and my comfy black pumps were tonight's ensemble. I wrapped a plaid shirt around my waist and ran my fingers through my hair. My curls were tussled and messy, though they still maintained a style. I definitely had the sexy tomboy looking going on tonight. I always loved how I could be cute and comfy with him. There was no need for extra. At first, I thought about throwing a dress on then decided against it. I wanted to keep the temptation level to a minimum tonight.

Not just for his sake, but of course for mine too.

I grabbed my diamond hoop earrings and slid them on right after I placed my watch on. I smeared some red lipstick on my lips. I threw the stuff I had dumped out of my purse earlier back inside. I loved big purses, but they drove me crazy at the same time. On one end I needed the space, while at the same I had so much space everything got lost. I picked up my keys and headed to my front room. He should have been on his way shortly so I decided to take a shot before he got there. Just as I poured myself a drink my phone rang. I took the shot and went to grab my phone off the island. I thought it would have been him, but to my surprise it was my mother. I swear she has the worst timing. I was really starting to believe she had a radar when it came to Cree.

I was deciding between answering or letting it go to voicemail. I didn't need any speeches tonight. I wanted to have a good night with my homey/lover/friend in peace. I wanted no drama, and no crazy conspiracies she had about he and I. At the point I was going to swipe to answer, I heard a knock at my door.

Thank God, I thought to myself.

I would call her back in the morning. I threw my phone in my purse and went to answer the door. I looked through the peep hole and saw it was him. I figured I would play with him a little before opening the door.

"Who is it?" I asked as I was trying to contain my laughter.

"Quit playing Ry and open the door. You know it's me."

I turned the locks and opened the door smiling.

"Yeah I know it's your ugly self," I said, laughing.

"Ugly huh?" he asked, smiling back.

I moved so he could come in.

"The extra bedroom is straight back to the left." As soon as I closed the door, he dropped his bag and pulled me to him. "What are you doing, Cree?"

"Something I didn't get to do before you left L.A."

He wrapped his arms around my waist and intertwined his lips with mine.

"Mmm," I moaned deeply as I inhaled his cologne.

This was not how this was supposed to go. It was going to be dinner, dancing, and then a conversation about how things like this could not occur. I had a boyfriend and it seemed like everyone was on level ten with their touching and feeling, including me. I broke the kiss and moved back. I exhaled. Hell, I needed another shot at this point. I looked up at him to see my red lipstick on his lips.

"What was all that about?" I asked in a confused tone.

"Well the last time I remembered it was called a kiss."

Smart ass! I thought to myself.

"I know what is called. I asked what it was about?"

"Well, it's about one of the reasons I came down here. I had business to take care of yes, although you were part of me coming down here too. You left without us talking about you and I."

I leaned against the door, trying to hold onto my footing. I didn't need him coming down here like this. I wasn't ready to face this side of him or of us. I needed more time to rationalize all of this in my head. I was fighting a battle inside my head of wanting to be near him, then again needing some space from him to sort through everything. I had to put a pin in this before the night escalated any further.

"Cree, I'm in a relationship," I blurted out.

He looked at me. I was trying to sift through the look he was giving me to see how he was going to respond. I wasn't trying to hurt him, though I didn't want to hurt Micah either. I was already in knee deep with Asha. I didn't need to add him to the list. Too many people became variables you couldn't control. With that came a catastrophe I had no patience to clean up. I wanted him to stay since were friends. However, I would have understood if he decided to leave. Hell, at this point it may have been the safest thing for both of us. He walked over to me. I realized I was still pressed against the wall. He lifted my hand and kissed my finger.

"As long as there is no ring on this finger, I still have a chance. I gave in and let the doctor hold onto you too long. I won't make the same mistake again."

He stepped back, grabbed his bag, and headed towards the room. I stood there completely speechless. His confidence had come full circle. I had awakened the sleeping lion. He was primed and ready for whatever he needed to do. A part of me got excited at the arrogance of his answer. The other side knew I had just started a war. I needed to figure out how to end it before it got out of hand.

I walked over to counter and poured another shot. The tequila went down smoothly. Temptation was a hard pill to swallow. I took a deep breath. This would only go as far as I let it go so no big deal. I made a mental note to ask him about the bouquets of flowers since Trent hadn't responded to the last text I sent him. I placed the shot glass in the sink, and I turned around to see him leaning over the island. *Damn he was sexy,* I thought to myself. I needed to get it together. I was already two shots in. I figured it was all I would need for the night. I needed to say alert since I was now being hunted. I looked at him and smiled.

"You ready to go dude?" I asked, grabbing my purse.

"Yeah, where are we going? I'm starving so I definitely need some food."

"I want to check out this new hole in the wall called *Sweet Cheeks* on St. Claude. It's not too far from the French Quarter so if you don't want to stay we can always go there."

"Hole in the wall? Still the girl I know," he said, grinning.

I was an old soul and I loved music to my core. It fed my spirit. In some ways, it offered therapy to my crazy mind. No matter how chaotic my thoughts would get, music would help calm the storm. He knew this since he often contributed to my concert habit. Whenever anyone I liked came to L.A., he would buy the tickets and drop them off. I don't think there were too many people I hadn't seen live. I think my favorite person was Jill Scott. I was in complete heaven during her concert. Her voice, the acoustic instruments, and being there with him was one of the best evenings. I literally sang every song she sang that night, while he looked at me in awe of how much I was enjoying myself. .

I giggled, and then said, "Part of me will always be that girl."

We headed for the door. He held it opened as I walked out. I locked the door and we headed to the elevator. We hopped on and I pressed the button for the 1st floor.

"So since you have a man is he cool with me staying with you?" he asked.

I was waiting for this question, although I figured it wouldn't come up. He basically just stated he didn't give a damn about me being in a relationship.

"He knows you're coming, however he doesn't know you're staying with me. I brought it up and he vetoed it."

He made a snide *humph* remark. I probably should have left the last part out. It was only going to add fuel to the fire. Not to mention, I gave him a peek into how I may be feeling. I wasn't trying to do that just yet.

"Vetoed it, huh?" he asked with a smirk.

"Don't get cocky. We're friends. I had already told you it was cool to stay so I didn't want to renege on my decision. Besides, Jayce and Tae will be here Friday so you'll have plenty of company. "

"Well it looks like I have two days to seduce you then. Also no worries because I'll grab a room Friday so you guys can have some space. I wouldn't want your sisters to find out how you really feel about me just yet. Maybe they already know."

The elevator opened and we walked out. I decided to ignore his *seduce me* comment. Addressing it will have only given him more ammunition. It was clear he didn't need any more of it. He was a loaded gun. All he needed was a motive and he was firing. I needed peace so I kept my mouth closed. I climbed into the car and he closed the door. *Always the gentleman,* I thought as he walked around to his side. The car was nice even though I knew he couldn't be modest if he wanted to. Taylor drove one of these cars back home. I remembered they were really nice once I settled in. I remember her screaming so loud when my dad pulled up at her culinary graduation with the car. The last six months of her degree, all she talked about was an Audi A6. So when she got a brand new white one that was fully loaded she was ecstatic. This convertible model was definitely in a league of its own.

I gave him the address of the spot so he could put it in the GPS. He dropped the top down exposing us to the open air. I leaned my seat back just enough to get comfortable. I wanted to enjoy the ride since I knew this was going to be an interesting night. He put some music on, and I began to zone out.

My mind drifted off. Let the games begin. Let our cares be cast into the wind, and the new memories we make last forever.

19 | Nineteen

*T*he ride to the restaurant wasn't long, yet it seemed like we had been in the car forever. We had literally been laughing since we left my house, and we couldn't stop. We laughed about everything we used to get into back home. We had good and crazy stories surrounding our Bonnie & Clyde moments. Pure, innocent fun anyone who enjoyed life would have experienced. Until now, I hadn't realized how much I had actually been around Antonio. We had a moment where the conversation had gotten quiet. I could tell he missed him. He was past the initial grieving, though I could see how his eyes would still go blank. They were best friends actually more like brothers. I moved pass the silence so we could go back to laughing about the good times.

"You remember when Tony tried to holla at Tae?" he asked, laughing.

I busted out laughing too because I did remember. Taylor had a crush on him and instead of letting him know, she played hard to get. For months they went back and forth until he finally threw up his hands and said forget it. At that point, she was all in with dating him. I knew she liked him, just not enough to actually be with him. She knew he was involved in the streets like Cree. Feelings or not, she really didn't want to be caught up in that. Once he realized she wanted to try, he literally bent over backwards for her. They were pretty consistent for almost a year. I never really got the official story on why they parted ways. Taylor gave us some I'm over him story so we dropped it.

I figured it either had something to do with one of them cheating or his lifestyle. Neither one of them could sit still too long so it was probably a combination of things.

"Yeah I do. I am curious as to what made them breakup though," I said.

"She didn't tell you?" he asked.

I looked at him with a confused look.

"No, she made it seem like they were over each other and decided to part ways."

He shook his head as if to let me know my version was not what happened.

"No Tony broke your sister's heart," he said, looking at me waiting on a reaction.

"My sister? Not possible," I said, dismissing his comment. .

I knew this version had to be fabricated some kind of way. Taylor was the ice queen and always moved through men in a stealth like manner. Involving her feelings was not something she typically did. I could see Jayce falling hard, but not Taylor. She prided herself on her bounce back mentality and untouchable heart. If Antonio got through it was definitely news to me. I needed to hear more of this story so some clarity could be made.

"I know your sister has a reputation for her voodoo ways with men. For whatever reason, Tony somehow dodged the bullet. They were a lot more serious than I had even known until it ended. At the time, Tony was facing some serious legal charges. I believe it was right around the time your sister had started culinary school. I think she had been in for about a year."

I was listening because so far everything he had said was correct. I do remember them dating during her being in school. I also somewhat remembered him getting into some trouble. During this time, I didn't think it was that serious since Cree made it seem like it was minor. I see now it may have been a little more serious than what he said. I wasn't sure how this had anything to do with Taylor though.

"Yeah I remember. What did her being in school have to do with their breakup though?"

"Tony was looking at ten years for something they were trying to pin on him. He wasn't sure about the outcome so he broke it off with Tae. He wanted to keep her from being caught up with any of it. He didn't want her messing up in school because of him. He ended up dodging the charges a year later. He figured she had moved on so he left well enough alone."

I thought about what he had just said as we pulled up. Taylor had never mentioned anything like what he just said. She made it seem like the breakup was no big deal even though I knew she was feeling him more than she let on. They were thick as thieves the moment they cut all the games out. When I think about it, she was really happy during their time together. I guess things work out how they are supposed to. Even though she really liked Tony, she couldn't be with him for the same reasons I couldn't be with Cree. The ending was too tragic and the cycle was never ending. Whether it was tears from a life snatched away or exhaustion endured from countless prison visits, life would somehow stop.

Time would stand still.

I didn't have it in me and neither did she. I listened to him tell me how Tony wanted to go back. He wanted her to give him another chance. He wanted one more chance to make their relationship right. He would have saw Tae as his way out, while fighting hard to be free of a life he had engrained in him.

There were so many decisions of love or profit, prison or freedom, street status or happiness. Then there were so many choices surrounding something as simple as having a peace of mind.

The ever turning wheel as you fight through the devil on one shoulder and the million people you are supporting on another. It all comes down to what you ultimately want. I hated to hear he didn't make it out. I had always prayed they both would. For months after I cut ties with Cree I would worry I would get the dreaded phone call. If not a phone call I would run into someone he knew and they would tell me.

The night he stood in my house covered in blood played through my mind for a long time. I never knew what happened and didn't think to ask. I figured it wouldn't get answered anyway so I left well enough alone. Now as we sit here, I embrace the fact it could have been him. He could be gone and Tony would be here. Better yet, they would both be gone. Taylor never mentioned anything about Tony being gone, which was surprising since she and Cree kept up with each other. I wondered if she knew about it.

"Wow, I never knew any of that. Tae never told mentioned all of what happened or how Tony had been killed. She knew we were all cool so it's kind of shocking."

"Well, for a while I didn't talk to your sister. When you cut ties with me, I realized you were done for good so I walked away. It was hard when we parted ways. I punished myself for so long about letting you get away. I knew you were good for me, but I was caught up. The fast cars, the money, and the notoriety had a grip on me. I knew I couldn't have both worlds for safety reasons. I needed to be on my guard at all times. When we were together I often wouldn't be with you. You were a breath of fresh air. I craved it more than I wanted too."

I listened to him as I stared out the window. I was trying to distract myself. He was sitting here pouring his heart out. I was fighting the urge to embrace him. Three years ago, I would have moved heaven and earth to hear him say this. For months I'd hoped my phone would ring with him on the other end. I waited so long for him to walk away from it all. I wanted him to throw in the towel and walk away so we could be together. I realized I held onto Trent because I knew he wasn't going anywhere. I knew when things ended with Cree Trent would still be there. Whether it was a healthy relationship or not, I knew he would be there. When I thought about it, he was my fail safe plan. The plan I knew I could hold onto when all else fails. At least it was until I lost the baby.

After dealing with the loss, I had come to see I was self-destructing. Staying with him was never going to work, child or not. Sitting here now, I was battling with ending this conversation or adding to it. I knew ending it would give me more time to suppress what was gradually rising to the surface. I could ignore its grip on me a little longer. I knew adding to it would only open more closets I would eventually need to control. I looked at him. .

"You ready to eat? I know you're starving by now," I said.

He laughed and shook his head.

"Still the same girl I know."

He got out of the car, and I watched him walk around to open my door. I could hear the saxophone playing as I held my hand out to him. I stepped to the side so he could close the door. I moved to walk towards the building. He pulled me back to pin me against the car.

"You can act like you don't feel anything for me all you want but I know better. You forget Rylee, I've seen who you really are. I know who's really buried in your heart. You can't hide from me."

I swallowed as I looked into his eyes. The seriousness that dwelled within them clarified this was no longer a game to him. I could run in a million circles, and he would still be standing here waiting for me to come to a stop.

"I'm not hiding, I'm just in a relationship."

He stepped back and rubbed his hand over his goatee.

I knew he was drumming up a question of some sort. I just couldn't figure out which one. The whole relationship scenario seemed puzzling to him. I couldn't explain it any better, and I didn't feel like doing it all night.

"Is there something on your mind?" I asked.

"Yeah actually there is. How long have you been in a relationship? I ask because it hasn't been long since you were home so when did this happen?"

"When I came back from L.A.," I answered.

He just looked at me.

"So you left my house, came back here, and jumped right into a relationship? Does he even know about the proposal? Does he even really know about me?"

"No. I didn't bother telling him since it had nothing to do with him."

"I know you Ry. You must've been messing with this dude for a minute to be in a relationship all of a sudden. I'm not buying the whole *I just met him* story. It's not how you move and we both know it. If you're in relationship it means some time and feelings have been invested."

He was right on all ends. I wasn't going to deny any of it. However, I was hungry and didn't want to do this out here. The mystery of my relationship decisions weren't going to get solved out in front of a club.

"Let's go inside. We can talk about it in there."

We walked inside and the atmosphere was perfect. Live music, dim lights, and the smell of good food greeted us at the door. The aromas took over my senses as the saxophone and acoustic guitar sounds wrapped their arms around me. Music was my aphrodisiac. These two instruments playing were definitely my favorites.

The perfect combination of hard and soft, sexy and tender. Their sounds were both erotic and passionate in the way they seduced you.

I was a sucker for jazz. Miles Davis, Nina Simone, John Coltrane, and a little Grover Washington would have me in a place of tranquility in no time. It calmed the soul so my spirit could replenish itself. We found a table in the corner with hints of lighting. I wanted to be somewhere between hearing the music and listening to him. I knew I wouldn't be able to avoid a conversation with him regardless if there was music or not. He wasn't leaving here or New Orleans without the answer he wanted. It didn't matter I had already explained to him that I was in a relationship. It made no difference how long or when it started. I was still in a relationship. I was already cheating with Asha. Adding Cree to the list would not make things any easier, no matter what my heart thought it wanted.

We sat down and the waitress came over to take our drink order. I ordered more tequila and so did he. The shots I had already taken were slowly circulating. My senses were mildly elevating. I wanted to slow my heart rate down. I needed to shift the focus to something else.

"So where are you looking to open another spot?"

A smirk formed across his lips. He was aware of what I was doing and I could sense it. I had hoped he would play along to balance out the intensity we were feeling.

"Well I'm actually going to be a silent partner versus an active body in all of it. I'd be more like an investor so I'll be going to look at the location tomorrow."

The waitress returned with our drinks.

"You ready to order?" he asked.

"Yes." I raddled off my order to the waitress and he followed suit.

She scribbled everything down and walked off. I turned to listen to the music. I could feel him staring at me. I was trying to avoid looking at him for long periods of time. He didn't know he was already breaking down my defenses. Bit by bit and piece by piece my self-control was fading away. Right about now I wish I had invited Asha. It would have eased some of the tension. Not to mention, he would be a bit more reserved. He was an open person, though when unknown dynamics were around he was more reserved. I heard his chair move. I looked up to see him standing in front of me.

"Would you like to dance?"

I looked up at him. The sane part of me knew I should keep my ass in the seat. Friends or not, being too close to him would only tip the scales. I held out my hand to him. He led me to the dance floor. The saxophonist had just begun playing *My Funny Valentine*. He wrapped his arms around my waist. I could feel his heart beating as I wrapped my arms around his neck. His breath on my neck caused me to exhale at a much faster pace. He smelled divine. Without even thinking, I wanted to inhale every ounce of him. I laid my head on his chest and closed my eyes.

Note after note, I got lost in the moment as we swayed side-to-side. His hands moved up and down my back as we submitted to the music. I could almost hear the words being sang as he hit each note perfectly. I was definitely adding this place to my return list. I would have to mention it to Micah so we could come back. The song came to an end. Without hesitation, I moved to head back to the table.

He pulled me back to him, and said, "I'm not done with you yet."

I looked over at the table to see if our food had arrived yet. It hadn't so I moved back in front of him. The guitarist began playing what sounded like Babyface's, *When Can I See You Again*. I looked up at him, smiled, and shook my head. He was trying to be smooth. I found it to be cute. After a few cords, the saxophonist joined in. It was a sweet cadence as I fell further into the spell they were creating. His hands slid down the curve of my back. After a few notes they found their resting place on my butt. I gave him a look to imply he was crossing into illicit territory. He was getting swept up in the atmosphere. The mood the instruments had set were deceiving. I was trying to save him from himself. This was not something he wanted to start.

He didn't want to do this here, and not right now.

My head rested on his chest. I could hear her voice loud and clear, *I only believe in intoxication, in ecstasy, and when ordinary life shackles me, I escape one way or another. No more walls.*

It was Anais. It was her truth, and my version of reality, absent monogamy.

I was in my element. The zone I felt comfortable with. I stood here with a man I wanted so bad, despite the fact I was with Micah. I was fighting what came naturally to me and I was struggling. I had created walls in a world they didn't belong in. I found myself caged, therefore breaking free had become a necessity. The way he was holding me, mixed with the music, and the tequila was taking a toll on me. The discipline I tried to display was fading along with my sober mind.

I was ending this as soon as this song was over. I needed to put some distance between us. Sitting across from each other with food between us would work just fine. We rocked back and forth a few more times before the guitar faded out. I moved back from him so I could walk back over to the table. I prevented him from trying to subdue me for another song. As I got closer, the waitress was walking out with our food. I thought it couldn't have been better timing. I needed some food to soak up this tequila, and my unwavering thoughts to make some bad decisions. Cree pulled my chair out and I sat down. He walked around the table, sat down, and held my hand. He blessed our food and we dove in. It was quiet for the first few minutes before I broke the silence.

"How's your mom? I haven't heard you say anything about her since you've been here."

I knew he and his mom were close. It had been just the two of them before she had gotten married to his stepfather. For a long time, he wasn't a fan of his stepfather, though he soon came around once he saw he really loved his mom.

"My parents are cool. They are traveling everywhere since my sister has finally left home. Guess they're experiencing independence again."

I laughed softly. I remembered my parents feeling the same way once Taylor and I moved out. Well at least my dad did anyway. He figured there would finally be some peace and quiet around the house. Not to mention, some freed up bedroom space. I knew he was secretly plotting on our bedrooms the whole time.

"Well, you know my parents were more than happy to have their house to themselves again. To only have a house full of people around the holidays was enough, especially for my dad."

We both laughed.

He had never officially met my parents. We had conversations about both sets. He knew how my mother felt about him. I had never kept that a secret from him. He didn't sweat her feelings too much, seeing he understood the place they were coming from. It doesn't take a rocket scientist to see how a parent would have unsettling feelings about his *occupation* so to speak. We had never talked about being anything other than what we were so I left well enough alone.

"So Rylee are you going to answer my question or act like I didn't ask it?"

I looked at him. I had hoped he had forgotten about it, though it was clear he hadn't. I knew what he was trying to do. He wanted to see how long Micah and I had been seeing each other. He felt it essential to establish some type of timeline. This was so he could see where he could poke holes. He was very cunning. I knew how his mind worked so I was clear how this was going to end. We had never had the type of relationship where we lied to each other. I didn't want to lie, nor did I want to be completely forthcoming. If I gave him too much information he would manipulate it to suit his purpose. I was stuck in the middle.

"Why does it matter, Cree? We're together so let that be the end of it."

"Okay, but we both know there's more to that story," he said.

I looked up at him as he stared at me. His response was way too easy. One minute he wanted to dig into why I was with him and the next he was like whatever. I wanted to ask what he was up too, but I knew it would be a waste of time. He sat across from me with a devilish smile plastered across his face. He had nothing else to say. I shrugged my shoulders and turned around to face the stage.

I leaned my head against the wall so I could drift off into the music. Rendition after rendition, the musicians played jazz and R & B classics. I watched a few other couples slow dance to the songs played, while others held hands and chatted at their tables. I wanted to dance again. I wasn't sure how it would make him feel. I knew he had something up his sleeve. During dinner, they had played a couple of fast songs so I figured I would wait for them to start those again.

"You want to dance again? I know sitting in that chair is killing you," he said, smiling.

He was right because I loved to dance.

"Maybe on a fast song," I responded.

"You scared of me Rylee Coltrane?"

I turned to see the mischievous expression he had on his face. He was trying to pull my chain. We both loved challenges so I knew what this was becoming. Calling me out would get him no further. I knew this game so catching me was definitely a rookie move I rarely fell for.

"Don't ask questions that you know answers to."

"Well, it seems like you don't want to get too close. You must be afraid those feelings you've been hiding for the last six years are going to push their way through. I mean I could be wrong, although I think I'm right."

He was right about my feelings, but wrong about me being afraid of him. I turned completely around so I could face him. I wanted him to get the full effect of what I was going to say to him. I wasn't afraid of him versus what I would do to him. I had the same reservations about Micah. I was fighting urges I didn't want to fight. I was holding onto someone else's heart, while wanting mine to be free. *I could sleep with Cree and then what?* We would be on this whirlwind roller coaster ride miles away. On the contrary, I wasn't completely sure he was done with the lifestyle I knew he was accustomed to. The lifestyle I knew had been engrained into him.

"You can stop with all of your reverse psychology. It won't work since I'm aware of what you're doing. My feelings are completely fine and under control."

So you're admitting there are feelings?" he asked, smiling.

I laughed because he couldn't help but be goofy. We were both silly people so the playfulness always emerged. We reminisced and talked for another hour or so. I listened to him tell me about his dreams, his businesses, and how he's happy he made it out alive. He admitted that after the death of Antonio he was enraged and full of anger. All he could see was revenge day in and out. He told me before he made a stupid decision his stepfather sat him down and had a serious talk with him. He said his family was done with his irresponsible choices. His chaotic lifestyle was jeopardizing a lot of lives, including his.

The realization of burying your best friend and possibly more lives finally hit home. I knew he had lost people before, though they weren't as close. Your best friend being killed is like losing a member of your family. They had come up together. Good, bad, or indifferent they had each other. Facing a loss like that didn't leave you with too many options. I thought back to that night he came over and wanted to know what happened.

"I've been meaning to ask you something for years. I never asked because I wasn't sure you would tell me."

He looked at me, and said, "What do you want to ask?"

"What happened the night you came to my house covered in blood?"

He leaned back in his chair. I gathered from the expression on his face that it wasn't the question he was expecting. I had no intention in making him feel uncomfortable. I was just curious. I hadn't bothered asking him the night he showed up. I had my own issues I was dealing with. Knowing what he had just done or been involved with would have probably pushed me over the edge I was already clinging to hold on to. I was submerged in madness, and adding acts of crime wouldn't have made it better.

"Nothing good and we'll leave it at that."

I nodded and left well enough alone. I knew it would be a vague answer, but thought I would try my luck. Whatever it was, he didn't want to talk about it. I had learned years ago to tread lightly when it came to questions about that part of him. He would confide in me about some things and others would go unmentioned. I knew if he didn't want to talk about it, it was best to leave it alone. To be honest, I'm not even sure I would have wanted to know if he took a life. From the looks of his shirt that night somebody was obviously hanging on to life somewhere.

"Okay that's fair," I said, and took my last shot of the night.

"So do I get my dance?"

The music had sped up to the New Orleans style jazz. I got up and headed to the dance floor. I looked to see he was still sitting at the table.

"Are you coming?"

He leaned back in his chair, while I made my way to the middle of the floor. I danced to the songs beat after beat. The tequila had fully penetrated my core. I was now in a state of bliss. My heart was racing and my body temperature had risen a few degrees. I had dove head first into the rhythm of the songs and was dancing my heart out. I faced him and moved my hips back and forth.

I was teasing him. I knew it, and he did too.

No words were needed. Our body language was how we spoke to each other. This was the game and we both enjoyed playing.

This was the game that would eventually get me into trouble.

20 | Twenty

nother hour or so passed by before we had decided to leave. I had really enjoyed myself. The music, the drinks, and the food were excellent. We took a different route home because he wanted to see the skyline. We hit the freeway and drove across the *Crescent City Bridge*. All of the buildings were lit up. The lights aligning the bridge bounced off of the water. Cree looked like he was in a peaceful trance. We had beautiful sightseeing spots in L.A., but it was always different when you were visiting somewhere else. Anthony Hamilton crooned through the speakers. I rested against the headrest and got lost in the music. I loved the soul nestled within each note he sang. His notes danced upon my earlobes and settled in the perfect place.

"I've got a surprised for you."

I turned to look at him. I wasn't sure I could take another surprise right now. The last surprise I got from my past I had to flee the scene. Seeing he was staying with me, escaping might pose a problem.

"Dare I ask what it is? Please be mindful I have no room for any more marriage proposals."

He started laughing, and then said, "Wow, that's cold Ry. You wrong for that."

I laughed too because I knew it was cheap shot. I could care less though, seeing that Trent was irrelevant to me. Besides, I was really in no mood for another one so I was exercising caution at this point.

"Well it's not a proposal. I can guarantee it."

He pulled into the parking lot garage and parked. His phone started ringing and he looked up.

I'll meet you upstairs."

I nodded and got out of the car. I made my way to the elevator and hit the button. I wasn't sure about this surprise, and then again I figured it couldn't be worse than my holiday experience. I wanted to hop in the shower before I crashed in my bed. It was way after midnight and I still had class tomorrow. I was glad it was a late class, otherwise I would be suffering. The elevator stopped on my floor. I stepped off to walk to my door. I figured I would leave it unlocked since he was right behind me.

I dropped my purse on the table and headed to my room. Once I sat down on the bed all of the shots hit me like at once. I was beyond sleepy. I couldn't climb under my sheets fast enough. Hopefully, his surprise could wait until tomorrow. I needed sleep and fast. I reached into my pocket and realized my phone was in my purse. Earlier in the car, I saw Micah had called four times. Apparently, my phone had been on vibrate all evening. I hadn't heard it go off. I wondered what was going on since we had talked earlier before we went out. I saw there were voicemails. I opted out of listening to them until the morning. I retrieved my phone from my purse, and I sent Cree a text that the door was open and went to hop in the shower. I placed my phone on the charger then laid it on the counter. I made my way to the bathroom.

I turned on the shower, stripped, and climbed in. The water felt good as the steam left the doors invisible. I inhaled the steam. With each breath, I exhaled the horniness I was feeling. The alcohol had come full circle and I wanted to work it off. My sweet spot was pulsating. In an instance, I remembered I had taken my toy back to my room. I moved my hand down over my stomach, slowly inching down until I reached the tip of my clitoris. I leaned against the wall. I closed my eyes so I could concentrate. I wanted to ease some of the tension my aching sweet spot was feeling. I had to relieve some of the pressure or Cree would be doing it for me.

I massaged myself until I realized I needed my toy. After a few frustrated strokes, it dawned on me I was spoiled. I hadn't used my fingers in quite some time. I washed myself, rinsed off, and then hopped out the shower. I grabbed a big tank and panties then slid them on. I heard movement in the front room. Cree had made his way upstairs. I closed my door a little so I could climb under my sheets. Sleep was upon me, and I couldn't wait to get swept up in it.

I buried myself in my pillow, rolling over to get comfortable. My clock read 2:30 a.m. My body was definitely in agreement with it. As soon as I closed my eyes to drift off, I heard a knock at the door. I had no strength to fight him off tonight. I was extremely tipsy and exhausted. If he made a move, I would probably be giving into it. I figured if I laid there without moving he would get the hint and come back in the morning.

Knock! Knock!

I guess not. Clearly, it was wishful thinking on my part to conclude after five shots of tequila and him professing his feelings that he would go to sleep. The only way I was going to get some sleep was to answer him and move this along.

"Yes Cree," I sighed.

"I told you I had a surprise for you or did you forget?"

"No I didn't, but can it wait until tomorrow?"

"No I want to do it now," he said, impatiently.

I sighed and climbed out of the bed. I needed to sleep this alcohol off or I would be paying for it in the morning.

"Ok, I'm all yours," I said, holding my arms out as if he was going to handcuff me.

"Close your eyes." I gave him a puzzling look as if I was trying to understand the game we were playing. "Close your eyes Ry. What, you don't trust me?" I rolled my eyes and played along. I couldn't fathom what kind of surprise he would have for me in my house. I felt him walking me to what I knew was the front room due to the direction. "Okay, stand here and don't open your eyes."

I stood in my front room in complete silence for a few seconds before I heard it. *I put a spell on you because you are mine—You better stop the things you do, I ain't lyin'.* Nina Simone was singing from what I knew was vinyl. The sound was forever implanted in my ear. I opened my eyes to see him standing there in front of a record player. He had brought me a record player. I covered my smile with my hands. I couldn't believe he'd actually bought me a vintage record player. I had one as a kid and it had somehow had gotten broken.

"So can I have my real dance now?"

Grinning from ear-to-ear, I nodded yes. He reached his hand out to me and I placed my hand in his. He twirled me around and kissed the nape of my neck.

"One more surprise," he whispered.

I looked over my shoulders and he had a smile big as day across his face. He gave me a look as if to say turn around so I did. He moved closer to me and placed a necklace around my neck. I could feel a pendant hanging so I rubbed my hand over what felt like a heart. He wrapped his arms around my waist to spin me around.

"So you can have a piece of my heart with you always, Happy early birthday Ry," he whispered.

I was at a loss for words. I knew I should have declined the necklace. The record player was one thing, whereas the necklace was something different. It was too personal. This moment between us had gotten too personal. The distance between us was closing in fast. I wanted to move a couple steps back, but the grip he had on my waist wouldn't allow me too. I searched myself for strength to move my legs, but found none.

We stared at each other for what seemed like forever before I laid my head on his shoulder. He smelled like home. The place where I could close my eyes, exhale, and everything in the world would be alright. Nina Simone belted out her, *I've Put A Spell On You,* lyrics as we swayed side-to-side. I remembered our nights like this back home. The peaceful moments buried within the chaos. Chaotic peace is what we would say our relationship was. To everyone in the outside world things seemed crazy, though to us everything rightfully made sense.

Our past, this moment, and everything dwelled within the unspoken silence nestled between us.

He tightened his grip around me and I moved closer to him. I was fanning the small flame already burning and I knew it. However, I wanted to be right where I was. He was warm and his hands felt good around my waist. I could feel his imprint growing every time we moved. He placed a kiss on my shoulders. His lips then traveled to the nape of my neck. I moaned softly. I was trying to control myself, while savoring this brief moment of intimacy. He moved his hands up my back until they landed on the sides of my head. He stepped back far enough to move my mouth close to his. The gap I had formed earlier was now closing. He started off with soft pecks on my lips. I responded with kisses of my own. He then traced the outline of my lips with his tongue. I licked my lips playfully, teasing him. He moved me closer and placed another kiss on my lips.

It was passionate and full of life. All beautifully disguised beneath a ferocious hunger.

There had always been a subtle obsession we shared. I always believed it was what fueled us. A need or a want that somehow held tight to us, hoping we would somehow get it together. In another life, time was rooting for us. I moved closer to him. My hands sliding up and down his back, while his held firm to my ass. For a brief moment, I had forgotten I was minus a few items of clothing.

150

He moved back, kneeled in front me, and pulled my shirt up. My breasts were exposed as the cool air mixed with his warm tongue sent waves of pleasure throughout my body. I held the back of his head as his tongue circled one nipple after the next. As I ran my hand back and forth over his head, and I could feel my sweet spot thumping. I was trying to ignore her invigorating pleas for pleasure. He had moved his tongue down my stomach and was circling the inside of my navel. His hands had shifted to the sides of my hips. He gradually pulled the top of my panties down with his teeth. He left just enough skin exposed to tease me. His moist lips settled at the top of my warm center.

My heart was beating fast. My sweet spot was pounding uncontrollably. My mind was racing nonstop.

My hands were on top of his head. I was torn between pushing him away and pulling him closer. My mind was telling me to push his head away and go to bed. My sweet spot was begging me to let him finish what he started. I hadn't had a chance to sleep some of the tequila off, and therefore my sense of judgment was not at its best. I knew I had enough rational thoughts flooding my mind to stop this. Somehow, the irrational thoughts were winning at this moment. They won every time.

"Let me taste her, Ry."

There it was. That was the trigger needed to conquer the remaining rationale I was fighting to hold onto. He pulled my panties down on both sides and licked the top of my sweet spot in one long stroke. The cool temperature of the room and the warm feeling from my body was causing my knees to buckle. I needed some support. Standing here in the middle of the floor with this man licking me was proving to be difficult. He moved further down, placing kisses on the inside of my thighs. He slid his hand directly between my thighs, separating them so his fingers could slide in. I let out a soft, yet deep moan.

"Can I taste her?" he asked.

His soft pleas were turning me on. They turned me on in way in which I could sense how he yearned for it.

I thought about how earlier I had given into the uncompromising predicament Asha had placed me in. Now here I was again, a slave to my sweet spot and a prisoner to orgasms. I was walking the line between good and evil. I was fanning a slow burning flame destined to become a wildfire. My no was stuck in my throat. My yes was at the tip of my tongue. No longer waiting for permission, he lifted me up and placed me on the island. My insides were screaming. A war was going on inside of my body, and I was searching for a way out. He moved a bar stool in front of me and sat down. He pulled me to the edge of the counter.

"Cree wait, we can't do this. I have a man remember," I muttered.

Finally! The words freed themselves from the grip ecstasy seemed to have on them. I had managed to get the words caught in my throat out. My conscience was trying to push pass my troublesome libido. My heart wanted a fighting chance. It needed one moment to win over lust. I sat up to look at him. The look in his eyes was intense. They appeared to be understanding, yet presented themselves as unwilling to give in to defeat. He kissed the inside of my thigh again. It was his way of responding to what I had just told him. He gripped my legs, and then pulled me closer so he could place a soft kiss on the entrance to my sweet spot.

"Crreee," I moaned as his name purred from my lips.

I wanted to move. He had my legs intertwined with his arms. I pulled my body in the opposite direction only to have him pull me back onto his lips. He continued to place soft, intimate kisses on my thigh on the tip of my clitoris and back to the other side of my inner thigh.

He was teasing me. He taunted me in the worst way possible.

He wanted me to want this the way he wanted it. His mission was to breakdown my defenses so I would let him in again. I could fuck him, and then where would we end up. I had boundaries now. There were lines that I was not supposed to cross. I realized I had caged myself. I had violated my golden rule, *Always stay free.* Now here I was caught between pleasure and principle. *I knew I could get away with it so why not?* No harm would come from this. By Saturday, all would be forgotten when he left. I had made my relationship disclaimer so no lies were told. If he left here with feelings they wouldn't be because I failed to disclose anything. I arched my head back and closed my eyes. I was ready to enjoy this. I wanted to submerge myself in this moment. This ideal fantasy fate had presented to me.

The kisses became more frequent, and his touches grew more aggressive.

The pace of my heart had increased. My heartbeat seemed to be in competition with the pulsating between my legs.

"Tell me how bad you want this, Ry. Tell me you love me."

He wanted me to beg for it, and confess a love I was unsure of.

At that moment, he took the first deadly stroke with his tongue. I was reminded of my reality. The vibration from my phone startled me and my past flashed across my screen.

I couldn't do this again. I couldn't open the door to my past again, no matter how bad I wanted this.

21 | Twenty-One

I lay in my bed as last night flashed across my mind. The words he said. The way he smelled and even the explosive amount of heat nestled between us. We were twin souls fighting to be one with each other. We were lost loves trying to find their way home again. I squeezed my pillow tighter and closed my eyes. The sound of the ceiling fan was echoing as my thoughts traveled throughout my mind. I rubbed my hand over the diamond heart pendant he had placed around my neck. The coolness of the metal and stones cooled the heat brewing beneath the surface of my skin.

I stared at it last night before climbing into bed.

It was truly beautiful, though it didn't belong around my neck. It belonged around the neck of a woman who would be able to reciprocate the kind of love he deserved. The kind of love he was trying to give me. *It has always been you Rylee,* Are the words that danced through my mind as I bit my lips. I could still taste him. I could still feel him. His touches and his kisses were just like I had remembered. They were full of passion. My Scorpio man came to claim what he felt should belong to him. What had always been his and life somehow got in the way. I wanted to run to him, but my reality prohibited me from doing so. I was a wanderer by nature, yet I was feeling this strong need to give what I have with Micah a fair chance.

My decisions, my responsibilities, my desires, and my freedom.

They all pulled at me in the worst way. Deep down I knew the time would eventually come for me to play this story between him and me out. Now was just not the time. I rolled over onto my back and stared at the ceiling. The air from the fan was cool and somewhat refreshing at the moment. I had one more night before my sisters arrived. My only prayer was to survive another night of his seductive ways. He was going to stay at a hotel once they were here so things wouldn't be awkward while everyone was visiting. I smiled at the fact he remembered my birthday after all this time. He was early with the gifts, however he did remember. Since flying home was not in my near plans, it was a good idea to bring them here. I was pretty sure my sisters would be doing the same. I was surprised by the necklace, though not as surprised as him pulling me into the living room to show me my first gift.

A beautifully restored record player.

I had one as a kid, and it had somehow gotten broken. To see he hadn't forgotten my love for vinyl and classic forms of music made me smile. I was mesmerized as we danced song after song. Nina Simone was one of my favorite artists. He had found three of her records. Not to mention, he made it even better when I saw a Miles Davis record on the table behind the couch. By this time, I was completely subdued and in heaven. I was so caught off guard I didn't even expect the necklace.

Candles and Jazz, and then the seduction was on high.

Streets or no streets, he knew how to make a girl feel special. I should have known the kisses were coming shortly after the necklace was fastened. Kiss after kiss was placed on the nape of my neck. His hands holding me close as I held his head in the palm of my hand. I inhaled him with each kiss he laid upon my skin. Before I knew it, I was on the counter straddling the line between pleasure and principle. The sound from the phone snapped me too.

I had gotten lost.

My lapse in judgment caused me to fall into a place I knew was sticky territory. Now I'm lying here and can't think of anything other than his lips on my mine. The tingling stroke of his tongue on my inner thigh disrupted my senses. Micah had called this morning. Somehow I couldn't find it in me to answer. He had called a few times last night. I should've sent him some kind of response, but my fingers still tingled from touching Cree. I told Cree I had a man once I gathered myself from the kiss we seemed to have gotten lost in. His reaction was not what was expected.

He looked at me, and simply replied, "As long as there is no ring on this finger, I still have a chance. I gave in and let the doctor hold onto you too long. I won't make the same mistake again."

I knew his response was a shot towards Trent. He always despised him.

He always felt like I was better than him. Like I didn't need the drama he bought along with him. When I had told him about what he did with Zoe he was furious. Talking him off that ledge was not easy. For days I was worried he would do something crazy to him. At first, I had considered letting him whoop his ass, and then decided against it. Trent was so vindictive I would have worried it would escalate to levels out of my control. Cree in jail for assaulting Trent was not the heat he needed. We agreed to let it go so he just held my hand and we moved past it. When I think about it, those moments may have been the moments that love manifested. Ironic how a few weeks later I ended up letting his hand go too. I was just so caught between two worlds of crazy. I couldn't focus too hard on either of them.

Now things have changed, yet have somehow stayed the same. I was with Micah now, though Cree was still here. I have played over-and-over in my mind whether us bumping into each other was fate or just bad timing. It always seemed liked bad timing with us. When we couldn't or shouldn't be with each other, there we were. However, when we were free to be with each other there was this blank space, a loss in connection. For years I have pondered off and on if I wanted Cree because I couldn't have him or if I truly loved him. Sometimes, when you are involved with someone on the side or part time, you feel this strong desire to be with them. It's like a magnetic force pulling you to each other and the other person seems highly irresistible.

They're like the forbidden fruit, and everyone wants it because it's unattainable.

I've come to learn that's the real aphrodisiac. It's the drug everyone constantly fiends for because it feels good. A high you only feel once. The trick is to know the purpose of the forbidden fruit. To know its aphrodisiac is solely created to lure you in. The magnetic pull creates a false sense of security. It wraps itself around you as it seduces you. When you're not looking you fall prey to something you will eventually have to let go of.

Was Cree my forbidden fruit?

My body craved him for sure. Like a light bulb, it would turn on as soon as we were within close proximity of each other. I laughed at the dynamics of our attraction. I remembered Jayce and Kira saying we were like a magnets around each other. I knew there was some truth to the statement. Funny thing was I seemed to have explosive chemistry with Micah too. I couldn't dismiss my feelings for Micah because they were real. I didn't love him, but eventually I believed I could.

He was my fresh start. The new beginning that something inside of me needed.

I moved here to get away from L.A. and somehow it has followed me here. I opened the door to my past and it was here front and center. The good, the bad, and the ugly portions of my past had resurfaced. I needed to put everyone back in their box. I knew I would need to reiterate to Cree that I'm in a relationship. He didn't care nor did he want to hear any parts of that conversation. Holding my arms behind my back and kissing me until my lips were swollen proved that much. I knew I was a lost because it escalated to my legs being spread wide open on the counter with his head buried deep between them. I had gotten to the edge before my rationale kicked in. My inner vixen was ready to play. For her there was no turning back. I had a flashback to what happened with Trent and moved back quickly. I couldn't do this again.

I could not open another door, and stick my hand into another cookie jar. Especially, since it was one I knew would not close so easily.

From the beginning, Trent had no real chance. Although, I knew Cree was a completely different story. My text alert snapped me out of my aquarium of thoughts. I picked up my phone to see who it was since I had already talked to Micah and made up with Asha.

It was Cree.

Cree was very competitive. He wouldn't settle for less than the winning slot. I needed him to know this is not a game. There was no race to be run, and no trophy to win at the end. I was taken and he missed his chance. I realize I came back and hopped into a relationship, and he may feel kind of cheated. However, the deed has been done. I knew this was going to be the longest 24 hours of my life. I entered my password so I could read the text. I clicked the message he sent, and there it was for me to see.

It was front and center in black and white words so there would be no confusion. It was His declaration and his stance on how he felt about everything I had said to him.

I stared at the message as if it would change to something else and nothing moved. There would be no changing of the words or his mind. He was making clear and wanted me to know where he stood. Relationship or not, he wanted me to know.

Tonight, this night, we will be finishing what we started last night.

22 | Twenty-Two

I managed to gather myself and make it to class. All throughout it, I thought about what his text meant. I thought about what it could mean for me and the status of my relationship with Micah. Up until this point, I hadn't really stepped out on Micah. Yes Asha and I were still messing around, but it wasn't as frequent as we were once were. Aside from my needs, she was beginning to really fall for Mario and I wanted to give her space to sort through all of her feelings. She and I would always be friends so everything was all good. It was kind of bizarre we were reliving the same scenario that brought him here in the first place. I wanted to inquire more as to why she was okay with this arrangement, but decided against it. I think her being cool and not flipping out made overcoming the awkwardness less weird. I honestly don't feel it would've been so easy had it been the other way around.

We will be finishing what we started last night.......

It played in my mind over and over and round and round.

Like a song I couldn't forget the lyrics to no matter how hard I tried. To be honest, I'm really close to staying at Asha's place tonight. I know he would never hurt or disrespect me so those weren't the issues. I just wasn't confident I would be able to keep my legs closed and my feelings under lock and key. Like always, he, I, and this story of adventures would have to remain unfinished. Starting something I couldn't finish would only result in more hurt feelings and broken hearts. I had already opened a heart only to have to close it abruptly. I

159

didn't want to do the same to Cree. I remembered I hadn't responded to the text and honestly didn't know how.

I could say something smart, or I could play dumb and act like I was oblivious to what he was talking about.

I didn't usually go the dumb girl route, though in this case it may serve me well. If I acted like I was unaware of what he was talking about, then I could gauge where this night was heading. I sent him a text asking what exactly needed to be finished. As soon as I pressed the send button an unwanted distraction managed to appear.

I had decided to come grab some gumbo from *Mr. B's Bistro* in the French Quarter for lunch. I had become addicted to it since I had been here. I had slowed up from eating it since it was beginning to add some curvature to my hips. He slid his slick ass my way and I fought the urge to roll my eyes to the back of my head. I sat up straight so he would have no room to put his lips on mine. He made his way to my table. Before I could stick my foot in the chair he snatched it out.

"Oh, come on now Reece, don't act like that. You know you're happy to see me."

I looked up from my phone to see him sitting down along with his friend who was quite handsome. I refrained from saying something smart to prevent him from being embarrassed. He made it too easy whenever I did see him.

"Titus, please spare me today. What do you want or need?"

He looked me up and down. I just gave bullets to someone holding a gun he was ready to fire. I hadn't really forgiven him for his little library stunt. I hoped he would remember that before leaping into the fire again.

"Oh Reece, if you only knew the many ways I could answer that question," he said, licking his lips.

His friend seemed to be trying to figure out the relationship between he and I, while trying to refrain from laughing.

"As big as this city is, how is it you manage to keep running into me?" I asked in an annoying tone.

"Don't you mean running into each other?" he asked, trying to correct me.

What he didn't realize was I had said it right the first time. I was in no mood for his craziness. I had other stuff to sort through. His added flirting or pursuit of me was not in the cards today. Just as I opened my mouth to answer him Cree responded to my text.

The text read: *You're a very smart woman Rylee, however if you need me to lay it out for you I will. When I say we're finishing what we started last night, I meant there will be no you running from me.*

Or better yet, no you stopping what I know you want just as bad as I do. This back and forth between us has been going on for years. It's over now.

I stared at his words as if they were going to step outside of my phone and pull me in with them. He had declared war. Whether I wanted to give in or not, he was determined to be the victor. Once again, I had opened the lion's cage. I could hear everyone now saying, *We told you not to let him stay Lee,* and so on. I needed to simmer this spark before it became a full blown blaze. I couldn't risk him doing too much. I didn't want him pushing me too far and expose my hidden feelings for him to Micah. A woman had a right to love as many people as she wanted.

I need to do so without restraints. I needed to do so with unwarranted confessions, and without boundaries others may place upon me.

I needed to respond. *I had to say something, but what could I say?* I did want this just as bad as he did. I could say I really wanted to stop last night, though it wouldn't be entirely true. Trent's face popping across my phone's screen at 4 a.m. was a gift and a curse. My hands were still somewhat clean, while I was still craving the temptation inside my walls. I hadn't bothered to call him back, seeing I was not interested in hearing what he really had to say. If it was about the flowers he could send a text, otherwise we didn't need to talk. I figured they were from him since Cree made no mention of sending them. Now that Trent has called I'm beginning to think he may be the culprit. I sent Cree a, *yeah ok,* and placed my phone down. I had no real energy to entertain Titus, though the free comedy was a perfect distraction.

"No Titus, I believe I said it right the first time."

"So how long are you going to play hard to get? I know you ain't really feeling ole boy. You need a real man to handle your feisty ass."

I laughed at him. He actually thought he could handle me. *Based on what?* Hopefully, it's not due to the library kiss he stole from me. He wanted a chance and I understood. His libido was in full force, and driving the lust that oozed from his arrogance. I was trying to give him a way out. I had spun enough webs. I didn't need to be caught in any more at this time.

"Titus, you're adorable and all, but it's not happening. I hate to bruise your ego since I'm sure you're not used to hearing no very often. Now, if you don't mind I would prefer to sit here and eat my food by myself without being harassed."

He gave me a look, and I wasn't sure how he was going to respond. I really did not feel like a scene. Most people came here because of the gumbo so I didn't want to have to switch spots because I clowned. He and his friend stood up. He looked at me with the same sinister look he had given me when I met him at the NYE party. He was sure of himself. I'd give him that much. He walked over to my side, and then bent over so no one else could hear the inappropriate comment I knew he was going to make.

"In the end Reece, ultimately they all say yes."

He pushed his chair up to the table, rubbed his hand across my shoulder, and then they walked off. Although I would be curious to see if his skills matched his ego, he really wasn't worth the trouble. The waiter returned to my table with my bowl of gumbo and bread. I was good and hungry. I prayed over my food then scooped my first bite into my mouth. I got excited thinking about my sisters coming to visit. I actually missed them. I wished Kira was coming with them, seeing I missed her too. I hadn't really planned out many activities since this was Mardi Gras week. There would be plenty of stuff to get into so we'd play it by ear. I scooped another spoonful in my mouth. This gumbo was beyond delicious. I was literally on the verge of relapsing into a regular patron again. People came in and out of here with bags of take home gumbo. I personally couldn't make it to the parking lot with it. I decided I would bring my sisters here once they came. With Taylor being a chef, she appreciated good food. My waiter came back to clear off my table and bring me my check. I turned to reach in my purse when I heard my phone ring.

Jayce came across the screen.

"Hello dear sister," I said as I handed the waiter the receipt and cash.

I signaled I didn't need change. He nodded, said thank you, and walked away.

"Hey Lee, are you busy?"

"No, I'm just finished eating. What's up?"

"Well, I've got some good news and some bad news. Which did you want first?"

I would swear this was a trick question. I would love to smack the person who came up with formatting news like this. No matter how good the news was, you only remembered the bad news. So in reality, it didn't matter what order you placed it in.

"I don't care Jay. You know I hate playing this game."

She laughed. She knew I could be easily annoyed, yet she'd toy with me anyway.

"Well, the good news is I got called back for a second interview in D.C. The bad news is I have to be there Friday morning."

She got quiet as she waited for my reaction. I wasn't mad even though I wanted them both to come. I was more worried about the fact I was being left at home by myself with a man who was trying to seduce me. I was banking on them coming so my self-control wouldn't buckle at another one of his touches. . I was one tongue stroke away from anarchy being declared inside of my body.

"Well, I am happy for you and sad at the same time. I miss you guys, but I know you really want this job."

"Yes, I am excited. I'm sad about not coming too. They want to move this process along pretty quickly so I'm heading out this evening to get settled and prepared. I will reschedule this ticket for the weekend of your birthday in a couple of weeks."

"Ok cool. So is Tae still coming or is she going to come with you later?"

"Yeah we're both going to come together. We told Kira we were changing our plans so she said she would probably come too. Guess we can come wreck some havoc on New Orleans like old times," she said, cracking up.

I was excited, though I had a new dilemma.

"Alrighty then," I said.

"What's wrong Lee? I can hear something in your voice. Is everything ok?"

I took a deep breath and told her what happened with Cree. I gave her the mild version, seeing I really didn't feel like hearing the, *I told you so,* speech. Once I finished telling her, all I could hear was her choking from her laughing so hard. I knew it wasn't that damn funny. She was enjoying this way too much.

"Wait until I tell Tae this. She is going to die laughing!"

"I didn't ask you to tell Taylor none of my damn business, ma'am!"

She was still laughing.

"Rylee, didn't we tell you this was a bad idea? I mean you are a horny toad, and we all know how you are around Cree. It seems like old times again. When we would be hanging out it would be like you couldn't wait to go home to jump each other's bones. Hell, as thick as y'all sexual energy was you should have been trying to sell some of it."

She was always the one for exaggeration.

"So what are you going to do? You're either going to give him some or put him out. Letting him stay there is only going to lead to my first option."

"I'll figure it out," I replied, sarcastically.

163

I knew I didn't have many options, and the truth be told I didn't want him to leave. I would just make it clear we we're friends. I wasn't sure what the future held for us, but for now I was with Micah.

"I've always admired your rebellious spirit Lee, but remember what I told you though. You're going to have to choose one. It's going to either be your heart or unlimited orgasms. I'll call you when I land in D.C."

We said our goodbyes, and then I got up to head home. I needed a nap and some time to think. With Cree running around, he wouldn't be back until later I'm sure. I made it two steps out of the door before my phone rang again. This time it was Cree. I guess my response wasn't good enough for him.

"Yes Mr. Nicholson, how can I help you?"

"Where are you?"

"I'm on Bourbon Street, why?"

"Meet me on Frenchmen Street. I want you to see something."

"Okay, I'll be there in a second."

I didn't have far to go since it was walking distance from where I was at. I could've walked, then again I didn't feel like walking back to get my car. My palates were satisfied. At this point, all I needed was a nap. I wasn't sure what he and I were getting into later. I did however know we needed to have a real conversation with our clothes on. I climbed into my car to make my way a few blocks over. He had texted me the address. I made a right turn and drove a few buildings up until I saw the address he'd sent. I parked my car and got out.

I could tell some rehabbing was going on though it seemed to be well on its way. I walked up to the building and saw the door was opened. I walked in and saw the inside was beautiful. Whoever he hired for the remodeling was doing a wonderful job. The interior almost resembled *Halo*, but you could still see the difference. It was L.A. mixed with that New Orleans flavor. The decor was modern, yet it resembled some southern flare engrained within it. I loved the deep purple hues he mixed with the teals, yellows, and white hues. With the lights off and the spotlights on it would be beautiful. The stage area was gorgeous. Clearly, it was designed for plenty of celebrity appearances. I was so caught up in the décor so I didn't hear him walk up behind me.

"So what do you think?" he asked.

I jumped, and then spun around. He looked at me, trying to figure out if I was okay. I flashed a smile at him.

"I think it's beautiful, Cree."

He smiled as if my validation made him feel better. He grabbed my hand.

"Come with me. I want to show you the best part."

I took his hand and followed him to the back. He opened some patio doors, leaving me in complete awe. There was a beautiful patio setup with a fountain, lights, and completed with a garden. The picnic style tables gave a more social feel rather than separate tables. The lights strung above the tables and couches seemed perfect. I wished it were dark so I could see just how beautiful the lights reflected off the flowers. Beautiful arrangements of succulents surrounded the base of magnolia trees. A walkway leading to the fountain was compiled of different stones. It was the perfect date or party venue. I looked at him. I was so proud of him and his accomplishments. He had gotten away from the life and did something positive and legal. If this never went pass us being friends, I was still glad we were able to find each other again. He always stayed in the back of my mind. After all this time, I was happy to see he was ok.

"Wow, Cree this is gorgeous. I just may have to patronize this place when you open it," I said, laughing.

"Oh really?"

"Yes really."

He showed me the rest of the building. Every spot in the building looked to have a special touch placed on it. Once we finished the tour, I told him I would catch him back at my place later. I needed a nap. I also needed to finish up the rest of my midterm paper. He had more business to finish up at the club so I said goodbye and headed to my car.

My drive home would be short. I could knock this paper out, take my nap, and hopefully be up by the time Cree got to my house. I started my car when I saw I had missed Micah's call again. It seemed like we were playing phone tag. I realized I hadn't talked to him. He knew it was midterms so he knew I would be busy. I sent him a text letting him know I was heading home to finish my homework. I told him that I would call him when I woke up from my nap.

Now that my sisters weren't coming I had to definitely figure something out. Micah wouldn't be back until Saturday, and Cree didn't leave until Sunday. There was no way he could stay at my house until then. I was thinking I'd refrained from telling him they weren't coming so he would still stay at a hotel. My phone made the alert sound. I looked down. *Okay baby* was his response. I figured he would understand. I turned into my garage lot and found a spot right next to the elevator. I grabbed my book bag and hopped out. The ride up the elevator seemed quicker than usual. I guess people hadn't really made home from work yet.

I made my way to my apartment. The breeze from the air conditioner felt so good. It was rather warm for February, and then again I was used to warm winters. I placed my phone on the charger then headed to my room. I had given Cree my spare key so I wouldn't have to get up to let him in. I flopped across my bed and buried my head into my pillow. It was 5 o'clock so I could take a mini nap. I set my alarm for 7 p.m. so I could get up and finish my paper. I closed my eyes and exhaled into the cold air.

Images of Micah stroking me flashed across my mind. The feeling of Asha's soft kisses buried between my legs caused me to tremble. The passion of Cree's kiss outlined my lips. I could feel all of them, even taste them. Their scents were layers upon my skin. I was in a conundrum of pleasure. It would appear I was on overload, though I wanted more. Ecstasy was a drug. Orgasms were the high you found yourself addicted too. Somewhere in my heart, they all had a place. I couldn't decide if it was because of feelings or if time eventually created this place we are all in. I knew in due time this all would unravel. I was on a roller coaster going up knowing the downward part was a few climbs away. .

My lovers were closing in. All of them wanted a fighting chance. I remembered what Jayce had said earlier. I contemplated on her words. At this moment, love would have to share the spotlight with ecstasy or jump off of the ride. I was simply going to ride this ride until the direction changed.

Men had their secrets, and women had theirs.

My secrets were wrapped up between them both.

23 | Twenty-Three

he moving around in the kitchen woke me up. I opened my eyes to see it was 9 o'clock. *Shit,* I thought. I had slept way passed my alarm going off. Apparently, I was catching up on the lack of sleep I missed last night. I rolled over to get up, and the aroma of food took over my senses. I inhaled what smelled like fried chicken. I threw the covers back and climbed out of bed. I heard another voice as I got closer. I hit the end of the hall, and I saw Asha sitting at the counter talking to Cree. They both seemed to have sensed my presence since they looked up at the same time.

"Well hello sleepy head," Asha said.

"Hey girlie, when did you get here?"

"About an hour ago. I came over to see if your sisters had gotten here yet since I hadn't heard from you. I knocked on the door, and this fine specimen of a man opened it."

She smiled, and then looked back at him. I don't know why I felt this sense of annoyance come over me. I had never been the territorial type, though at that moment I felt a tinge of it. Asha was a tiger when it came to flirting. For whatever reason, Cree was off limits. I shook it off before my face reflected my thoughts. I knew I had to keep it together, seeing I was involved with her brother. I didn't want her to become suspicious of anything.

"I wouldn't say all that about him," I said, laughing.

167

I moved towards the island and pulled one of the stools out to sit down. He looked at me with a slight smirk on his face. He wanted to say something, but seemed a bit hesitant in doing so. I wasn't sure what had been said while I was sleep, though I was pretty sure she'd told him she was Micah's sister.

"So what have you two be up here doing?"

"Oh nothing. I've been chatting his ear off, while he was cooking and telling me about his new club called the *Orchid Lounge*. It sounds dope so we definitely have to go check it out when it opens."

I looked at him again. I was so caught up in how good his lips looked I didn't even realize my phone was buzzing. I got up to see it was Taylor calling. I couldn't do this with her right now. I knew she was calling because Jayce had opened her damn mouth. She couldn't hold water and I knew it. I sent her to voicemail and texted that I would call her back later. I didn't want to chance either of my guests hearing that conversation. She responded, *You better,* before I could even put my phone down. I knew I would have to call her later, otherwise she would blow me up until I did.

"Is everything cool?" he asked.

"Yeah, that was Tae."

"Oh okay. What time are they coming tomorrow? I can grab them from the airport since I know you have an early class."

I paused because I wasn't going to say anything until he had already left. They were both staring at me, waiting on my response. I could have strangled Jayce right now for bailing on me at the last minute. I knew she had an interview and was happy for her. This was just a huge dilemma.

"Well, their plans changed. Jayce had a last minute interview in D.C. so they decided to come for my birthday in a few weeks."

"Well that sucks. I was looking forward to partying with them. By the way, when is your birthday?" Asha asked.

Cree, on the other hand, stood there with this look of mischief on his face. I could tell he was excited. He was trying to hide it, but it wasn't working. His excitement was plastered all across his face. I wanted to say something, but I decided to save it for later. I thought it would be nice to spare Asha and her ears.

"Yeah, I was too. It's March 5th," I responded.

"Well, it looks like it's just me and you buddy. Just like old times when we were home," he said.

I knew he was baiting me.

I gave him a look and moved passed his comment to ask, "So what else were you two talking about?"

"Well, Asha here was telling me her brother lives here too. They moved here from D.C. I believe it was."

Her brother huh, I thought shaking my head. He knew who he was. Seems he may have skipped a few details. I wasn't too sure if Asha had told him who he really was. I knew she was pretty good with keeping secrets. Considering he danced around it, he probably didn't know who he really was. I had already told him I was in relationship. There wasn't much of a secret there. "Yeah, her brother Micah and I are together."

I made sure I said it in front of Asha.

I was forever being strategic, and forever covering my bases. I was always in need of an alibi.

My public disclaimer was to shield me from any suspicions in the event it appeared there was more between us. If I kept Micah in front of me then Cree being on top of me wouldn't come up for question. I knew Asha wouldn't question the nature of our friendship, but still I had to be sure. Yes, I rode her tongue on occasions, but I couldn't get too comfortable. No matter what the situation was they were brother and sister. I had to keep the way they were connected in the forefront of my mind at all times.

I watched her laugh as he told her some old stories about us. My legs trembled at the very thought of slow grinding on her lips. I wanted to feel her lips on me. The other day had me wishing I could take her on the couch right now. I remembered when we pulled Trent into our little sex circle. Oh, how it backfired on me. Cree probably wouldn't freak out, but I couldn't chance it. Besides, I wasn't sure I wanted to share him with anyone else. Trent was irrelevant, though I wished he would've fallen for Asha versus me. Guess we can't have everything we want in life.

"Wow, so how long have you known each other?"

I glanced at him with a smirk on my face. I knew he was trying to gather information. I never answered his question from the other night so he was using Asha to get the information.

"Well, I met Ry the same day she moved into the building. I'm not really sure when she met my brother," Asha said.

Now she was being slick.

I never told her when Micah and I officially met, just the fact we knew each other. If I wanted to lie, I could say it was at her house party. She and I had talked about our whole relationship, yet I still managed to leave a few things out. I saw no need in telling all of it.

"I believe it was probably in class or your house party. It's been a minute so I'm not sure of the exact date."

"Oh I forgot about my house party. Well in that case, meeting him there sounds about right," she said.

He observed me inquisitively. I knew he was trying to see if we were together before I came home or when I came back here. I wasn't going to have this conversation with him in front of her. Up to this point, all my little secrets had been kept separated. No matter how hard it seemed I intended for them to remain as such. We traded a few more stories before I glanced at the clock to see that it was creeping up on 10: 30 p.m. I still had two pages left to type for my midterm paper. Having Asha here actually worked to my advantage. She was my distraction from Cree. I could type my paper and be done before midnight.

I gave him a goofy expression as I stuck my tongue out. I made my way over to the couch to finish my paper. I only had a few more details to plug into it, and I would be good to go. I flopped down and grabbed my laptop out my bag. My headphones were at the bottom so I slid them out too. I had to block everyone out so I could finish this up. It was my last project before I could go back to regular homework life. I knew Asha would be leaving soon since she had midterm stuff too. I just needed her to be here until I finished. I logged my computer on and plug my headphones into it. As soon as everything popped up, I started scrolling for music. I needed something I knew wouldn't have me in here singing, while not putting me to sleep. I scrolled until I landed on D'Angelo's, *Brown Sugar*. I loved everything about that album. I pressed play and opened up my paper.

I could hear them laughing in the background while they were eating. I never remembered Cree cooking at all when we ran together. Hell, I didn't even know the man could cook. Guess we were so busy running the streets that neither one of us had time to be in a kitchen. Not even ten minutes after I started typing, he was bringing me a plate of food. It was fried chicken and waffles laced in syrup. Clearly, he was missing *Roscoe's Chicken & Waffles* from home.

I gazed up at him, and he said, "Try this. It's a new recipe I'm trying out for the club."

He was making it really it hard to cross him off my list. The man was an entrepreneur, attractive, hustler, good friend, and now a damn chef. Good Lord what else! He seemed to be a modern day Superman. Too bad Micah beat him to the punch. Honestly, it worked out for the best. I knew I wouldn't have been faithful, especially living in two different states. Shit, I was struggling with Micah and we lived in the same complex now.

Micah, I thought to myself.

I realized I hadn't talked to him since Cree arrived. Hopefully, he would understand me having house guests and not be too upset. He was coming back Saturday so we would catch up then. He didn't know my sisters weren't coming anymore so we could spend that time together. I reached for my phone so I could text him. The text read: *I can't wait until you come home. I miss your lips, your tongue, and you know what else.* I attached a tease pic and pressed send. I took a bite of chicken and scarfed down a piece of the waffle. I had to say it was delicious. I was impressed.

I managed to go between the food and my computer for the next thirty minutes. After another thirty minutes, Asha tapped me to say she was leaving. It was close to 11:30 p.m. I was halfway through my paper by then. I placed the finishing touches on typing and proofing my paper. I caught a glimpse of the clock, and it was now after midnight. Although I wasn't exhausted since I had napped earlier, I was still a little tired.

I closed my laptop and placed it back in my bag. Since Cree fed me, I got up to see if he needed help cleaning. I walked around the island to see a spotless kitchen. It looked to be cleaner than it was before he started cooking.

"Wow, I would've cleaned the dishes since you cooked."

He dried his hands and placed the towel on the counter.

"No problem, baby. I knew you were finishing up your homework."

Baby? Something about the way he said it made me want to smile, while ducking for cover at the same time.

"Well, thank you. I appreciate it," I said as I moved to grab a glass out of the cabinet.

I wanted some wine, but since it was so late I would settle for water. I needed clear and coherent thoughts. There was no room for judgment altering vices. He was on a mission and I knew it.

"So when were you going to tell me your sisters weren't coming?"

I chuckled, and then said, "If you must know, I just found out earlier. It wasn't a secret or anything. I hadn't realized you were looking for them to come."

He rubbed his hand through his beard.

"I wasn't, though they are cool to hang out with. I was just curious," he answered.

I filled my glass as I turned to peek at him. I lifted the glass to my lips so I could drink the water. Apparently, I was thirsty because I gulped it down and filled up again. He waited until I put the glass down. I moved around to walk passed him. I had almost made it around the counter before he grabbed my arm and pulled me to him.

The kiss came so fast I had no real time to block it. Our tongues intertwined with each other until he broke the kiss.

His eyes held a serious look of contentment. He was searching for the right words to say. He was vexed with where he fitted in my world of lust and love. I had no real answer for him other than the one I had given him. *We could fall back into our little game of sex and then what?*

He was in this for the long haul and those two words were not something I could hold onto.

"How long are we going to play this game, Ry?"

"What game?"

"This little game where you act like you don't have feelings for me. Better yet the game where you act like you're not in love with me."

"I never said I didn't have feelings for you. I said I was in a relationship. Don't confuse the two because they are not the same."

"Since when did you start being faithful? Come on Ry, you forget how we started out I see."

I didn't forget, however I hadn't realized he wanted to continue to remain as such. Truth be told, it made me question if he was even single. I didn't know very many men who would voluntarily be a side piece unless he already had a home life set-up.

"No, I did not forget. I'm just curious as to why you would be okay with it. Is there a Mrs. Nicholson back home that I don't know about? Otherwise, why would you be cool with me cheating to be with you?"

"No there isn't and I think you know it. Now before I answer your question, can you tell me you haven't already cheated on him? You keep forgetting I know you, Rylee. I know damn well ole boy back home wasn't acting a fool for no reason. I wasn't going to say anything because it wasn't my place to. Now, whether you crept back is your business, but don't stand here and play the innocent role. We're better than playing each other like this. Why would I be here if I had a chick back home?"

"For the same reason you're here right now and you know I have a man. You forget I know how you used to play the field."

"Well, if I remember correctly, you weren't a stranger to the playing the field either," he replied.

He had point, but it really didn't matter. I had enough lovers to juggle. I wasn't trying to add anymore. He would require more than sex and I knew it. Trent had created a mess I had no intention of cleaning up again.

"So what's up with you and ole girl?"

172

I gave him a puzzled look. I hated he was so damn observant. It was a gift and a curse at the same time. Mostly, it drove me nuts when we used to run together. I honestly believe it's why we never really lied to each other. We both possessed the trait so we could fish out bullshit easily. It was so much easier to tell the truth versus endure a million annoying questions.

"We're just friends, Cree."

It wasn't a lie, but it just wasn't the whole truth.

"Yeah okay, Ry. If you say so. Well, if you are *just* friends your friend is obviously into you."

I looked at him as I slid to the other side of the counter. He followed right behind me, pulling me back to him.

"I told you there was no more running. We're finishing what we started last night, tonight. Now, if you don't resist just maybe I'll go easy on you. I've given it a lot of thought and there's no need for me to tire you out tonight. I have two more days to remind you of how powerful our lovemaking used to be."

He placed his lips over mine. In a matter of seconds, I'd dropped my defenses. *It would only be this one time,* I told myself. *After this I will act right. I will give my body what it wanted and then close up shop. No more exes, no more mixing my past with my present, while jeopardizing my future.* I placed my arms around his neck. He replied by lifting me up. We walked over to the couch and he sat down. The room was completely silent as the sound of our breathing competed with our heartbeats. He slid his hands up my shirt to unsnap my bra. My breasts felt a sense of relief as I lifted my arms for him to remove my shirt. His hands cuffed my breasts as he placed kisses on them. His tongue circled my nipples. The air blew across my back as I slow grinded against him. I moved to lift his shirt over his head. I stood up to slide my shorts down as he unbuckled his pants and removed them. He pulled me back down onto him.

"Come here."

I followed suit, sitting back down. My knees positioned just right on both sides of his legs. I could feel his dick hardening with each stroke of our tongues. His hands went up and down my back. He cuffed me tightly, sliding us onto the carpet. He pulled my panties off, tossing them to the side. My legs spread apart as he placed them onto his shoulders. He looked into my eyes. He was searching for permission. I knew I would have to face this in the morning. For now, my body wanted this. I smiled, softly biting my bottom lip. A grin appeared across his lips. My lip biting was our signal. No matter whom we were with or where we were, my lip biting meant playtime.

He brushed my inner thigh softly with his lips. He was teasing me. With each second passing, the anticipation mounted. I rubbed the top of his head. He finally kissed the outside of my sweet spot. His lips were warm. The tip of his tongue was slowly breaking me down. I was at my breaking point. I couldn't take the torture anymore. I pushed his head into my sweet spot softly. In one long stroke to the inside of my walls I exhaled.

"Shh," was all that escaped from my lips.

His tongue twirled round and round against my clitoris. My legs trembled. My breathing increased. I was trying to control the pace of it. I wasn't ready to cum. I wanted to savor each stroke as he went up and down. The heat from his mouth mixed with the heat from my sweet spot was making it very hard to do. I rubbed my hand up and down against his head. It seemed he had decided to go bald and the surface was incredibly smooth. I rolled my body against his tongue, and within seconds my first orgasm escaped me.

"Ohh," I moaned.

He looked up at me as if to say he wasn't done. I arched my back as his next lick caused me to jump. I moved back a little with the jump. He gripped my hips to slide me back down. The pull was forceful, pushing his tongue deeper into me. I wanted to scream, pull something or anything! I knew he had a serious tongue, though I did not remember it being this skillful. I was on the verge of releasing another orgasm when someone started banging on the door.

I looked up at the clock and saw it was almost 2:30 a.m. *Who could be at my door this late?* Asha had left earlier. Micah was gone until Sunday. I lay back down, signaling for him to ignore it. I moved his head to keep going, but the banging continued. I promised to God to myself that if this was Trent again, I was committing a crime tonight. I got up, and slid my clothes back on. I irritatingly marched to the door. I watched Cree grab his stuff, heading to the spare room. I was glad he hadn't put his clothes on right there. We were finishing this tonight. Without even thinking, I swung my door open with an attitude.

"What the fuck!" he shouted.

I stood frozen as he stood at my door with his eyes glaring.

"Micah, what are you doing here?" I said, hoping I'd disguised the shock in my voice.

"What do you mean what am I doing here? I've been calling you for two days. I've got no call back. When I do call, all you've sent me was text messages. What the hell, Ry? Is there something going on? I was starting to get worried since you don't normally dismiss my calls like this."

I had no response to his question. I was searching my mind for something to say.

As I opened my mouth to answer, Cree walked out with no shirt on, with tats and body on full display.

"Ry is everything ok?" he asked.

It was as if he timed it perfectly. I knew he could hear the commotion going on from the back. Micah turned to look at me. In an instance, I knew shit had just gotten real. I had a half-naked man in my house in the middle of the night. There was no real way to explain this.

"Who the fuck is he, Rylee?" Micah asked.

I saw Cree open his mouth to answer. Micah's tone didn't sit well with him and I knew it. I signaled for him to chill, and that I could handle it.

"Baby this is my friend Cree that I was telling you about."

Micah shot a look of anger at me.

"I know mutha'fuckin' well this isn't the person I told you couldn't stay here. You let this nigga stay up in here after I specifically said not to. Really Ry? Is this how we acting now?"

He moved closer to me, bridging the gap. I stepped back to put a little space between us. Cree looked as if he was going to say something again. I knew from his past he wasn't going to let too many more shots be fired before he fired back. I also knew with Micah moving towards me he would somehow take that as a threat. I was trying to keep this as peaceful as I could for 2:30 in the morning. I knew he was angry at me so I was trying to keep it between us.

"Micah wait," I said, reaching for him.

"Don't touch me Rylee! I don't want you to fuckin' touch me!" he yelled.

He stormed out the door and I ran after him.

"Micah wait! I can explain!" He took off down the stairs with me right behind him. He pushed the door so hard I thought it was going to break off the hinges. "Micah wait! I can explain!"

He spun around a little too fast for me. I stopped mid-stride since I wasn't sure what he was going to do. This was our first fight. We were still learning each other's temperaments. I knew I had fucked up. I hadn't planned for him to come home early. I suppose if I had answered one of those calls I would've found out.

"What is there to explain, Rylee? You're home alone with a nigga in the middle of the night. That your man asked you not to let sleep here. I think the real question is what would have happened had I came

175

home on Sunday? Would you have even told me he stayed here?" he asked.

Well, any logical person knew the answer to that question. I wasn't sure what type of women he was used to dealing with. Never in history would I voluntarily snitch on myself. Getting caught was one thing, but confessing was something entirely different. I had to pick my battles right now. This was not one I was going to deal with tonight.

"Micah he got in late tonight and couldn't check in. I told him he could crash here until the morning."

He just looked at me.

Now I was standing here telling another lie, and keeping another secret I had to bury deep.

I wasn't sure if he was buying any of this. He had no proof Cree didn't arrive late tonight except for Asha. I was pretty sure she wouldn't drop a dime on me. I moved closer to him so I could wrap my arms around him.

"Baby I missed you. Let's not spend your first night back fighting."

He leaned down, and pulled my face close so he could kiss me.

"Goodnight Rylee. If I stayed with you tonight I might hurt you. You lied to me so right now being next to you is not good for either of us. Truth be told, I believe you would've lied about tonight had I not showed up. I need to clear my head. We can finish talking when I'm not pissed off."

He moved my arms from around his waist, and then he moved to head towards his building. I looked at him and saw how pissed he was. He stopped midway down the walkway before he turned around.

"Oh, and so we're clear if that nigga is still at your place in the morning you'll be answering for it. Just so you know, I won't be anywhere near nice about dragging his ass out of there. If you don't want your friend fucked up, I suggest you have him leave now."

I stood silent and in shock. He walked off. I turned to head back to my place. I took the elevator up. The entire ride I thought about how close I had come to giving into Cree. I thought about how things could've been so much worse if Micah would've been louder. Everything went back and forth, and in and out of my head. Despite all of it, one thing remained constant. I tried shaking it and couldn't. I was who I was so I accepted it. It was all I could do to keep it together. I pushed it to the side, but it came back full circle.

There was no fighting it because my sweet spot was still throbbing.

He left me here in this state with a man I couldn't resist.

24 | Twenty-Four

walked back to my condo. I opened the door to find Cree standing in the middle of my front room completely naked. I thought to myself, *You can't be serious,* I closed my door. I was already trying to calm my hormones down. All the while trying to calm a highly pissed off boyfriend down. I wasn't sure if Micah was actually going home or was he going to patiently post up to see if Cree left. Either way, having him standing in the middle of the room naked was not the remedy I was searching for. I leaned against the door and shook my head. I was shocked to see after all of this he still wanted to have sex. It was as if Micah busting us meant nothing or better yet, as if it didn't happen.

"What are you doing Cree?"

"What do you mean? Did you not hear me when I said we were finishing this tonight? I don't care about that nigga. Whatever he's feeling is his problem. The fact he left you knowing I was still here is stupid on his part. Tell me right now you don't still want it. If you don't, I'll put my clothes on and be out of here in the in the next few hours. "

I glanced at him. I hated ultimatums. I despised being on the spot even more.

By now it was creeping up on 3:30 a.m. I was tired, not to mention horny as hell. I didn't know what Cree wanted from me. This was beyond sex and we both knew it. Sleeping with him right now was segueing to something else. I wouldn't begin to stand here and play

177

naive. Micah was pissed. Cree was standing here stark naked. I was standing here ready to put my relationship in even more trouble. All to free a couple orgasms my body held captive. He moved towards me. He was so close to where his breath fell like a cool breeze to my earlobe.

"Tell me to leave Ry. If it's what you want I will leave now. Tell me what you want. I'll do whatever it is."

He kissed my cheek. The movement of his lips silenced me. He sucked on my earlobe, and then little by little moved down to my shoulder. *Who could rightfully think clearly when someone was licking, kissing, and sucking on them?* I opened my mouth and he slid his tongue inside. He had me pinned against the door with my hands over my head. I wanted this. I wanted him. I had fought it long enough. His hands slid down my shorts and found their way to my center. His fingers caressed my trigger spot gently, moving it in sync with our breathing. Our kisses became deeper. Forceful as if this would be our last time. I couldn't decide if the sneakiness made it hotter or if it was the fact we had both been fighting this urge for far too long.

Him trying to respect my boundaries, and my conscious self-trying to remember I now had some.

His body pressed against mine felt good as he moved to whisper something in my ear.

He blew softly on my ear before saying, "Looks like you've been outvoted. Your sweet spot seems to agree with me."

He still remembered.

He would always call it my sweet spot when were together. He said it so much I started saying it too. I was hot and wet. His fingers moved back and forth until fighting it was no longer an option. I exhaled and gave him the orgasm he was fighting so hard for. He pulled his hand up and licked his finger. He traced the outline of my lips before he slid his finger inside my mouth. I swirled my tongue around it before sucking it. I pulled back, sliding his finger out of my mouth. I stared at him as if to say your move. He pulled me off the door and picked me up. I wasn't sure where we were headed. He moved towards the island, easing me back on top of it.

"Now without interruption, let's finish where I left off last night."

He slid my panties off, pulled up a stool, and buried his head between my thighs with no warning. There was no chance for me to stop him. He had grown tired of the interruptions. He wanted my sweet spot. The resistance I put up had made it worse. I held onto the sides of the countertop as he ravished me. I felt violated and vindicated at the same time. My entire body was on fire. His tongue was the match to start the blaze.

"Ohh my God Cree—"

I started to say before another orgasm mounted, deliberately pounding through me. He held on firm to my hips. He had no intention of giving into my ecstasy pleas. My clitoris was throbbing nonstop as his tongue continued the assault on my sweet spot. He showed no mercy. He gave no indication of a white flag being waved mattered. The cool countertop provided me relief from the sweat beads beginning to form. I placed my hands on top of his head. Holding onto the counter proved to be difficult as each climax I freed weakened my grip. I rested my leg on his shoulder.

"Cree plleease—"

I begged, and he ignored the mercy I searched for. He was leaving his mark. He wanted this memory forever etched in my mind. He wanted traces of him left upon the walls of my swollen sweet spot.

I moved his head in the same wave motion as I moved my body. I tried to control the outcome. He wasn't having it. My Scorpio man fed off of control. It ran through his veins. It gave life to the very being whose face was buried deep inside me. I wrapped my legs around his neck. My body gave him the last orgasm I was holding onto.

"Ahh," I belted out.

I hoped my neighbors hadn't heard me. The moan came from my soul. He raised his head as he moved to lick the inside of my thigh. I shivered at his touch. He caressed my hips. My entire lower half was sensitive to touch. He got up and walked off. I was lying on my back contemplating how good I felt. Caught in deep thought, I hadn't realized he'd come back. He walked up to me. I turned over to see him holding his hand out to me. I lifted up carefully to slide off the counter. My legs were still a little weak, though I managed to stand. I noticed he had put protection on. We moved back to the area we had started before. He sat on the couch. I lowered myself down on top of him. He pulled my shirt off exposing my breasts again. He buried his face between them. As he took one in his mouth, I lifted up just enough to slide him in.

"Ohh Ry," he moaned.

I swallowed hard, feeling him expand inside me. Deeper and deeper he slid inside. I allowed the whimper I held onto to fall on his earlobe. I scraped my fingernails up his back as he sucked on my neck. He felt good. His lips felt good. The heat from his body mixed with mine sent me over the edge. He cuffed my cheeks, grinding my sweet spot back and forth. So many memories flooded my mind. The many nights we'd have sex, talk, have more sex, and then fall asleep. The extreme nights that welcomed pleasurable mornings. Flirtatious laughs, leading to uncontrollable orgasms. He leaned his head back. His lips exhaled the high he was traveling on. I was caught between a place of beauty and blasphemy. I had just gotten caught by my man, yet I was here riding this man into sweet euphoria.

The irony of it all, I thought to myself.

"Ry, you feel so damn good."

I leaned forward. With my hips, I pushed him further into me as I took hold of his mouth. Our tongues competed with each other as I bounced up and down. He wanted to pull back. He was trying to free the moan I was holding captive. I pulled his mouth closer to mine, forcing him to relinquish the pleasure into me. I squeezed tighter, rocking my hips. I wasn't the girl he thought he remembered. I was in a different arena. A far cry from who I was when I first opened Pandora's Box. I had experienced eroticism in many ways since being here. I moved to give him a little control. Somehow I couldn't find it in myself to free it. Over-and-over, I gyrated on the tip. Massaging the shaft, then up and down until all he could do was fight to hold on. He looked at me only to realize this was a different me. He grabbed hold of my waist firmly. With my legs wrapped around him, we slid back onto the floor.

I wrapped my legs around him tighter. He stroked me with everything he had. Each time he went in, I felt a piece of my guilt slip away. Freeing me from the shackles, I allowed to be placed on me. Soft moans escaped both of us. The sweat smothered our skin. The ceiling fan gifted us with breezes of air as our bodies overheated from the sensual gratification we had submitted too. I felt him hardened more. I knew he was nearing the edge. Lying on top of me, his moans provided comfort to the voices in my head. His lips brushed my earlobe. I kissed his cheek. I pulled his ear close to my lips.

I whispered, "Give me what belongs to me. What you so desperately want me to have."

His strokes increased, and my insides quivered.

He drew closer to the edge, pulling my orgasm with him. My fingertips dug deeper into him. My legs were holding on for dear life. I buried his face into my shoulder. The whimper caught in my throat grew into a full-blown moan. Without warning, I released the last piece of energy I had left. His leg started shaking and he had exploded inside me. His breathing was heavy, and mine was chaotic as I tried to steady it. He collapsed in the entanglement I had wrapped him in. I hugged him as he rolled us over onto our sides. Our once exhausted moans faded into faint breaths. Our erratic heartbeats steadied. He looked into my eyes. I tried to hide the satisfaction, but I couldn't. The ounce of guilt I felt walking back in from arguing with Micah had disappeared.

I closed my eyes to fully embrace what had occurred. He leaned over to place another kiss on my lips. I released my grip on him and rolled over on my back. His hands caressed my stomach. Staring at the ceiling, I instantly drifted off to a different place. The fan cooled my body, while my mind raced a million miles per minute. I was addicted to hedonism. I could no longer fight it. A smile nestled itself against my lips.

There were so many secrets buried within my lips, and so many sins hidden within my walls.

Sex was plastered everywhere.

25 | Twenty-Five

*B*ang! Bang! Bang! The sound of someone banging on my door woke me up abruptly. It had been a long, yet short night. I sat up completely frazzled at what was occurring. I looked at my clock. It was 7:15 a.m. I had 45 minutes left on my alarm clock. Whoever was at the door had clearly robbed me of it. I knew who it was before I had even jumped up. He'd made an idle threat last night. For a moment I didn't think he would follow through with it. I got up since he refused to stop the damn banging. On my way, I saw a note and my spare key on the counter. Cree was gone. He had snuck out in the middle of the night.

No kiss goodbye, and no money on the nightstand. It was who he was, and it was how we were.

My body was in a state of bliss. My mind had a million thoughts floating around. Micah showing up out of the blue threw me for a loop. A part of me knew he would be here this morning just to see if Cree had left though I'd hoped it would be later. I rubbed my hand over the necklace I still had around my neck. It was two carats of diamonds placed in the shape of a heart. It really was beautiful. I walked over to the counter and picked up the note.

Ry,
Last night was amazing. One day when all is said and done, you will be mine. We were meant to be. Keep my heart close to yours. Catch you next trip...Cree.

I opened the drawer, placing the note and key inside. By the sound of the crazy person on the other side of the door, I didn't need to throw any more fuel on this mild wildfire.

"Ry open the door! I know you're in there!" he yelled.

I snatched the door open and pulled him inside.

"What the hell Micah! Its seven o'clock in the damn morning! Are you trying to get me a noise complaint?" I screamed.

He stormed passed me.

"Where the fuck is he?"

I closed the door before my neighbors heard anything else. I knew he was mad, but not smell like a whole liquor bottle mad. I wanted to ask if any was left, but dismissed it. I was too tired, and I knew I would need to find some kind of energy for this fight. I was wrong about everything surrounding Cree being here. I knew it, which is why I didn't feel like the argument. Apparently, he needed to yell so I would be the apologetic girlfriend and listen. I had class in two hours, which meant he had an hour to clear his chest. I walked pass him to head for the kitchen. It was clear I wasn't going back to sleep so I might as well make breakfast. He nearly stared a hole through me. I wasn't sure if he expected me to kick this off, but it wasn't happening. Seeing he woke me up banging on my damn door, it was his show. I opened my refrigerator and pulled out the fruit I needed for my smoothie.

"So you're going to walk pass me and say nothing Rylee? You could at least say you're fucking sorry!"

I rolled my eyes in the direction which he was standing.

"If my memory serves me correctly, I did apologize last night. You were just too pissed off to hear it. However, if you need to hear it again then fine. I'm sorry, Micah."

"Is that all the fuck you gonna say? No my bag Micah? No I really fucked up? Or No attempt to sound like you know you fucked up? I mean damn Rylee you straight did the complete fucking opposite of what I asked you not to do. It's like you didn't give a shit about anything!" he yelled.

I pressed the button on my blender so my fruit could blend. I needed something to boost my energy and fast. I was exhausted mentally along with physically drained. Whether he realized it or not, he needed to calm down. I only had one class today. I just needed to get through it without passing out. Cree made up for lost time last night. After the third round, I was literally in dire need of sleep. After hanging out, class, and then arguing with Micah sleep was all I wanted to do later on. He moved closer to me causing me to look up. His eyes were red from either no sleep, alcohol, or both. He grabbed my arm and pushed me up against the cabinet.

For whatever reason, I didn't move. We had several conversations about domestic abuse so he knew I didn't play that shit. I wasn't sure what he was going to, however I wasn't in fear of it. He pressed his body against mine. The closer he got to me the more I smelled the liquor on his breath. He bit my cheek hard. He wanted to inflict some kind of pain. He licked the side of my face, moved down to my neck, and then back up to my ear. He cuffed my neck as I looked into his eyes. They were their usual smoky gray color except something else was hidden beneath them.

It was anger, passion, and love I presumed.

He gripped my neck harder as he pressed himself up against me. I inhaled a deep breath. His hands slid down my shorts. I wanted to move his hands away, and tell him he needed to sleep off the liquor. Only I knew it would set off another trigger. His hands entered my sweet spot and I released a soft moan. Soft pleasures mixed with minor waves of pain. I was still sore and needed a warm bath. I couldn't start the morning off like this.

Remnants of my old lover's fingerprints were left upon my skin. The very traces of last night's indiscretions left clinging on the tip of my tongue. Our many sins buried beneath the outline of my lips. All the while my man is standing here wanting to fuck away the anger he was feeling. The sense of betrayal I somehow caused him. His finger moved quickly against my clitoris. I bit down on my lips as I leaned against the wall defenseless. I wasn't sure if he was setting me up or trying to get some. I had to play this right. Otherwise, I would be setting off World War III in my house. I couldn't endure a round of sex I knew would possibly turn into two. An outcome I knew weighed on how angry he really was at the moment. He needed a release so I would give him one and send him on his way.

I moved my hand against his dick. I could feel his hardened imprint against my leg as he continued to pull an orgasm out of me. I had released everything I had a few hours ago. I needed time to rejuvenate so he would be all morning trying to make me cum. I knew I had 30 minutes to get him off, me showered, and off to class. I pushed him off me so I could turn him around. I pulled his hand out of my sweet spot. I tauntingly licked his finger. He released the grip he had around my neck. I slid his dick out of his pants. The coolness of my hand caused him to jerk. Bit by bit, I moved my hands sensually over his shaft. He leaned against the wall. His eyes penetrated mine as I pulled his pants down. I moved the rug from under the sink so I

184

could kneel down in front of him. The tip of my tongue swirled around his tip. I could hear him release a soft breath before I slid him into my mouth.

"Ohh," escaped his lips as my tongue tormented every inch of him.

The heat from my mouth incited him further. I pulled him out of my mouth, teased him with my tongue, and swallowed him again. His fingers moved smoothly through my already messy hair. He was searching for a grip of some kind. A reminder he was still in touch with reality. I swirled my tongue around and around, while the wetness of my mouth increased. He moved my head back and forth as he released memories of last night.

My mouth moved in sync with his rhythm. Quick licks turned into deep strokes.

I gently massaged his soft spot. I pulled him out of my mouth. They danced on my tongue as I sucked on each of them. His dick was in my hand being stroked ferociously as my tongue pleasured other parts of him. He moaned loudly and I knew he was close. I entered him back into my mouth, holding the other pieces of him in my hand. I moved my mouth back and forth, faster and faster until he had nothing left to hold onto. I could feel him shaking. I moved so he could free himself. He needed to free the tension he obviously came to give me last night. I grabbed a towel. Within seconds, he let out a loud groan. He moved the towel, pulled up his pants, and leaned back against the wall. He needed support, and the wall provided it.

He reached his arm out to pull me close to him. His heartbeat was still quick. The tempo hadn't slowed up just yet, giving his breaths a chance to balance themselves. He drew me in and wrapped his arms around me tightly. He kissed my forehead as I lay my head on his chest.

He exhaled slow breaths, and said, "Rylee, I am a dangerous man when my heart is involved. One thing you need to know is I am *very* territorial about what belongs to me. When I say I love you, I mean it. Don't make me lose myself if you're not all in. I don't want either of us to get hurt."

There it was. The jealously I saw buried inside the look he gave me earlier. I exhaled.

Ownership even in love was an illusion. A fantasy doomed for failure if truly believed in. There was no such thing as a man owning a woman or vice versa. Anyone who believed in such a theory left themselves vulnerable.

They were blinded to the truth, and exposed to pain.

A dream destined to be shattered.

26 | Twenty-Six

S *o how did everything go with your little company? Hopefully, you stayed out of trouble Lee,"* she said.

The weekend was over. All of the Mardi Gras tourists had faded out. Another week had come and gone as if time had no real agenda. Life as I knew it seemed to have gone back to normal. Cree had left, Micah was back on the road, and I was lying across my couch talking to my nosey mother. I decided once I found the energy, I would go cruise the French Quarter. I figured I could see if Asha wanted to hang out.

"Mom, everything is fine. Cree and I hung out. It was no big deal."

"I'm sure it wasn't," she said, sarcastically.

She knew better and so did I. Regardless, there was no way I was telling her we slept together. Hell, I wasn't even going to tell my sisters. I was keeping that entire sinful secret to myself. I didn't need the lectures or constant probing. Everyone was a counselor when it came to my love life or lack thereof. I was unclear on where he stood. I didn't need any outside voices in my already loud head. He had literally texted me every day since he had left. I answered a few and ignored the rest. I didn't want this to turn into a thing, which was a situation I knew wasn't going anywhere, anytime soon. I still had the necklace on. My eyes would catch reflections from the diamonds every time the light hit them. It truly was a pretty necklace. I hopped up to place a vinyl on my new record player. He managed to lace me with quite a few classics that I loved so much. I slid a Miles Davis record on and headed back to my couch.

"I would really like to know why you still have an issue with Cree mom. Trent and are over so what is the issue?"

"Rylee, I grew up with men like him. I've known his type my whole life."

"Mom, he's done with all of it. He put it behind him and has moved on."

"No he hasn't baby. He's just found better ways to disguise it. It's not easy leaving that kind of money behind. They live and breathe everything surrounding the street lifestyle. I just don't want you to get caught up with the craziness. Been there, done it all, and it's not easy to walk away."

She had my full attention now. I knew my father was a somewhat of a bad boy in his earlier years. How bad could he have been I didn't know. I wanted to know more. I knew I had to tread lightly since we would be talking about my father. They were both very open with us, but still they protected pieces of each other. Pieces of themselves they would never want their children to know. I understood it, and I respected it. I knew there would come a time if I had children that I would have my secrets. Many of which I could never let see the light of day.

"Are you talking about dad?"

"No Lee. I am not talking about your father."

"Well then who was he mom?"

"There was a guy before I was involved with your father. His name was Lamar. He was much older than I was. The only person who knew about him was your Aunt Mia. I knew what he was into, but during those times just about everyone in Brooklyn was in that lifestyle. I was being fast and almost paid dearly for it."

My heart was pumping, while my ears were on fire. My mother, the Trinidadian beauty, had been in love with darkness and danger. Never in a million years would I have pegged my mother as a dope man's girlfriend. It seemed so cliché of her. Now everything was coming to light when it came to her feelings about Cree. All of the animosity, the worry, and the warnings she would give me made sense. All of it stemmed from a bad experience. I couldn't believe my Aunt Mia held out on me. She was always the one spilling the goods. She was actually an older version of Jayce when I thought about it. She and my mother were close, however she was quick to point out how my mother wasn't always this person we'd come to know. We always thought it was funny and laughed when they argued about it. I guess my MeMaw didn't know about this little escapade surrounding Lamar.

"So what happened to you mom? Did you get hurt?"

"I literally dodged a bullet."

She said it as if she was in the moment all over again. I couldn't have imagined what happened although I understood. Regardless of how much fun I would have with Cree it would constantly be this silent feeling of worry. He never sensed it because I hid it, but still it was always there. My sense of awareness stayed on high alert. On top of being on guard, I never got too lost in our fun. If we were home that was one thing, but never when we were out. My ears were tingling as I waited for her to finish her story.

Miles Davis was in one ear, while my mother was in another. At this moment, she seemed so real and so vulnerable. She was a woman who knew variations of love. In another life, it was the dangerous kind of love. A love she so desperately wanted to protect her child from. I cuffed the heart pendant in my hand as she finished her story.

"Lee, I know what it feels like to be in the wrong place at the wrong time. How you fall in love with the wrong kind of man. I was caught up in materialistic stuff. Yes, I was 17 and still it was no excuse. I knew better. Had I gotten hurt or caught with anything, my life would have been over. It is so true when they say God protects babies and fools. I was on my way to Lamar's house when time seemed to have stopped. If would have I arrived where I was heading ten minutes earlier I would be dead. Time heals a lot of things, but not everything baby. There is no coming back from seeing someone you love dead. Your heart doesn't heal from that kind of loss. Your mind does not erase those memories. I never wanted you to experience that kind of pain."

I gasped and she paused. I thought about Antonio, and I imagined how it could have been Cree.

I could hear the sadness in her voice. It was no longer disdain for Cree, yet a broken piece of her never to heal. It was a part of her past never to be forgotten.

"After I attended his funeral, I swore I would never date someone who was involved with the street lifestyle again. When I met your father, he dabbled in it for a bit. Once I threatened to leave him, he let it go. We moved so we could start over."

I listened to her tell me more as I took heed to her warnings. I texted Asha to see if she wanted to hangout, while she finished talking. I felt like I needed some girl time since I had my share of men lately. My sisters hadn't confirmed what time they were coming so I made a mental note to double check with them. I got up to head to my room. I needed to find something to wear. Whether she was coming or not, I was getting out of this house.

"Cree is starting over mom. He's opening legal businesses of his own. I know you don't believe he can change, though he has and it shows. You just said dad changed so how come someone else can't?"

Now I paused.

For the first time in all of the years I had known him, I was defending him. *Why?* We weren't together, nor did I have anything vested in him. I had never cared what she thought about him before. I needed to change the subject before this got too far or she got suspicious.

"It doesn't matter any way. I'm in a relationship with someone else. Cree and I always have been and always will be just friends."

"Do you have a boyfriend?" she asked, surprisingly.

I filled her in about Micah as I put on my clothes. Asha had said she was in so I needed to get dressed. My mother seemed excited about Micah, which was just the distraction I needed.

"So when do I get to meet him?"

"Probably during spring break if he doesn't have any games. Hey, did Jay get the job she was interviewing for?"

"Yes she did," she replied, sadly.

I knew she was bothered that we were all moving away. All she had left was Tae, though she rarely stopped by since she was trying to start her catering business. I had a year and a half left here then it was onto my next adventure. I hadn't decided if I was going back to L.A. or somewhere else. A piece of me missed home, though now that I have left it seemed backwards to return.

"It's okay mom. You still have Tae there with you," I said, giggling.

I was being funny and I knew it. Jayce was the closest thing to sanity she was going to get. Tae and I were always floating on the wings of prayer.

"Yeah ok, Rylee. I'll talk to you later. I have some work to do. Be sure to call more often. We are your parents you know."

I laughed, and we said our goodbyes.

As soon as I slipped on my shoes, Asha knocked on the door. She was just in time because I was hungry and in the need of some adventurous today. I grabbed my purse and keys then headed for the door. I opened it to see her standing there looking extremely devilish. I laughed since I knew she was up to no good.

"Do I even want to know?" I asked, locking my door.

We headed down the hall, and she started laughing.

"I'm just being goofy. What are we getting into today?"

"I don't know. We can check out the French Quarter. I'm hungry so definitely some food. After we eat, I'm open for anything."

I knew saying *open for anything* could get me in a world of trouble. To be honest, I welcomed a little trouble. Even though Micah and I made up, there was still this sense of awkwardness between us. An uncertainty of some sort he couldn't put his finger on. I had a feeling he suspected something regarding Cree, yet he kept quiet about it. I knew Cree would probably be in and out of town due to this club so I kept quiet about it. He didn't trust him. Honestly, I wasn't sure where I stood at the moment. I would just stick to my rendezvous with Asha. At the end of the day, staying under the radar while floating high on orgasms was my end goal. Anything outside of him and her was pure trouble. We headed for the car and my phone rang. I popped the locks and we climbed in.

"Hey Jay," I answered.

"I got the job!" she screamed.

I yelled and almost scared Asha. We started laughing, and she shook her head.

"Oh my God, sis! I'm so happy for you! So when do you start?"

"Well, see that's the thing. I start in three weeks. They wanted me to come early so sis I won't make your birthday. I was thinking of switching my ticket to your name so you can come here for your spring break. What do you think?"

I started up my car. I wasn't happy about her not coming again. I did think D.C. for spring break wouldn't be such a bad idea. At least I would still get to see Asha and Micah. This way, I wouldn't have a lapse in sex. Spring break was two weeks after my birthday. It wouldn't be the same without them being here. I would manage, seeing Asha and Cree were here. The Greek weeks were starting up so I would have enough parties to attend. It wasn't a milestone birthday. I was just turning 27 so I could forgive this one.

"Okay, spring break is fine. I'm getting ready to hang out with Asha, though I do have a question to ask. How does Jordan feel about all of this? I know you two are glued at the hip these days," I said, laughing.

"Well, since you asked, he's coming too. He worked it out and his company is going to transfer him to their headquarters in D.C."

"Of course they are transferring him," I said, sarcastically.

"Stop hating hussy. You can have a man too if you let that playa lifestyle go," she teased.

"Whatever. Not in this lifetime or the next. Look, I'll call you later so we can finish chatting."

"Dang, ok rush me off the phone, bye."

We hung up. I turned around so I could back out.

"Looks like I'll be in D.C. for spring break."

"Aww hell! I was gonna hop in your suitcase to L.A.," she said.

I knew she was joking, seeing she knew I wasn't going anywhere near L.A. after the holidays. I would consider going during the summer, but definitely no time sooner. I couldn't chance Trent catching wind I was home again. He had sent me little subliminal texts here and there, though nothing alarming. He had yet to own up to the flowers. I knew they were from him so I didn't care if he acknowledged them anymore. To be honest, not speaking to him was better. We wouldn't find ourselves in an argument. I had no energy left to argue with him.

I missed my sisters. I didn't miss L.A.

Lately, it seemed I didn't have to go back there to be reminded of it. I was happy for Jay, yet sad at the same time. She would be further than I was from home. I knew it would not be long before Tae moved. She already moved around with her catering so she would probably be uprooting soon too. The question was where she would go.

"Well, you know me going home is not up for question," I said, laughing.

She looked at me as if to say she felt the same way about D.C. I knew going home was somewhat of a headache for her. Her parents had a way of driving her crazy. We bonded on that level. I'd hoped she would consider going home since she would have me as an escape. I'm sure Jay wouldn't mind one more houseguest. Jordan was another story. A house full of women was only ideal if it benefited the man.

"Yeah, I know," she said.

We laughed and chatted about her family coming to visit next week. She was excited about seeing them. It appeared they were a close knit family which could be good or bad, depending on how you looked at it. Sometimes the closeness was what drove everyone crazy. I had it with my family. I loved them, but distance served all of us well.

"So who all will be flying down for Micah's game?"

"I believe it's just the guys in my family for right now. My mom is coming because of course she's our mom. Other than her I think my aunts will be sitting this one out."

"Well, at least you'll have plenty of company. Micah seemed excited everyone was coming," I said, looking for a place to park.

She gave me a mischievous smile.

"I just bet he is."

"Why you say it like that?"

"Let's just pray New Orleans is in one piece when they leave," she laughed.

"Asha, they can't be that bad."

I pulled into a parking spot and parked. She was so tickled by my response that she couldn't stop laughing. I remembered Micah saying his family was wild. I figured it was an exaggeration at best. Clearly, Asha's laugh proved something different. She shook her finger at my naive comment. The innocence buried within my response evoked the naughtiness within her.

"Well, I'll tell you this and count these words as your warning. Please steer clear of all of them if Micah or I are not around. I would hate for you to become the next family victim or holiday story."

I laughed at the hypocrisy of her comment. I was already a victim or villain. It depended on which end of the spectrum you were looking out of. In the beginning, I was indeed a victim. A slave to the catastrophic way they seduced me. A slave to the unwavering spells their tongues casted on my sweet spot. My sugar walls were painted with the countless orgasms they brought me. All of these things pushed me closer the edge. I was so far over that I fell into this trance of becoming the villain. I had already committed the cardinal sin. I was clearly in the same boat as his ex. The only difference was he was a she and she was his sister. We hopped out the car and headed to the streetcar station. Neither of us had ridden them since we had been here so we decided to enjoy them today. I was hungry. Oddly enough, I had no real taste for anything in particular. I figured after our tour I would know what I wanted to eat.

"Do you know what you want to eat? I'm clueless on what I want. I'm trying to resist the urge to stop by Mr. B's before we go home. The gumbo is addictive, yet I can't fight the urge."

She nodded her head in agreement. She understood my plight when it came to the crack in a bowl. I had wanted to take my sisters there. I figured once Jayce got settled they would come to visit in the summer if I decided to stay here. Cree had texted that he would be down here more in the summer to really promote the club. I don't know if us hanging out was a good idea. We had talked about what happened when he was here. There were no regrets in his words anymore. I couldn't say there was much on my end either. His tone was laced with intent to seduce me again. A clear indication the pursuit would continue. I hadn't told anyone what happened when he came here. I felt that secret should be kept buried deep inside the walls of my mind.

"Yeah, there's this spot on Iberville Street I heard has the best shrimp po'boys. We can stop there when we finish."

"Ok cool," I said, handing her a ticket.

We walked over to the bench to sit down. The streetcar was due to be here in a few minutes. It was a beautiful day. The trees were full and green. The flower blooms were an array of colors. There was something so beautiful about the south. The richness intertwined in the layers of Mother Nature. Even with all of the dark holes history had dug, there was still something very different here from Los Angeles.

L.A. provided eternal sunshine, where New Orleans was soul food. Together my spirit was engulfed in the harmonic vibes I absorbed.

"So are you going to tell me what happened with Cree or not?" Asha asked.

I snapped out of my daydream. Her question came out of nowhere. I had no intention on telling anybody about Cree's visit. Especially not Asha! She was my friend, but she was Micah's sister first. I kept that in the forefront of my mind at all times, no matter how close we got. Yes, she would keep her secrets. However, I couldn't totally trust she would keep mine.

"What do mean? What makes you think something happened?"

"Well, for one the way he was looking at you when I was there. Ry, that man had so much lust seeping from his skin I almost got a contact high. If nothing happened I would be shocked."

Her words were assumptions. They were simply letters laced with suspicion and curiosity. She had no proof, and with no proof there was no real truth.

I laughed of her accusations.

"Cree and I are just friends Asha."

"Well, I guess I believe you, though I think my brother feels otherwise."

I gave her a confused look. She knew something, and I needed to know what it was. It seemed like there was something she was trying to tell me. There was something she knew, while she attempted to piece this puzzle together.

"Ry, is there something you want to tell me?"

Just as she asked the question, the streetcar pulled up to the station. We got up and made our way on board. We found a seat in the middle and sat down. The streetcar was beautiful. The interior had a vintage feel to it.

"I only ask because my brother showed up at my house pissy drunk. He had been blowing me up all evening. Since I was at your place, my phone was upstairs so I missed his calls. I went upstairs and crashed after leaving your house. The next thing I know he's falling over his own feet at my door at 4 a.m. He went on and on about how you lied to him about Cree. I assumed something happened since he was in such an uproar."

I took a deep breath. It appeared I had to offer some form of clarity. She knew something was going on, yet she didn't have a complete puzzle from what I could hear.

"He showed up at my house around 2:30 a.m. and saw Cree was there. Before he left he told me not to let him stay there, but I dismissed it and let him stay anyway. Naturally, he was angry and we got into it."

"So he caught you guys in the middle of something?"

"No he didn't other than the fact he was at my house at 2:30 a.m. in the morning."

"So have you guys worked it out?"

She had no idea how far off her question was right now. Yes we had worked it out, though I still felt like he wasn't quite passed it. Nothing had been brought up again so I left well enough alone. There was no need to poke the sleeping beast.

"Yes we're cool now."

"Cool, because I like us all getting along. It would be awkward if you guys were at odds. I would feel like I was caught in the middle."

She rubbed her hand over mine. Her hands felt good going back and forth. My legs missed her touch. The sensual way she would caress them as her tongue wreaked havoc on my sweet spot. She slid her hand up my thigh. My romper sat mid-thigh giving her easy access. I knew what she was doing. I had no intentions on being wet this entire ride. I looked around to see there weren't many people on the streetcar. An older couple sat in the front, while a family sat a row or two behind them. She had worn a t-shirt dress. It accentuated her hips perfectly, providing the right amount of coverage to her rounded derriere. I moved her hand onto her own thigh. I looked her directly in the eyes as I moved them up her thigh. I leaned over so I could whisper in her ear.

"Do exactly as I say. No more, no less. Do you understand?"

She smiled and nodded.

I leaned forward, placing a kiss on her lips. Our tongues began to tussle with each other. The sound of the streetcar and driver talking drowned us out as I moved my hands up her dress. I could tell by the material she had on lace panties. The lips of her center were warm as my fingers crept downward. I pulled back from our kiss to give her some instructions.

"Leave your hands here. Don't move them one inch. If you do I will stop."

I moved her panties to the side. Staring in her eyes, I inched my fingers between her lips. She was wet, throbbing against my finger. I slid my finger in and out as my thumb moved against her clitoris. I could feel her breaths against my cheek as she exhaled slowly. I moved close to her lips.

"You like this? Tell me you like this."

"I like this Rylee," she muttered.

"Now I want you to slide down just a little bit. Move very slow, Asha. Be sure to keep your hands in place."

She slid down further as I pushed my finger deeper into her. My thumb caressed her a little harder. A soft moan escaped her lips. She swallowed her urge to touch me. I smiled as I enjoyed the control she wanted so badly. I looked to the front to make sure no one was watching us. I turned back around to her. I placed another kiss on her lips.

"I'm going to move my head down. I want you to spread your legs open and place your hand on my head. Do you understand?"

She nodded. The instructions were arousing her.

Her lips only moved when she needed to let gasps of pleasure escape. I saw the streetcar had passed by Canal Street. I leaned down slowly as I slid her dress up just enough. Her fingers were gripping my hair. I took the tip of my tongue and teased her clitoris. Her free fingers dug into her thigh. She fought the need to break the rules. She wasn't ready for the game to end. I buried my face in her lap as she rubbed her fingers against my scalp. Moan after moan fell from her lips. Her essence trapped between my lips as her nectar covered my tongue. The scent of her invaded my senses. I spread her lips further, giving my tongue the chance to devour more of her. My head moved in a back and forth motion. I slid my finger deeper inside of her.

Her grip became firmer. My tongue moved faster.

She was competing with my finger for the orgasms she was on the urge of releasing.

I made figure 8's as she swelled around my finger. I sat up to feed her the nectar covering my lips.

"Rylee please," she pleaded.

"Do you want me to stop?"

She leaned her head back. I licked her neck and nibbled on her earlobe. I wanted her to free the orgasms or beg me to stop.

195

"Tell me what you want, Asha," I whispered.

The children playing in the front drowned out her raspy moans. Moans tangled in the grip ecstasy had on them. She wanted to be free, yet she was trapped. Pleasure had casted her into purgatory. Each sound imprisoned by the need to cry out. She was hoping not to cause a scene. The antique homes behind her were decorated with beautiful landscaping. I had never realized how beautiful this place was. I was glad to see it like this. A backdrop of historic buildings with tree lined streets. My hand was inside her center as she released silent pleas disguised as erotic moans. Her lips separated and I slid my tongue inside. She tasted so sweet. Her hands were the soft to my hard and complicated life. I moved back down to end this game. To free her of this sweet hell she was nestled in. I spread her legs as far apart as they would go. I separated her lips and entangled my tongue with her center.

My head went up and down, and my finger in and out as my tongue circled round and around.

Each stroke pulled away at her sanity. She gripped my hair with everything she had, while her juices covered my lips. I sucked every ounce of her until the throbbing slowed to a steady tempo. I moved her panties back over and placed a kiss on the top of her center. Her face had a light layer of sweat on top of it. I softly bit her bottom lip as she slid her tongue in my mouth. We kissed each other passionately until we felt the streetcar stop. She smiled at me as she got up to get off. I smiled knowing I had her right back where I needed her to be.

Free from suspicion, and back to keeping our secret.

With no worries about Cree or her brother.

27 | Twenty-Seven

*W*e rode the streetcar back to where parked. By then we were starving so we grabbed our po'boys from *Acme* and headed to continue our afternoon out. I had to give it to Asha because they were delicious. We found ourselves in the *Voodoo Museum* while on our afternoon tour. I'd had to admit I was quite fascinated. I had never really thought there was much beauty to the art form. I was intrigued by the darkness it contained. Asha walked around to read the information scattered throughout. She gave me a sneaky look. I licked my lips to remind her of the havoc recently wreaked upon her.

"So do you believe in any of this?" she asked.

I thought about her question before answering.

"Yes, I believe there are other realms spirits wander in."

"Do you think its devil worshipping?"

"There are certain elements of darkness within it. I wouldn't necessarily say it was devil worshipping. Honestly, I find it quite intriguing and would like to know how it really affects someone," I answered.

She nodded as if to let me know she agreed with me. I didn't know enough about it to call it devil worshipping. I knew it dealt with possession and control over someone's person, which could be interpreted in many ways. We walked through a little longer and then

197

left. The sun had gone down a little. The sunset was slowly scattering itself across the sky. Shades of pink kissed the layers of orange and yellow hues. Bourbon was its typical spirited self. It was full of life and personality as the laughter and music filled the air.

"Let's grab a drink," Asha said.

"Okay."

We walked into one of the bars. There were a few seats opened at the bar. The bartender walked up to us and asked us what we wanted. Before I could respond she ordered two shots of Jose. It was obvious she and her brother had a thing for tequila. I think they liked the fact it was quick and potent. It provided an immediate response to the desired feeling you were searching for. The perfect reveal to whatever secrets you are trying to bury.

Sins that were left ripe for the picking.

The bartender came back with our shots. I sucked on a lemon then took the shot to the head. I don't think the glass touched the bar before I spotted Titus across the room. I quickly dropped my head, hoping he didn't see me. I had no desire to deal with his arrogance today. I signaled for two more shots from the bartender.

"So tell me about what's going on with you and Mario?" I asked, being nosey.

"We're still cool for now. Of course we have the bomb sex. I know he's been seen with Arrington so I fell back to give him some space. I don't do drama, groupies, or chase men. I saw enough of that craziness with my family so I'll pass on it."

I felt relieved she knew about Arrington. I had never got around to telling her because of my own madness. I figured Micah would since they were siblings so I stayed out of it.

"Yeah, I feel you. I hadn't heard you say anything so I figured maybe you guys called it quits."

"No we're still good. Just playing the roles we agreed on."

I understood that very well. The bartender placed our second round of shots in front of us.

"$15.00 ma'am," he said.

"I got it," Titus said, pulling out his wallet.

I rolled my eyes, signaling I was totally not in the mood. I wanted to drink with my friend in peace minus his overkill of flirting.

"It's okay Titus. I'm paying for it," I replied.

"Ry, if the man wants to pay for the drinks let him. Hi my name is Asha and you are?"

"My friends call me Bishop," he said.

She looked at me puzzled. She was trying to figure out why I called him one thing and he introduced himself as another. I wasn't his friend so there was really nothing to figure out. Not on my end anyway.

"Wait a minute, your name is Rylee? I thought you said your name was Reece?" he asked.

"Reece is my middle name. I go by both if you must know. My friends call me Rylee"

The bartender handed him his change, and he dropped the tip on the bar. He walked around to the other side to sit next to Asha. He wanted to taunt me into submission. Using Asha as leverage to fuck me would never work. I had no desire to fuck him so it would be a waste of time. I had enough lovers and I didn't need anymore. I shook my head in disbelief at the extent in which he was willing to go. The realms he was willing to extend his arrogance was remarkable.

"So Asha, how do you two know each other?" he asked another question.

He was digging and I knew it. I hadn't given him any information regarding me. It seemed he thought asking my friend was going to push him closer to his goal.

"We're friends who share a common interest," she answered, winking.

"Is that right?"

"Yes that's right," I snapped.

"Well, I will say this Asha. You are a very beautiful woman. It's such a shame we don't have the pleasure of your presence at *Southern*."

Asha laughed.

He was laying the flirting on thick. I took my shot then sucked on my lemon. It actually tasted better than the bullshit he was serving. I heard my phone ring. I reached in my purse to get it. I pulled it out to see it was a text from Micah. He wanted to hang out and watch movies tonight. He didn't know it, but his text was perfect timing. I'd had a long day and was ready to get rid of Titus.

"So we're heading to a party at *Loyola*. Did you guys want to join us?" Titus asked.

"I'll pass," I said.

"I'll go," Asha said.

"Cool, you can ride with me," Titus said, smiling at me.

He wanted a reaction so bad. Sadly, I wasn't going to give him one. I didn't care enough to do so. The notion he fiend for one was satisfaction enough. I gave Asha the *are you sure* look. She nodded and I got up. I whispered for her to text me when she made it back. I grabbed my purse and headed out. The sunset was fading out. The variations of dark blue smothered the assortment of other colors from earlier. I walked back up Bourbon to get to my car. As I was attempting to cross the street an older lady mumbled something. I turned to see who she was talking to and she stared directly at me. I crunched my forehead to reflect my confusion.

"Excuse me," I said. She pointed to a chair as if to signal me to sit down. I walked over to her, curious as to what she was going to say. "Were you talking to me?" I asked.

She pointed to a chair again.

"What is your name, chile?"

"My name is Rylee."

I sat down as she reached out for my hand. It was then I realized she read palms. I had never had my palm read before. People did it back home all the time. I had never indulged in the curiosity surrounding it. I wasn't sure if I even believed in the meanings interpreted behind them. She held my hands in the palms of hers. She traced the inside of my palm with her finger. Her face held a look of discernment. I could only imagine the stories my palms told. The tales of love, lust, and ecstasy captured between them. Fingerprints that hid scandals, secrets, and sins left behind. I was nervous by her silence. Some parts of me were tormented by the steadiness of her breathing. I searched her face for some kind of movement. She held my hand tighter as she looked up.

"Your pain is your strength. Your resistance to love is driven by your fear of losing yourself in it again. You are a lover of many Rylee though you love only one. Your loyalty to freedom causes you to shun love. Your past has forced you to believe you can only have one or the other, but never both. Your desire for pleasure is going to be the trap that ends it all. A new year is shortly upon you. For you, it will be full of exposure. Your worlds will soon collide. Be wary of the reflection you will soon encounter."

I stared at her as she released my hands.

I stood up to turn around and head for my car. I quickly walked to next block and found my car. I opened the door and climbed inside. So many thoughts ran through my mind. There were so many unanswered questions that she left me with. Her words nestled themselves in my spirit. There was an unsettling feeling about them. Each syllable, and each word uttered from her lips wrapped around me in an eerie way. Everything she said made some kind of sense.

Everything, but her last words, *Your worlds will soon collide. Be wary of the reflection you will soon encounter.*
What worlds? Whose reflection?

28 | Twenty-Eight

"ow could you do this Rylee? I fucking loved you," Micah said.

He slammed me against the wall. The notes I had hidden were on the floor in front of me. The impact from being slammed penetrated the back of my head. My throat was contracting in the palm of his hands. My heart raced at a rapid pace. I was holding on to the air I so desperately wanted to exhale. The grip of his hand reflected hurt and betrayal. His eyes a dark gray as the anger seeped from his lips. His love was apparent, though it seemed to be gift wrapped in venom. I looked over to see Cree standing next to me. My name ever so visible on his chest stared back at me. The reflection caught me as I reached for him.

He moved closer to me. His hands gripped the heart hanging from my neck.

"I thought you loved me Ry. I thought we were forever," Cree said.

She was my savior. She knew the secret I was keeping. I reached for her to save me from his grip "Tell him about us Rylee. Tell him about all the times I stroked you to the edge of pleasure. Tell them how we rode each other's tongue until we came everywhere," Asha pleaded as the tear ran down her face.

The reflection from the ring caught my eye. His stance was as if I had never ran out on him.

"Rylee, will you marry me? You are the only woman for me. I want you to be my wife," Trent said.

They were all here. Each of them exposing the secrets I had hidden. They were exposing all the sins I had committed in the name of pleasure. They were pleading for me to carry their burdens. Hoping their love is the love I confess too. All of my lovers were reaching for my heart, while I cradled theirs in my hands. All of them, stood in front of me searching for love somewhere between the lies told.

"How could you? Tell him, no tell her, please marry me? Rylee, Rylee, Rylee!" they all shouted.

I jumped up from the startling dream.

Sweat covered my body. The echo of the ceiling fan drowned out the voices in my head as the cold air dried the moisture my body was consumed in. Two days later, her words were still etched in the back of my mind. I looked over at Micah. He was sleeping peacefully. I watched him, unclear if he was to soon be affected by the brewing earthquake. The pendant was stuck to my wet body. My breathing was somewhat stagnant. I climbed out of bed and headed to the bathroom. I closed the door. I stood in the middle of the floor, pulling the t-shirt over my head. I stepped in the shower and turned the water on. I stood under the shower so the water could run over my face. I leaned back slowly against the wall. The lukewarm drops ran down my body as my thoughts raced through my mind. I buried my head in my hands. All of my past and present sins were pulling me in opposite directions. Each of them stood, begging me to choose them. My worlds surrounded me in one place.

I searched myself for the love the old woman spoke of. It was clear to me I clung hard to freedom. The ability to move around without rules and without restraints had become my drug. I loved Micah, but I loved being single too. My feelings for Cree were clouded, while the thought of Trent created a sick feeling in the pit of my stomach. Asha was a temporary factor soon to end when the demands of our sweet spots grew tired. They were phases simply passing through time.

Another ten minutes went by before I grew chilly.

I stood up straight to turn off the water.

I stepped out in front of the mirror. I was naked as I could be with no cover to shield me from the truth. I wrapped the towel around me and opened the door. I walked out of the bathroom to see he hadn't moved. His breathing sounded serene. He was truly a gorgeous man. I was indeed a lucky woman. For whatever reason, it didn't seem to be enough. A void buried itself beneath my surface. The natural part of me constantly fighting with the new persona I had taken on. I walked across the room making my way to the window. The sky was a blanket of black. The stars lit up spaces within the darkness. There was so much open space to move around in. I stared at the sky as my reflection caught my eye. I saw the girl I was and yearned to be. Twenty-seven was on the horizon. A new year that would bring me new adventures, orgasms, and memories to last forever.

Love would unfortunately have to wait.

29 | Twenty-Nine

arch 5th had finally come as 27 wrapped its arms around me and I embraced it. I was ready for dinner with my man. It was my birthday, and he was treating me to dinner somewhere nice. I was going to throw on a little black dress and some spiked black heels. My inner rebel was in full bloom tonight. Micah and I had somehow come full circle again. We were in a happy place. Asha was still bringing me pleasure, while my past had managed to disappear. I managed to even be nice to Trent when he called to wish me happy birthday earlier. The conversation was decent until he went off into his, *You'll come back to me,* rant. He rambled on about something I couldn't make out. His words held no weight anymore. I did all I could to hold off the laughter. I was done with the conversation when he said he had a birthday gift for me. I didn't need any more gifts from him. One unwarranted proposal per lifetime was enough for me. I told him thanks, but no thanks and said goodbye.

My parents, sisters, and everyone else called me as well. Cree had two dozen peonies delivered with a sweet note. All in all my day had been good. Hopefully, my night would be even better. I wanted to end my night skin-to-skin, releasing orgasms with my man. I stood in the mirror with my lace unmentionables on. I rubbed my hand over the outline of my hip. My tattoo had healed perfectly. It was a gift to myself that I snuck off to get yesterday. I traced the outline of the letters and smiled. There could be no better description of my life than the ink on my hip.

I lived it, I breathed it, and somehow I could not escape it.

I stared at myself until my phone interrupted my thoughts. I grabbed it to see it was Kira. We hadn't talked since after Cree left. She had tried to grill me about him being here. All of them seemed suspicious with what occurred, but still I wasn't giving up the goods. I was keeping our dirty little secret a secret. The less people knew the better. If I started telling people I would have to keep up with the pieces I told. I swiped the answer key.

"Well, it took you long enough chic," I said.

She laughed off my comment.

"Girl, you know I work crazy man hours. Not to mention, I live with a grown child who needs attention too."

By day, she was an intern at a prestigious law firm. By night, she was a law student at UCLA. Kira was working her way up the ladder, and I was beyond proud of her. Her life was demanding, yet she juggled it well.

"Yeah, yeah," I said in a sarcastic tone.

"Whatever! Happy birthday old lady," she teased.

"Old? Ma'am, we're only three months apart or have you forgot that little detail?"

We laughed. The Pisces and the Sagittarius, we were quite the dangerous duo. I'd have to say our personalities often brought out some excitement. We were two outspoken people who didn't have a care in the world. Who at any given moment would rock yours if need be, good or bad.

"No, I remember when I was born, hussy. It still doesn't take away the fact that you're old too."

"I'll remember that when November rolls back around," I said, laughing.

"So what are you getting into this evening? Your lovers taking you out on the town or are you playing indoors tonight?"

We both laughed at the irony of what she asked. I had told her the scoop on who was who when it came to Asha and Micah. I could tell her mouth dropped to the floor when I said I wasn't cutting either one of them off. I had planned to end things with Asha, but she didn't want to. She had her thing with Mario, yet still she wanted us to continue. I was apprehensive at first, though I really didn't want it to stop either. The way she manipulated my orgasms, pulling pleasure from parts of my soul I didn't know existed. *Who could honestly walk away from all of it?* Not me and I couldn't even lie and say I would. I was in a place where life could not get any better. My body still tingled every time Cree texted. The memories of that night flooded parts of me I knew I needed to control. He had offered to fly me home for the weekend several times and I declined. I knew accepting his invitation would lead to me coming in more ways than I could count. Every time I walked passed my counter I shivered. The erotic massacre he reined upon my sweet spot would be unforgettable. Time had definitely improved his skill as well as his stroke.

"For your information, I will be having dinner with my man tonight. Thank you very much."

"Oh, so your misses is okay with not seeing you tonight? Wow, I should definitely consider having girlfriend on the side," she teased.

She knew Asha wasn't my girlfriend. Maybe my lover, but she definitely wasn't my girlfriend.

"Well, not to cramp your birthday, but you know I couldn't let the Zoe thing go. I found out about Trent and the mysterious baby situation."

I had forgotten all about him, her, and that baby. I managed to push it to the back of my mind. Thinking about it would only bring up memories of a life long forgotten. I wasn't sure I wanted to hear it, not today anyway. I knew her telling me was her way of protecting me. Safeguarding my feelings from what was soon to come. The future could be a bitch. Betrayal had a way of making sure she was a cold one. Kira wanted to be the warmth I needed. The guard I had let down years ago. I couldn't tell if she was worried about me falling back into him or she just felt I needed to know. Either way, the band aid had to be ripped off.

"Do I want to know?"

"Yeah you do," she said.

I listened to her tell me how after she had run into Zoe, she received a phone call from her a week or so later. Zoe told her seeing her reminded her how much she'd missed her. How much she missed it being us. She went on to say how even though she knew I could never forgive her, she missed me too. Once they obviously got passed the formalities, she told Kira her daughter was Trent's and he didn't know. The guy she is engaged to believes the child is his and she had been carrying the secret around forever. Kira told me she wanted to mend the broken fences between them, however felt she needed to come clean first.

I listened as the words went in one ear and out of the other. From the moment she brought it up, part of me knew it was his. The other part of me didn't want to believe the betrayal could reach so far.

Sleeping with my man was one form of betrayal. Having his child was an entire different form. Kira could make things right with her all she wanted. There would never be a day in my life that I would. I wasn't even the type of person to hold grudges, but she'd done the unforgiveable. Hell could freeze over, reheat, and freeze again before the words, *I forgive you,* would come out of my mouth to her treacherous ass.

"Well, looks like I dodged two bullets then, huh?"

"What do you mean?" she asked.

I wasn't in the mood to get into my miscarriage story. I would save it for another day, and another time. Today I was going to enjoy dinner, wine, and multiple orgasms with my man. I would deal with Trent later. The next time he called, he would know not to call ever a-fucking-gain. My phone had beeped and I could see it was a text from Micah. He was on his way so I needed to finish up. I would have to deal with this nut later.

"Okay hooker, he's on his way so I need to finish getting dressed. I'll call you tomorrow."

"Ry, you cool? I didn't want to ruin your birthday."

"Kira, you didn't and I'm fine. I promise."

"Okay cool. Oh, I almost forgot I'm going to meet you in D.C. for spring break. Jayce asked me to come so we can tear up a new town for your birthday and her new gig."

I perked up quick. I was ecstatic now and definitely looking forward to spring break. It would be the four of us all together again.

A new town, new memories, and more trouble to get into.

We said our goodbyes. I promised to call before D.C. so we could finalize everything. I threw my phone down and headed to the bathroom. I had straightened my hair and it was hanging long. I'd added some honey blond to it a week ago. It mixed perfectly with my chocolate roots. I added a little eyeliner, mascara, and some lip gloss. I slipped on my diamond studs to wear with my pendant. *Keep my heart close to yours,* his note said. I looked at the necklace and smiled. I gave my hair one last once over and headed to put on my dress.

As soon as I walked out of the bathroom, I heard a knock at the door. *Shit,* I thought. I was trying to be ready before he had gotten here. I ran to the door to open it up and let him in. I looked through the peephole only to see more flowers. He had remembered I loved peonies too. I dashed to the bouquets Cree sent. I snatched the note out and threw it in the drawer with the rest of the notes. I didn't need any drama today. Then I opened the door for him to come in.

"Hey baby, come in real quick. I needed to throw on my dress."

He walked in and placed the vase in my hands.

"Happy birthday, baby," he said, leaning over to give me a kiss.

I blushed as he closed the door. I placed the bouquet on the table by the door since the other ones were on my dining table. He gave me a once over and I made a slight grin. I gave him a *don't try it* look. I was looking forward to dinner and catching up. We had been hit or miss since they had made it to the tournament round. March Madness was due to begin and would become more intense if they kept winning. I had promised I would make the home games. I wanted to support and cheer him on. He had said some of his family was going to come down for a few home games as well. Guess I would get to meet some of the *wild bunch* as he called them.

"Two seconds baby and I'll be ready."

I dashed to my room, and threw on my dress and shoes. Within a matter of minutes, we were out the door. I wanted to ask where we were heading because I was hungry and definitely wanted something good. I leaned my head back against the headrest and got lost in the night. My mind drifted off to what Kira had just told me. It was typical Zoe, though. It appeared as if she somehow perfected her gift of secret keeping. I couldn't believe it. Trent was a father. He was a father and he didn't know it. I guess one betrayal for another. He screwed me and now he was being screwed. There was a part of me that wanted to tell him, but then again I had no intentions of getting in the middle of their drama. For my own pleasures, I would pay mad money to see the look on his face when he found out he had a daughter. I couldn't do anything but shake my head. After all the hell he had put me through, one of his children still managed to get here. Whether he knew it or not, the sight of him would sicken me forever. Forgiveness was short lived. It became shorter when the memories still haunted you. My past was my present. The ghosts seemed to keep resurfacing. I was so caught up in the madness going on I hadn't realized we arrived at our destination.

"Baby, we're here," he said.

I looked out the window and my stomach dropped. My entire body froze to the point I could have sworn my entire soul climbed out of my lap. I tried breathing. This was no coincidence even though I knew it was. I turned and looked at him.

"What are we doing here?"

He looked at me, and gave me a confused look.

"What do you mean? We're having dinner here. My coach is one of the owners, and I asked if he could give me a good spot to take you to.

He suggested here, and since they aren't open to the public yet, we've got the place to ourselves," he said, climbing out the car.

I swallowed hard. I knew any sudden reactions would cause him to become suspicious. This night couldn't get any crazier. I sat in the car as he came around to open my door. My world was getting smaller. My secrets were slowly surfacing. He intertwined his fingers in mine and we walked inside. The sign was beautiful as it read: *The Orchid Lounge*. We walked in and the man who I presumed was his coach walked towards us.

"Hey Micah, glad you could make it. This must be the beautiful young lady you were telling me about. Happy birthday, Miss," he said, holding out his hand.

I placed my hand in his as he kissed it.

"Yes, this is Rylee and thank you again coach," Micah said.

"Thank you," I also stated.

"Well, we have the patio set up for you whenever you're ready," he said, holding out his hand.

We followed him out to the patio. The inside renovations were complete. He opened the patio door to a table fully decorated just for us. It didn't seem like it was almost a month ago I stood out here with Cree. Everything was a beautiful as I remembered it. The strings of lights were lit up, while the night air was clear and crisp. I could see they added cushions to the benches. The entire table looked lush. I walked over to the table and sat down.

"Thanks Coach. Is your partner here? I want to tell him thanks as well," Micah said.

The hairs on every ounce of my skin stood up. Cree hadn't said he was back in town, though that didn't mean he wasn't. After the last time, I assumed if he came back for business stuff I probably wouldn't know about it. I looked at his coach hoping he would relieve the pressure building up in my chest.

"No, he's not here. I'll be sure to let him know you said thanks. Enjoy your evening and let the waitress know when you're ready for your food."

We nodded and he walked back inside. I took a deep breath. This night would have been over before it even started if Cree would have walked out of here. The waitress came outside to take our drink and food orders. I ordered the brown sugar chicken & waffles with bourbon syrup. I was hungry and excited to be here. It was a beautiful space. Part of me felt sneaky for enjoying the atmosphere, knowing who it belonged to. The last time I was here I didn't get a chance to view the back fountain area. I got up and followed the stone walkway to the fountain. Plush trees and bushes lined the walkway giving it a rainforest feel. The fountain was secluded and lit up as well. A couple of benches were against the wall. I leaned over and ran my fingers through the water. The reflection of the light beneath the water lit up brightly. I stood up to turn around and bumped into Micah.

"Whoa, you startled me."

"Oh did I? Well, who did you think it would be?" he asked.

He always asked such loaded questions.

"Nobody, you just scared me. What's up? Is our food ready yet?"

"No, it's not. I told her she didn't have to rush anything. We were enjoying the evening so we were cool."

He was up to something. I could see it in the sultry look he held within his eyes. He pulled me closer to him. He placed a soft, intimate kiss on my lips. I looked at him and smiled.

"What was that for?"

"I love you, Rylee. I mean, I really love you. From the first day I met you, something about you caught my eye. I know we started out just having sex, but somewhere along the way I really fell for you. I haven't felt this way about anyone in a long time."

He pulled my lips to him and kissed me again. I sat him down on the fountain so I could straddle him.

I leaned to his ear, and said, "I want you right here, right now."

I sat up enough to unzip his pants, sliding a portion of him out.

"Rylee, she's going to catch us."

I didn't care. I was so overwhelmed with emotions, I needed a release. My blood was pumping and I just wanted to feel him inside me. He realized I wasn't going to stop so he moved my panties to the side and I slid down onto him. I covered his mouth with mine. His breath was warm and his hands added some extra heat to my body. I moved back and forth on him as the water splashed behind him. I needed a different memory here. A memory other than the one I had of Cree and me standing out here. This entire place reminded me of him. Tonight, I wanted to forget about him. I needed to forget about him. He was becoming too prevalent within the confines of my mind. The dangerous side of me wanted him to walk outside tonight. The side of me I fought to cage and control. I was indeed a wild spirit who was on the verge of breaking free. Free from this grip I had on her. Images of Asha, Cree, Trent, and Micah flashed before my eyes. I rode him harder and faster, hoping all of them would disappear.

Wicked smiles and sultry eyes constantly raced through my mind. Eight hands and four tongues took over my body. I was here, 27 and free, somehow held hostage by all of these degrees of pleasure. Love, lust, obsession, revenge, and pieces of anger consumed me. They were all momentary highs looking to be exhaled. I cuffed the back of his head so I could release the chaotic pleas my body needed to free.

"I love you too, Micah," I cried out.

It was a new year. I was going to give my body what it wanted, and then starting over.

30 | Thirty

e stood up, fixed ourselves, and headed back to the table. Our food had arrived after about ten minutes of sitting down. We chatted the entire dinner. He was excited about the tournament and his family coming. I told him I was going to D.C. for spring break. He wasn't sure if he was going back since he had games. He told me his plans for the summer, while I mentioned I was still figuring mine out. He asked me to stay with him for the summer back home. I told him I would think about it and let him know. I had already considered staying with Jayce for the summer so I needed to weigh my options. We talked about everything under the sun for another two hours before his coach told him they were closing up. He paid the bill and thanked him again.

I was ready to get round two going before we called it a night. We made our way to the car. I loved how the city was so lit up at night. The lights and different colors all illuminated the streets. We held hands on the way home. I caught my reflection in the side view mirror. I felt beautiful, seductive, and powerful. My inner vixen had truly evolved. I was living in the moment. I was living my life by my rules and on my own terms.

Micah's hand in my hand, Cree's heart around my neck, and their kisses buried deep within my sweet spot.

Micah rubbed my hand.

He meant well. He loved me. I was a person who was torn between two worlds. I had become a woman who turned her back on

213

monogamy a long time ago. With him I believed I could be that girl again. I could be the girl who believed in love, happy endings, and forever. Then there was the other side I knew craved freedom and playing with fire. If only my two sides could live harmoniously inside me. I knew that was a dream, a reality never to come true. We pulled into my parking garage. He put the car in park then turned to look at me. He leaned over and kissed me.

"Happy birthday, baby. Let's go finish your night."

We got out the car and headed towards the elevator. As we walked in my neighbor was coming down.

"Hey Rylee, someone was banging on your door earlier. I just wanted to give you a heads up in case you get a noise complaint."

She walked off, and he hit the button to my floor. I had no idea what she was talking about. I looked over at Micah. I just figured someone had the wrong door. The elevator stopped and we walked off. I swallowed hard when I saw him slumped over, completely drunk in front of my door. He looked up to see us standing in the hallway.

"Rylee, Rylee, I love you! I love you so much. Where have you been? I've been sitting here waiting for you."

Micah looked at me and I stood still. I was frozen in time. If I could have moved my feet I would have. Here it was, clear as day. One of my *dirty little secrets* as real as can be.

"What the fuck Ry! Who is this and don't lie to me!" Micah yelled.

I felt like a deaf, paralyzed mute. My voice was gone. All movement had ceased in the lower half of my body. I looked at him, and then back at Trent's drunken ass. If I had a gun he would be shot dead right now. He stood up and moved towards me. I stepped back. Micah moved in front of me as if he was protecting me from the madness.

"Dude, who in the fuck are you? Why are you here?" Micah asked.

Trent stood up, trying to gather himself. He looked at me as he reached into his pocket.

"Excuse me man, but I don't know who you are. It doesn't matter because I'm here for Rylee. I asked her a question over the holidays and she didn't answer. I'm here on her birthday to ask again. We're meant to be together. I realized it after I left from visiting her last year. I just came to claim what I feel should be mine. So who the hell are you?"

My world was crashing before my eyes. My breathing had come to a halt. Everything was happening right in front of me, and yet it seemed so unreal.

"I'm her man. That's who the fuck I am. What question over the holidays?" I was fading away by the minute. Micah had turned to look at me. "Rylee, you better start talking. What the hell is he talking about?"

I swallowed hard. As I opened my mouth to answer, Trent beat me to the punch.

"I asked her to marry me and gave her this. She ran out without answering. I figured she needed more time to think. I figured all of the flowers would have softened her up, seeing she loves peonies and all."

He was such an asshole. Not to mention, a goddamn snitch. He managed to keep the fact he knew about Cree a secret, but this he couldn't shut up about. *Who in their right mind wouldn't equate running out to a damn no?* Micah turned around and saw the four point five carat ring I ran out on three months ago. My past had reappeared with a vengeance. The ghosts would not leave me be. I realized this had to literally be the worst birthday ever.

Micah looked at me as he was moving closer to me, and repeated himself saying, "You better start talking right goddamn now."

I was caught. *I could lie, but why bother?* I had nothing to lose when it came to Trent.

I stood in the middle of the hall, and told him what I had been avoiding for months. I told him about the proposal and how I hopped on the first plane back after it happened. Since Trent felt the need to mention the flowers, I skated pass that portion. Micah moved closer to me. His eyes were glaring, holding his anger captive. He walked passed me and left down the stairs. I knew he was pissed beyond words. I turned around to look at Trent. All of the rage I had pinned up had now spilled over. I moved closer to him so he and only could hear me.

"Get the fuck away from me. I will never marry you. If you ever come within ten feet of me again, I will personally make sure you stop breathing. Good fucking bye, Trent."

I pushed passed him, opened my door, and slammed it closed. I dropped everything on the floor, including myself. Happy goddamn birthday to me.

31 | Thirty-One

he only place it is safe for you to be is within the walls of my mind. The layers of my heart cannot contain you. The inner dwelling of my sweet spot is too dangerous. My body is at war with so many emotions. I am afraid you have become a casualty. The promises my lips held for you will be broken in the name of lust. Passion will hold me hostage until I give into its demands. Sex has somehow made me its slave. Love has tried to save me, and still the orgasms won't allow me to be free. I give into them knowing they are a part of who I am and who I will always be.

"Ohh," I muttered.

My body was on fire as his tongue engrained O's inside the walls of my sweet spot. Imprints that would prove he was here. My leg rested on his shoulder as I gripped the rope, moaning in utter pleasure. I was fully submerged in the wetness of his tongue, dampening my inner thighs. He slid his finger inside, wanting to feel me contract against his touch. He massaged my clitoris, teasing me into submission. I wanted to feel him deep inside me. Deep inside the places I kept hidden. I wanted him to touch my soul. Pulling ecstasy through my entire body.

He pushed himself inside of me forceful so he could make a point to announce his presence. My sweet spot contracted to his engorged member as he moved in and out. The headboard hit the wall loudly as he pounded inside of me. His eyes harbored anger. His lips had been dipped in betrayal as he sucked and licked all over me. I wanted to cry out, but no one would hear me. I wanted to beg for his forgiveness, but somehow he had no more to give. My body belonged to him and the unadulterated pleasure he was punishing me with. I fought to hold onto my orgasm. It was the only control I had left.

After each stroke I crept closer to the edge. Minute by minute, my resolve diminished. I wrapped my legs around him bridging the obvious gap between us. My orgasm lingered and I was on the verge cumming. I arched my back and in a matter of seconds my phone rang waking me up. I jerked as if the sound had scared the hell out of me. I moved to see who it was when I realized the inside of my thighs were wet. I grabbed my phone to see it was Asha. She was texting me to say some of her family had arrived. She wanted to know if I was coming to the game with her. Secretly, I had hoped it was Micah calling.

A week and a half had passed by. We still hadn't talked. Not a text, not a phone call, or even a glimpse of him near Asha's. The silence was killing me. I needed to see him. I had called him several times. A couple of times he answered only to hang up. Other times he sent me straight to voicemail. My texts went unanswered. My apologies went unnoticed. We didn't have classes together this semester so I couldn't see him there. I wanted to ask Asha about him. I toggled with putting her in the middle. Seeing she and I were still enjoying each other's company, her spying for me wasn't smart. I had told her Trent showed up and what went down with that situation. Her entire face reflected disbelief. I was completely outdone at the fact he tried it again. Whatever stress I had felt, Asha stroked it away with her tongue. I told her I would catch her at the party afterwards. The possibility of him ignoring or isolating me was infallible. I couldn't chance him making a scene in front of his family. We would sort this out another time. His game was definitely not the place.

I buried my head in my pillow.

I was angry with no real outlet. No real way of expressing what was going through my mind. I had fucked up. No better yet, Trent had fucked up! The moment I opened the door, a door I unlocked, my entire world changed. I was trying to process all these raw emotions. One moment I was enjoying my birthday, on my way home to start round two, the next moment I was trying not to commit a homicide. It was as if he was trying to sabotage my life. Force me to be with him no matter how I felt. I had literally stood there trying to process everything I heard going on. I wanted to reach out so I could grab Micah. I just couldn't move. It was surreal. My mind couldn't process what he was saying fast enough. Numbness took over me. A cruel joke was being played out, and I was the punchline.

It was hard to explain the energy in the hallway.

There was silence, tension, and chaos on the verge of escaping behind the many secrets exposed.

I had no clear view into the future. The control I held in the palm of my hand had slipped from my grasp. I could hear pieces of his heart crack as he stormed off. I wanted to run after him and plead my case. I had no real explanation other than what I already confessed to him. In the end, it wasn't the truth being exposed that mattered. It was the fact I wasn't the one to expose it. I reached in my drawer to pull one out. The lighter gave life to the sanity I was in desperate need of. I inhaled again and again as the smoke filled my lungs. Giving into Trent was a foolish move. A move I should have sidestepped. I opened the tiger's cage and the bastard bit me. Silly of me to think I could pacify a wounded soul. He had been more trouble in these last few months than in our entire relationship. I thought back to what Kira had told me on my birthday. I wished I had blurted it out right then. Destroyed what was left of his pathetic ego! Had it not been for putting Kira in an awkward spot, I would have. I gave no shits about Zoe's feelings or keeping her secret. My only concern was Kira. I didn't live in L.A. so I felt somewhat obligated to keep drama away from someone else's doorstep. I knew Zoe would never jump off at her, though people seemed unpredictable these days. The dilemmas I faced forced me to rationalize my present state. There was no one I wanted to talk to about this. No one who could help sort this madness out.

I inhaled again.

The old woman's words wrestled within my spirit. She had predicted the tragedy at my door before it even happened. *How did I not see it?* My worlds had somehow collided. In one single moment, I was caught between heaven and hell. Trent laid waiting in the background for another chance to pounce. Like a predator on the hunt for his prey, he lingered. He waited long enough for me to think he had faded off. Long enough for me to think he no longer cared. The flowers were a way to slowly torture me. The point of them was to drive me to the brink of crazy. He wanted a reaction. He wanted validation. A man in dire need of both was indeed a dangerous man or just reckless. I opened my lips allowing another cloud of smoke to escape. With each contraction, I left room for the narcotic to penetrate my core. Momentary relief came over me as the high settled itself within my thoughts.

218

I exhaled my sour feelings. Every one of them faded with the smoke hovering over my head.

I was glad to be heading to D.C. next week. I was looking forward to hanging out with my sisters. We were going to paint the town, drink a plethora of wine, and catch up. I was unsure if Micah would be returning home for the break. I would love for him to return so we could talk, but the option was not within my control. For now, I had forfeited any control or opinion I may have been privy too. I was standing on the outside waiting for him to open the door. Our reconciliation would be on his terms. I thought about where this would leave us. What state we would need to recover from. I was torn between whether I would be hurt if he ended things and if I would fight for this. Part of me cared deeply for him. Small fractions of me would even say I loved him. Neither of those feelings provoked the urge to fight. I was a wanderer by nature. I had accepted that fact. Problems only arose when I suppressed the notion to conform to something else. Someone I knew after a while would return to her true self. Cree saw this in me, yet he still desired me. I often wondered if he was okay with it because he was able to have a piece of me. I knew all would change if I were to ever become his. I was only extremely desirable to the man that couldn't have me all to himself.

The clock read 2 o'clock. I had slept most of the morning away. I wanted to wake up and last night have been a horrible dream. I needed Trent at my door to be a figment of my ever twisted imagination. However, it wasn't a dream. It was a real life nightmare, my real life nightmare. I understood change was inevitable. It was a part of life. For this reason alone I couldn't understand why Trent couldn't let it go. I knew I hadn't wounded his ego to the point he had to have the final say. If he thought about it long enough, he did have the final say. He ended whatever future we had when I walked in on him and Zoe. Ever since that day, I silently thank God for delivering me from him. I laughed at the irony of him being Zoe's problem now. I thought about her daughter. How I actually felt sorry for her. I was close to my father. We had a bond no one could sever. Now, because of her selfishness, her daughter would never have the opportunity to have that with Trent. Yes, he was a jackass, in addition to being a horrible boyfriend. Although, if given the chance I believed he may be a good father.

I reached in my nightstand to pull out the only photo album I packed. I flipped through each of the memories. All of us, the five of us with smiles as big as the city we lived in. My sisters, Kira, Zoe, and I were embracing each other. Our faces reflected innocence, unknowing of the corruption they would soon be tainted with. A tear formed in my eye when I flipped to a picture of me, Zoe, and Kira. It was our junior year in high school. My sisters had already graduated so it was just us. The three amigos everyone knew were thick as thieves. A bond I never imagined would break. A bond I never knew would suffer unimaginable amounts of betrayal. Each memory caused a smile to form across my lips as the tear I held hostage with my eyelid fell.

I loved her and she loved me, but somehow it wasn't enough.

Ever since the day it occurred I played so many things through my mind. *Why me? Why not Kira? Why not Jayce or Tae? Better yet, why not a complete stranger?* I would never wish that betrayal on anyone, though it never sat right with me as to why she fucked my man. Now here she was with a baby and another secret. The irony of it all was they lived in the same city and he had no clue. He was so busy trying to start a family with me that he didn't realize he already had one. Another tear fell as I flipped the page landing on a picture of us with Cree and his friends. Antonio was holding Taylor. I was snuggled with Cree, while Zoe and Kira were on the side being goofy. All of us were sitting in the park on top of cars with not a care in the world. I remembered this day so vividly. We literally hung out in the park all day. We were eight people hanging out then it unexpectedly turned into a full-blown party. Three cars grew to twenty and we allowed the night to carry us away. Snacks turned to dinner and dinner turned to breakfast. I literally saw the sun go down then come up again. My favorite part of the night was when Cree and I abandoned the group. We headed up the mountain to watch the sunrise. I remembered falling asleep shortly afterwards, though that moment was everything.

It was peaceful and it was pure.

For those brief moments, our business paused. His life demands waited, and my madness became obsolete. Time stood still as we enjoyed the things we so often take for granted. I flipped through a few more beach, bonfire, and carnival pictures before placing it back in my drawer. Life had a way of being so cruel. The unwavering way it could tarnish something so innocent. At that point, trust became a matter of why versus who then monogamy soon followed.

I climbed out of bed. I hadn't cleaned my house real good since Cree left. I figured since I was skipping the game, I could at least do that much. This way, I wouldn't have to worry about doing much before I left for D.C. I gathered all of my clothes, threw them in the basket, and headed for the laundry room. This would be the only reason I would consider moving out of this building. It was bad enough I hated doing laundry, but to leave my house to actually do it made things worse. I threw my towels and rugs in a different basket. Since it was a Saturday afternoon I concluded most people would be out of the building, therefore leaving me with enough washing machines to wash everything at once. I pulled my basket of clothes to the door, grabbed my keys, and made my way to the laundry room. I wished I would get a glimpse of Micah, though he was probably at the stadium. I would have to settle with seeing him at the party. I opened the door to the laundry room. I glanced around to see it was empty. I pulled my basket to the machines. I loaded up two of them then made my way back to get other basket. I probably needed four to get everything done. I cracked my door open, pulled the towels out, and made my way back to the laundry room. On my way I heard what sounded like a familiar voice.

"Hurry up, Asha. We're going to be late."

I leaned over the balcony to see what looked like my man walking down the outside sidewalk. I wanted to yell out, though I knew he would just ignore me. He wasn't dressed in his game clothes, which explained why he was rushing her. I headed to the laundry room to throw the rest of my loads in the washing machine. I looked around the room and remembered it being where I embarked on this path. This path of countless orgasms, untapped portions of my soul disguised as unparalleled amounts of pleasure. I grabbed my basket and made my way back to my place. I left the baskets by the door. I walked over to my entertainment system so I could turn on my iPod and speakers. I had a few hours to clean, eat, and then get ready for tonight. I filled my bucket up with water, placing the mop inside. Jhene Aiko's voice harmoniously echoed throughout my speakers.

I lit some candles and started cleaning.

Without uttering a word, I had made the decision that I was not leaving town with this gap between us. Whether he realized it or not, we were making up tonight. It was happening no matter what it required and with no questions asked.

32 | Thirty-Two

I rolled over to the sound of Beyoncé's voice singing Superpower as my phone rang. I realized I left it on my dresser at the point I reached on my nightstand to stop the ringing. I opened my eyes to see it was already dark. The red numbers flashed 9:15 p.m. across the screen. I'd slept longer than I anticipated. I was sure the missed call was Asha trying to figure out where I was. After I had cleaned my house, folded my laundry, and fixed some food I was tired. I had laid down at 5 o'clock only with the plan to sleep no more than an hour or two. I still needed to do something with my hair. I already knew what I was wearing so that issue was out of the way. I figured a plaid shirt dress layered with a leather jacket was enough to pass for cute. I had some black military boots I could slide on and top it off with a snap back.

Simple, chic, and comfortable is all I cared to be tonight.

I had no plans on staying all night. I was going to party with Asha, meet a few of her family members that she was bringing, and then on to make up with my man. I missed him. I understood he was angry, and he needed time to sort through said anger, however it was going on two weeks now. We hadn't argued, screamed, or even talked about what happened. I stared at the ceiling hoping he would at least hear me out. I wasn't sure where we stood. I had no clue if we were still together or not. I climbed out of bed. My phone light was blinking, which meant there were messages. I grabbed my phone to see that I had five missed calls and a couple missed text messages. Two of the calls were from Asha, one was from Jayce, and the other two from a number I didn't recognize. I checked the text messages before calling the number I didn't know back. Asha had texted to see what time I was going to the party. She wanted to ride with me. I already knew what that meant. She had some good Kush and wanted to share. The second text was her again saying she would just me meet there.

I guess my lack of response caused her to change her plans. I sent her an *ok* back. I scrolled my phone log for the number I didn't recognize. I tapped the number and it started ringing. I had no clue who could've called. I didn't remember giving my number to anyone recently. The phone rang a few times before someone picked up.

"Hello," he said.

"Hi, someone called me from this number. I was trying to see who it was calling."

"Well, hello sexy," he responded.

I couldn't make out the voice. For a brief moment, an angry feeling came over me. I thought it was Trent calling from a different number, hoping to catch me off guard. In that case, he picked the perfect time because I was ready to give him the tongue lashing of his life. I was in no mood for his antics. I stood behind my threat I made that night. I had no desire to ever hear from his ass again.

"Look, I'm in no mood to play games. Either you tell me who this is or I'm hanging up," I snapped.

"Still feisty as ever," he said.

At that very moment I knew who it was. *How did he get my number?* I never remembered giving him my number. *I knew no one who could have given it to him, so how?* I rolled my eyes thinking this was the moment I was trying to avoid with him. I knew him having my number only meant he would go full speed in pursuing me.

I would have to ignore him that much harder.

"How did you get my number, Titus?"

"I have my ways," he answered.

I sighed. I knew all too well what his ways entailed. He had a goal in mind and I was it. There was nothing else he wanted from me other than to be able to say he conquered me. I knew I was a conquest and so did he. Men like this were predictable. Their moves were easily anticipated. They would stop at nothing to get what they wanted, and once they obtained it they disappeared. It was human nature. It was the essence of a man.

"Well that's evident, though that wasn't my question. I asked how you got my number."

"If I tell you I would be giving up my source."

"Fine Titus 'cause I really don't want to play games with you. What is it you want or called for?"

"Are you going to the Q's party tonight?"

"Yes why?"

"I needed a date for the party and you're the only person I wanted to go with."

He never let up.

"Titus, what about that's not going to happen did you not understand?"

"All of it," he responded.

In the midst of me snapping at him my phone beeped. I moved it from my ear to see it was Asha texting me that they were heading to the party. By *they* I hoped she meant her and Micah. I had no real interest in anyone else being with her. I walked into the bathroom to turn the shower on. I thought about flat ironing my hair, but I really didn't have the time. I would have to wear it in its natural state tonight. I twisted a tendril around my finger.

"Umm, hello," he said.

"Oh, my bag," I said, completely forgetting he was on the phone.

I had gotten lost in thought about Micah, and then my hair.

"So was that a yes to my question?"

"Look Titus, I need to get ready. If I happen to see you at the party I'll speak. Any and everything else you are talking about won't be happening. You have a better chance of hooking up with someone else."

"Oh, like your girl Asha?" he asked.

I laughed, because he actually wanted a reaction. Unfortunately, he wasn't getting one. He wasn't important enough for one.

"Goodbye Titus. Hopefully, I don't see you tonight."

I pressed the end button. I walked to put my phone on the charger and headed for the shower. I stripped down. I looked at myself in the mirror. I traced the outline of the letters. My life plain as day in Latin; *Quod me netrit me destruit* engraved in black ink across the front of my hip. Five words representing this newfound journey I had embarked on. The self-revelations I had come to embrace. My truth I had permanently engrained in my skin. These past few weeks had summed up the words I stared at in the mirror. I climbed in the shower and turned the nob. The water ran over my face as the rest of my body absorbed the drops covering it. Water always calmed me. It always gave me a sense of renewal. A fresh start so to speak. It was the Pisces in me. I thought about what I was going to say to Micah tonight. *How was I going to make him see I was truly sorry?* I needed him to understand I knew I fucked up. I wanted a chance to right my wrongs or at least explain how everything went left. A small part of me wanted to say fuck it. I knew walking away would probably be best for everyone involved. I knew him forgiving me would only lead to another fuck up. I would behave for a while, just long enough for him to let his guards down, then were right back here again. Forgiveness had always been a gateway drug to me. You take hit after hit until you overdose and can't take anymore. At that point, you either wean yourself off or you give into the addiction until it destroys you. Either way, it all stemmed from the second chance given.

The possibility or hope for change.

I turned the water off. I grabbed my towel and wrapped it around myself. I plugged my blow dryer in so I could dry some of my hair. I didn't want to dry it completely. I liked the way it curled when it had a little dampness to it. I blew the warm air through the strands as my fingers combed through. My curly afro expanded perfectly as I placed the dryer back on the counter. I rubbed lotion all over my body. My makeup and jewelry would be light tonight. I turned off the bathroom lights. I grabbed my purple lace panties and bra out of the drawer. Since I was going on a mission afterwards, I wanted a little hidden sexiness underneath. I pulled my dress off the hanger and slid it on. I could see it was 10:30 p.m. by now. I wanted to make it to the party before 11 p.m. L.A. had ruined me and I was in no mood to stand in line all night. I slid my boots on and laced up. I threw my jacket on, grabbed my phone, and made my way to the door.

I figured by now Micah would be at the party. I didn't bother asking Asha, seeing she would be curious to know why I didn't ask him. I prayed Titus would be nowhere in sight by the time I made it there. I was in no mood for his antics. I had a goal in mind, therefore all distractions would have to pause for the night. I made my way down the elevator. I walked to my car when I heard my text alert go off. I climbed in my car then pulled my phone out. The message was from Cree. I swiped the message to open it up. He wanted me to know he would be in town tonight. As much as I would love to see him, I had other priorities to attend to. I responded with, *Catch you later,* and threw my phone back in my purse. I started my car up, backed out, and made my way to the party.

Let tonight begin.

33 | Thirty-Three

*T*he *parking was ridiculous.*
I managed to find a spot not too far from the building. I could see people standing in line as I walked up. My watch said 10:55 p.m. as I made way to the door. I would have gotten here sooner had it not been for me trying to find a parking spot. The music got louder as I made it to the front. Once I got to the door, I could see they were charging to get in. I only had $20 dollars in cash so I hoped it wasn't more.

"Excuse me, how much is it to get in?" I asked the girl in front of me.

"I'm not sure," she responded.

"Ok, thank you," I said.

I rumbled through my purse to grab my ID and money. I finally made it to the front only to see the person I had planned on avoiding all night. Too my surprise he was wearing an Omega shirt. *Figures,* I thought to myself. I shouldn't have been surprised he was a Q-dog. His entire demeanor made sense now. I knew this was going to be a long night once a smirk was plastered across his face. I was going to try and be nice. All I wanted to do was smoke a little weed, grab a drink, and have some fun with my homey lover friend. Once the night ended, I wanted to go home and fuck my man. Normally, I would say, *Make love* or *have sex,* however we were way passed both. I just wanted him to forgive me and we spend the rest of the night having incredibly, satisfying, disrespectful sex. My body craved the kind of sex that included throat grabbing, hair pulling, and ass smacking deep strokes until the wee hours of the morning. No words needed to be exchanged, only the echoes of our breathing against each other's earlobe. I was on a mission to get on my level then persuade him to leave. The people in front of me appeared to be having some admission issues. In the midst of me waiting, my text alert went off several times.

I grabbed my phone to see it was Asha and Cree. She was looking for me, while he was asking me to swing by once he landed later on tonight. He was supposed to get here around midnight. By then, I had planned on being halfway home to burn off some alcohol. I texted them both back as I walked in the door.

"I need your ID and it's $10.00," the guy at the door said.

I handed him my ID first then my money.

"She's good D. She's with me," Titus said.

He looked me up and down before handing me my license back. I looked at him, and then at Titus. I forced a smile across my face long enough so that I could say thank you.

"Thank you, Titus."

"Anything for you Reece or is it Rylee? Which one can I call you?"

He always had to be the sarcastic jackass. He could never just take the response as is. He always had to add something in the mix. He already got on my nerves, yet he seemed to enjoy that very fact. If we were being honest, I didn't want him to call me anything. I would be perfectly fine never hearing or seeing his face. He had never done anything to me, though his arrogance irritated me. I think it was that he reminded me of Trent, which was probably what didn't sit right with me.

"Reece is fine," I said, smiling.

He laughed at my dismissive tone.

I knew it was the fact that I didn't give in so easily that made him come harder. He liked the pursuit. I loved the chase. Sadly for him, there would be no conquest for him in the end. I knew where we began and where we ended. This right here would be all we ever were, and that is subtle exchanges of sarcasm laced with sexual frustration. He was attractive, but he was trouble. We both knew it so there was no need to go any further. I wasn't sure what his goal was since I'm sure he made some kind of move on Asha. He was too forward not to have tried something.

"Can I get you something to drink?" he asked.

"Do you cater to all the female guests like this?"

"Well only when they're pretty girls from Trinidad."

"I'm not from Trinidad. I'm from Los Angeles."

"By way of the islands," he responded.

I looked at him. He was definitely on a mission. He had a goal in mind, which is why he was working ever so hard to accomplish it. He didn't want me. He was just curious to see if the chase was worth all the fight I put up. I looked at him smiling.

"So you're a Que, huh?"

"Yes ma'am I am. I crossed the sands last spring."

"Dare I ask what your line name was?" I asked, laughing.

"It's Purple Haze," he said.

I gave him a confused look. He leaned closer to me so only I could hear his response. I wasn't sure why he had that name other than for one reason. I could guess though I knew I would be wrong on so many levels.

"They gave me that name because all it takes is one hit, and well you can figure the rest out."

Of course, that was definitely not what I was going to say.

He handed me a cup of something they scooped out of a keg. It looked like grape Kool- Aid, though I knew it was far from it. I sipped a little bit and found it to be really good. It was so good I took the entire cup to the head. I handed my cup back to the guy scooping it out for some more. I had an agenda so I needed to get on my level, have some fun, and then bounce. Titus watched me down the second cup in a matter of seconds. By the time we walked off I had drank four cups of it.

"You might want to slow down, Reece," he said.

I looked at him as if he was accusing me of being a *lightweight*. Thanks to Micah I had been fully acclimated into drinking tequila on a regular now. I was more than capable of drinking whatever this was they were serving.

"I'm a big girl, Titus," I snapped.

"I'm sure you are, but I've seen this drink bring grown men down."

"Thanks for the head's up. I'll remember your advice when I'm drinking the next cup. Well, thanks again for your hospitality. I need to find my friend now."

"If you're speaking of Asha, she's out back with a couple of guys she came with."

I waved him off and headed for the back. I hoped to see Micah here since I hadn't in almost two weeks. Once I arrived outside, I saw Asha surrounded by two extremely fine ass men. Unfortunately, neither of them were Micah. These must have been those delicious cousins she told me about before. I could see the resemblance across all three of them. I walked over to her and could immediately smell the weed.

"Hey girl," I said, walking over to hug her.

"Damn, I didn't think you were ever going to get here," she said.

"I've been here. I was being held hostage by Titus."

She laughed because she already knew the headache he was to me. I couldn't help but laugh at the fact she told him we were girlfriends. His response to joining in only proved my stance regarding his arrogance. I looked at her, and then at the two guys standing next to her.

"Oh I'm rude. These are my cousins Tyson and Kendrick. Guys this is Rylee," she said.

They both looked me up and down. I was quite fascinated at how bold they were. Taylor would eat this up. I still hated she couldn't come. I was, however, excited about the fact I would be headed to D.C. in a few days.

"Hello," I said, returning their stares.

Asha passed me her bong. I took the lighter, lit it, and inhaled. I passed it back to her as I slowly exhaled the smoke. I could feel the effects of the drinks I had start to take effect. I wanted some more. I figured I would take a few more hits before making my way back inside.

"So you're a party girl too, huh?" Kendrick asked.

"Depends on what you consider a party girl," I answered, smiling.

"So are you from here party girl?" Tyson asked.

Asha glanced over at me, shaking her head. I could see the grin forming across her face. I knew what they were up to, and she did too. They were feeling me out to see whose bait I would bite. We looked at each other to see who was going to break the news to them. No need for them to work this hard and not get anywhere.

"No I'm from L.A. I moved here to finish school."

"So you're a Cali girl. Well, Cali did you move here with someone or by yourself?" Tyson asked.

Wow, they were really forward, and straight to the point. There wasn't an ounce of chaser added.

"Well, that's a very forward question to ask someone you just met," I said.

"Not really," he said.

I raised an eyebrow.

"I'm just trying to find out if I need to be looking over my shoulder tonight. I don't want your man walking in and stepping out of line. I'd hate to put a hurting on him in front of his girl," he said.

They were definitely cousins. I wondered if they were all like this. From the three I've met, they seemed to all have that high confidence mixed with a mild dose of arrogance. Tyson's arrogance was pretty high. I don't know if it was because he was fine as hell that made it okay or what. Either way, he was definitely laying it on thick.

"Well Tyson, I hate to disappoint you, but yes my man will be here tonight."

"Too bad, you could have had one hell of a night with me Cali," he said.

Asha and Kendrick jerked their heads and belted out a laugh. It was clear this was not new behavior to them. I wondered if he was the cousin Micah had got into a fight with over his ex-girlfriend. He definitely seemed like the, *Mr. Steal Your Girl,* type. He had the looks, swag, and mouthpiece to pull it off. The question was did he have the same skills as his cousin. Too bad I would never find out.

"Rylee, excuse my brother. Sometimes he acts like he has no home training. He doesn't know any better," Kendrick said.

"It's okay. I just know your cousin wouldn't be too thrilled about you all over me if he walked in here."

Their eyes bucked open.

"Oh, you're Micah's girl?" Kendrick asked.

"Yes."

"Like I said, too bad," Tyson said, laughing.

They both shot him a look as if to say, *not again with the bullshit.* I wasn't sure if he was the one since neither of them ever said a name. After looking at them and listening to him, I was pretty sure he was. I passed Asha her bong back after taking another hit. I could feel the high settling within in me. Tonight was definitely going to be a fun night.

"Speaking of your brother, where is he?" I asked Asha.

"They went back to his place to shower and change after dinner. He should be on his way."

She didn't bother asking why I asked her. I suspected she already knew since I told her about Trent. I didn't update her on if we were still on the outs, although it was pretty obvious. I figured with us being in this setting and him seeing me, he would loosen up for us to talk. We passed the bong back and forth a few more times. I had grown thirsty again and wanted some more of the house drink.

"Come grab a drink with me," I asked her.

"Okay."

She handed the bong to Tyson and we walked off. The crowd outside had grew, which meant the inside had become packed. As we headed into the house, we saw Arrington then Mario. I looked at Asha, unsure if she was going to make a scene or not. Under different circumstances she would have been cool, however she currently had liquor and a narcotic festering within her. The outcome could be unstable and unpredictable. As soon as he saw us he walked up to us leaving her behind him.

"What's up, baby?" he asked, pulling Asha close.

I took a deep breath of thanks. It was clear both of them would be acting like adults tonight. I could only hope for the same results.

"Hi Mario," Asha said.

He eyeballed her. Obviously, he could tell she was already on one. I waved at him and made my way back into the house. The DJ was bumping and everyone inside was dancing, talking, or drinking. By now it was after midnight. I was tempted to text Micah, but didn't out of fear he wouldn't respond. I walked over to the dude serving the drinks. I held up my fingers for two drinks. I put one cup to my lips to drink when Asha made her way over to me. The second cup was for her, but I went ahead and downed it since she could get her own now.

"I see you guys are behaving tonight," I said to her.

She rolled her eyes as if I was saying something foreign. I knew she really liked him no matter how much she hid it. I had overheard a few conversations with them to know they were way pass sex at this point. Her feelings though still distant were entangled with him. I could see it because it was a reflection of what I was looking at. The inner battle we both struggled with.

The battle between if we should love or not to love? If we should show feelings or no feelings? Both are clear signs of control slipping away.

"Yeah we're good. We worked everything out and agreed to chill on the extra shit."

"So you guys are together?"

"Something like that, though it doesn't change what we have going on."

I felt a sigh of relief come over me. Asha was my outlet. She was my occasional fix when I needed something different or something soft. Her gift was my curse, and I enjoyed every minute of pleasure it gave me.

"Well, I'm glad you two came to your senses. Arrington wasn't in it for good reasons anyway."

"I know right. Let's dance," she blurted out.

"What about your cousins?"

"Girl, they fine. They'll have company soon enough," she said, grabbing my hand.

We took another drink to the head and headed for the dance floor. The DJ was on fire as he played hit after hit. Countless tracks from Bad Boy, No Limit, Cash Money, UGK, and Death Row blasted through the speakers. It was summertime in Cali for me all over again. Each song brought back a memory I shared with the people back home. Everybody on the dance floor seemed to be in their element. People were just vibing to good music. I didn't have anything against new hip hop, but it just wasn't the same. It didn't give you the same groove as the old rappers did. The old hip-hop tracks made you want to dance. You could feel the beat and you understood the words. Being an old soul, I would always choose the old over new. After a few more songs, Asha and I took a break. We were heading back outside before she pulled me down an empty hall. She leaned against the wall and put something in my hand.

"Try this."

I opened my hand to see half a pill.

"What's this?"

"It's ecstasy. Mario gave it to me for later. I didn't want to take a whole one so I'm giving you half. If it kicks in before we go home, maybe round two in your car?"

I looked at my hand. I was drunk and very wrapped up in my high. I figured this pill would do no more than make me more ready for what I was going to put on Micah later on so I figured what the hell. At least it would be a really fun and intense night for both of us. I threw the pill in my mouth and swallowed. She swallowed hers, and then leaned over to kiss me. We tongued each other down for what seemed like minutes before we headed back outside. I looked around, hoping Micah had slid pass us on the dance floor. Once we got back outside, I could see her cousins had found other distractions. I looked around and still no Micah. Asha didn't seem to be phased since she was indeed high on several levels and soon to be on more. I checked my phone. The only text I had come from Cree saying he made it. It was 1:30 a.m. and the party would be shutting down soon. I looked up to see Titus staring at me. Once we locked eyes, he made his way back over. He looked to have a piece of paper in his hand.

He stopped in front of me, handed me the paper, and said, "In case you're interested in finding out how I got my name."

He walked off. I opened the paper to see an address. I assumed he was inviting me to his place tonight. I slid the paper in my purse. I walked over to Asha and her cousins. The speakers had been turned on outside so the crowd there was now dancing too. Mystikal's song, *Danger,* was playing. I loved this song. I had always been a fan of his. All of the people from New Orleans got really hype when the No Limit and Cash Money songs came on. They were representing for their hometown. I felt the same way when Cali artists came on. I wanted so badly for Micah to come. I could hear the echoes of laughter as my body became elevated to another level. The crowd was slimming down, though there was still a decent amount of people left.

We inhaled all of what was left in Asha's bong. A few more songs came on and before we knew it 2:30 a.m. had reared its ugly head. The DJ started playing slow jams, which let everyone know the party had come to an end. I was high and beyond intoxicated. I saw Asha in the corner with Mario, and I knew what kind of night it was going to be. I pulled out my keys, waved her goodbye, and headed for the door. I passed on the option of saying bye to her cousins. Tyson was already on a mission, and I didn't want to provoke him any further. I headed to my car thinking about how Micah really didn't show up. I wondered if it was because he knew I was going to be here. *Was he really trying to avoid me? Better yet, were we done?* I made it back to my car and climbed in. I pulled my phone out to see there were no texts from Micah. There was the unopened message from Cree staring back at me. I swiped the message to open it.

It read*: Ritz Carlton, room 2208.*

His hotel and room number lit up my screen. The message had only been sent 30 minutes ago. I put my phone down to pull the paper out of my purse. The address stared back at me as the ecstasy circulated. I was torn between right and wrong. I carried the decision of giving in or giving up. I placed the address in the cup holder and started my car. I responded to the text, and then drove off.

I was horny, and I be damned if I went to bed that way tonight.

34 | Thirty-Four

wasn't sure if I should be here. I was standing in front of this door horny as hell. The numbers stared back at me as if I was making the wrong decision. The goal I had set out for tonight fizzled when Micah didn't show up. Cree texting me his room number was more temptation. I tried to block him being here out of my mind and couldn't do it. Titus's attempts of seduction enticed my already high sex drive once he slid his address in my hand. Micah and I hadn't spoken since Trent showed up at my door. I missed him and though Asha had a way of making me of forget my problems, I wanted some dick.

I needed some dick.

I knocked on the door and there he stood. God he was beautiful. All I wanted was for him to lean me against the wall and fuck my frustrations away. He looked me up and down as if he was surprised to see me. I pushed him inside, closed the door, and forcefully took his mouth under siege. At first I noticed a bit of hesitation, but I had a solution for that as well. I pushed him against the wall and removed the towel wrapped around his waist. I gave him no opportunity to refuse as I took him inside my mouth. He moaned in pure pleasure as I sucked the life out of him. The grip he had on my head was a bit stronger than usual. I didn't mind since we both wanted this.

I liked it rough at times. I wanted to make him moan.

I playfully danced my tongue up and down the shaft. He moved my head back and forth before seizing control. He pulled himself out of my mouth, picked me up, and headed for the bedroom. I heard the shower running and remembered he had a towel wrapped around him when I first walked in. My legs dropped to the floor. He kissed me with such passion. I felt the wall against my back as he pulled my panties down. In one tug my dress was ripped and thrown behind him. His hands slid up my back as he unsnapped my bra. In one swift move, my bra slid down my arms exposing my breasts. The shower door was covered in steam. He opened it to push me inside. The warm water felt like heaven rolling down my back. He lifted me up and I wrapped my legs around his waist. I loved moments like this. When there was no conversation needed. Spontaneity always went to the top of my list. I could live in these moments forever if given the chance. My fingers slid across the door. Each time he went in inside of me was with a bit more force. His strokes contained hunger and inflicted control. He took one of his hands from around my waist and put it around my throat. I was becoming more enticed by the minute. I could feel the heat rising from within. He bit my earlobe, while I gyrated my hips in response to the intense thrust he was giving my sweet spot. He pushed my legs down, and then pulled out so he could turn me around. He pressed my face against the shower wall, entering me again. I held onto the towel bar firmly. I felt myself at the edge of the cliff. I was ready to jump head first.

"Is this what you came for?" he muttered.

His voice seemed raspier than before. I could smell the alcohol on his breath. I couldn't even move my mouth to answer. I was trying to savor whatever oxygen I had left to breathe. Between the heat from us and the steam from the shower my lungs were searching for some air to breathe. My heart had never beat this fast. He had never been this rough. He bent me over. I cried out when he smacked my ass. I was overdosing on ecstasy. If I didn't slow down I would need to be resuscitated. He looked at me with something different in his eyes. There was passion I saw lingering upon the surface. Then there was a hunger, a possessiveness lying beneath all of it. At this very moment, we weren't making love. We were flat out fucking.

It was carnal and raw. It was unconcealed and unwilling to be caged, It was unforgiving and left no questions asked.

He entered me with more force behind each thrust. Our sex had never been this violent before. Nevertheless, my sweet spot responded to each aggressive stroke he gave. I was inhaling a new high destined to leave me with dangerous withdrawals. I was riding a wave I knew would soon carry me away. A new standard was being set. A new standard I would be expecting every time we gave into our desires. He pulled my head back, sliding his tongue in my mouth.

Sultry eyes were staring at me. Water ran down his chocolate skin. Well defined muscles contracting as he forcibly held me up.

My airway was fighting for relief. My chest was pleading for me to slow down my breathing. My eyes were blurry as the water fell on my face. I wanted to wipe the water from my face, and then decided it wasn't important. I used the strength I had left in my arms to hold onto him. He pulled out of me so that he could continue the assault on my sweet spot with his tongue. I stood under the water gasping for air as he lifted my leg, licking me until I yelled out in sweet surrender. My eyes rolled to the back of my head. My feet were clinging to what balance I had left. I exhaled the deep moan I had been holding onto. If it proved to be the last breath I would ever release I would be utterly satisfied.

I looked down as his head moved in and out, torturing what was left of my resolve. I blinked a couple of times to make sure I wasn't seeing things. I was tipsy and high as hell, though I never remembered that tattoo being there before. It had been two weeks since we had crossed paths. I figured maybe it was new. I managed to acquire one too so I gave it no more thought. I closed my eyes, drifting into euphoria as the orgasmic cloud I was on carried me away. Something about this, about him seemed undeniably different. Somehow I didn't care. I gripped what I knew to be my lover's head as he pulled out the demon buried within me. Graciously, I subdued her power, while he took complete control of her. All of the lies, the secrets were being casted out. Whatever happened after this no longer mattered.

I could die right now and be a happy woman.

The assault I thought was coming to an end was only the beginning. I couldn't hold it any longer. I came harder than I could ever remember. My entire insides were vibrating. Fiending for strength, I could barely stand. As if my lack of balance was obvious, he picked me up and we headed for the bedroom. Normally I was all for round after round, however that last orgasm took everything out of me. I could have put my thumb in my mouth and went to sleep as relieved as I was right now. I had poked the beast dangling Cree in front of him. Witnessing Trent's little stunt simply released the monster. At this moment, abruptly coming over here like this made it no better. He laid me on the bed, and tied my hands to the bed posts with a scarf I must've left. He kneeled on the floor and dove back into my sweet spot. His mouth, his tongue, his mouth, and then his tongue was all I could think about as he ravished the feeling remaining in my clitoris.

My body had become a slave to numbness. I had no energy to fight him off. My hands being tied up didn't make it any easier. My breathing was out of control. I was slipping into another dimension. He was fucking me like he was hurt. Like somehow, some way, I had violated whatever was between us. I couldn't fathom him feeling that way, though I understood. After months of countless sex, he probably felt like my sweet spot was his. His response made it clear that in no way should another man be sniffing around his territory. He would never openly admit it, but there were moments of possessiveness. I usually felt it when we were fucking.

"Oh my goodness," I mumbled.

His tongue went deeper and deeper. He was searching for something inside of my hand. I knew what it was. He wanted my all, though I was unable to give it to him. It was too much control for any one person to handle and I knew it. I had somewhat relinquished it before and the dumbass messed it up. So I promised my heart it was never happening again. I could feel the shots, the marijuana, and ecstasy pill I took flood my body. At this point, everything was mixing together. I felt intoxicated and paralyzed at the same time. There was no life left in my limbs, though that meant nothing to him. As each moment passed, he made me cum over-and-over again. I wanted to beg him to stop. This was not the way I saw this going. I hadn't planned on this type of fucking.

I played my hand, and he called my bluff.

He turned me on my stomach. His lips kissed me from my shoulders all the way down to the small of my back. Each kiss provided a small relief from the savage way he licked my sweet spot. He entered me again, this time slowly and less intense than the first few rounds. He slow stroked me into sweet surrender. He held my hands tight as he trembled, releasing the orgasm he fought so hard to hold onto. He collapsed on me before he rolled to the other side, releasing my hands. I shifted myself to look at him. Something in his eyes was different. I couldn't tell exactly what it was. *Maybe it was just me?* Everything was fully circulated in my system. I laid back to catch my breath. I grabbed my chest, while he kissed my lips softly. I didn't think we would ever reach gentle after fucking each other like savages.

"Baby, I don't know who you are, but you are my kind of freaky."

I looked at him completely confused. I didn't understand what he meant.

"What do you mean you don't know me Micah?"

He looked at me with a look of bewilderment as if I said something wrong. I was coming down from the highs I had been on. I knew we had been at odds. I knew I had betrayed the purity of our love. However, it didn't call for utter dismissal of who I am. I looked at him again, triggering his need to stop the bullshit. I looked at his arm and it somehow became clear.

My throat immediately snatched my breath.

I hopped up, and stumbling out of the bed. I grabbed the loose sheet, wrapped myself up, and backed against the wall. I slid down with my hand over my mouth. The narcotics I partook of earlier came crashing down at full speed. I had just fucked up in a major way. My heartbeat was racing. My sweet spot still throbbing from the catastrophic mayhem he reined upon it. I was searching for something to say.

He looked at me, and then I looked at him.

His eyes had the same lustful look after countless orgasms had been released. He sat up on the side of the bed. I could see something different was buried beneath them. There was a darkness to them. A hidden, sinister look indicating this moment was not over. This here, what I had done was beyond forgivable. No amount of explaining would fix this.

What was he doing here?

Where the hell was Micah?

He never showed up to the party. Asha had said they came back to shower and change. I assumed he had come home, no one else. I was high, completely under the influence of alcohol. I let my judgment escape me, while walking into this house. I slept with who I thought was my man, though he wasn't.

I would say it had been an honest mistake, but nothing could be further from the truth.

He looked like him, exactly like him! I searched for a moment, any moment for when he or Asha said it was just them. I remembered Asha saying she had been hanging out with her family. I never contemplated another sibling. *Earlier when I looked over the balcony it was Micah or was it?* They weren't twins, they were triplets. I remembered Micah saying multiple births ran in their family. However, he never really elaborated on it. All of the pics she had in her place I figured were of him. I never remembered seeing a family pic of all of them, so how in the hell could I have known. *How could they not mention they had another sibling?*

I held my head down.

In one night, and after countess orgasms I had repeated the same mistake his ex-girlfriend made years ago.

I was completely in my own thoughts when he opened his mouth to speak.

"Sorry baby, you have the wrong brother. My name is Niko."

Also Available by

SHADRESS DENISE

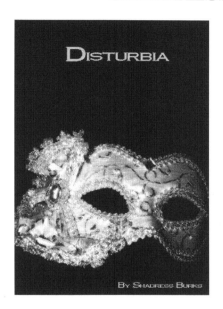 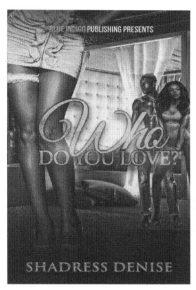

www.iamshadressdenise.com

Made in the USA
Columbia, SC
16 November 2021

48930420R00139